Two Women

TWO WOMEN

CHRISTENE A. BROWNE

Second Story Press

Library and Archives Canada Cataloguing in Publication

Browne, Christene, author
Two women / Christene A. Browne.

Issued in print and electronic formats.
ISBN 978-1-927583-20-3 (bound).—
ISBN 978-1-927583-21-0 (epub)

I. Title.

PS8603.R697T86 2013   C813'.6   C2013-903865-5
                    C2013-903866-3

Editor: Colin Thomas
Copyeditors: Kathryn White and Julie Wallace
Design: Melissa Kaita

Cover: Illustration © Janice Kun/www.i2iart.com

Printed and bound in Canada

Second Story Press gratefully acknowledges the support of the Ontario Arts Council and the Canada Council for the Arts for our publishing program. We acknowledge the financial support of the Government of Canada through the Canada Book Fund.

Canada Council   Conseil des Arts
for the Arts   du Canada

MIX
Paper from
responsible sources
FSC
www.fsc.org   FSC® C004071

Published by
SECOND STORY PRESS
20 Maud Street, Suite 401
Toronto, ON M5V 2M5
www.secondstorypress.ca

For Leonie and Merle,
and all the others who have suffered silently

CHAPTER 1
Bernice, the Teller of Tales

BY THE SUMMER of 1970, Bernice Archer had experienced the comings and goings of sixty-nine summers, but somehow, she still hadn't grown accustomed to the season's many irritations.

One sultry July evening, she cursed the heat as she prepared to bathe. Anxious to wash away the day's grime, she lifted off her sweaty dress—a garment the size of a small tent—and flung it to the floor. Her king-size drawers were next.

"Oh," she squealed when the plump toe of her right foot met the cold water. The initial shock was followed by a satisfying moan.

Holding on tightly to the side of the tub, she maneuvered herself downward.

"Fifty-nine gone, only thirty-three to go," she mumbled.

Counting down the days had become a nightly ritual. This time of year had become synonymous with sorrow, since all of the most traumatic events of her life had occurred then. Each time the Earth was the farthest point from the Sun, it felt as if nature was forcing her to relive all of her terrible moments.

The faucet continued dripping even after it had been forced off. Not wanting to look at the crumbling plaster or ugly leak spots, she closed her eyes. Her muscles relaxed, but there was no peaceful surrender.

As she tried to find a comfortable position, her daughters in the next room began to sing an aria from Puccini's *La Bohème*:

> *Sì, mi chiamano Mimì,*
> *ma il mio nome è Lucia.*
> *La storia mia è breve.*
> *A tela o a seta*
> *ricamo in casa e fuori…*

Their voices resonated like a heavenly chorus. As the music washed over her, her mind began to wander back to the summer of 1907. She was seven. Her mother had just died.

Dressed in a cotton slip, she kneeled at the foot of her bed preparing to say her evening prayers. Her older brother Charles fanned her with his hand. She looked up at him with frightened eyes.

"Charles, is it okay if I ask you something?" she whispered.

"Sure, Bernie, anything you want. Go ahead."

"Why did Mama die?"

"Well, you know she was very sick, and she was also very sad too, I guess."

"Was she sad because Papa left?"

"I suppose so."

"Do all papas make mamas sad?"

"Not all."

"Is Mama in heaven now?"

"Yes, honey, her soul is there."

"What's a soul?"

"It's a piece of God that's inside of us."

"Is it inside everyone?"

"Yes."

"Even Papa?"

"Yes, even him."

"Should I pray for Mama now?"

"Sure, Bernie, go ahead."

After her prayers, she snuggled up and listened as Charles read a bedtime story. By the time it was done, she had fallen asleep. In her dream that night, she saw the translucent face of her dead mother surrounded by a swarm of flies. She woke up sobbing.

"Charles, Charles! I saw it again. I saw it. I keep seeing it."

Charles told her another story as he cradled her in his arms and rocked her back to sleep. He slept on the floor beside her that night and many more to follow.

A few weeks later, under the shade of their apple tree, she stared up at the sky through the blossoms and imagined her first tale. It was told only to the wind and a host of invisible friends.

"Once upon a time, a very long time ago, there was a little girl who was the strongest and most beautiful girl in all the land. Her name was Blossom. Blossom was not happy because an evil monster had come to town and killed teveryone who lived there. The monster made Blossom so mad that she picked him up and threw him in the ocean, and that was the end of him."

The tales born under the shade of the apple tree had been her constant companion throughout her life. As she matured, they also matured. They benefitted greatly from her steady consumption of the classics—everything from Aesop to Zola. When her daughters were born, she began sharing her creations with them in the form of bedtime stories. She recounted the first one as she held them in her arms hours after their birth. Fifty-three years later, the practice was still in place.

The aim of Bernice's stories was to protect her daughters and maintain their innocence. She did this in other idiosyncratic ways as well. To minimize their interest in the opposite sex, she often told them, "Bowel movements can give you much more pleasure than any man ever could. They leave you feeling nice and light and free and easy, while men leave you feeling all heavy and bothered. So always choose the movements."

Bernice's daughters weren't very worldly, but they knew enough to know that they would never be faced with a situation where they would have to choose between a man and a bowel movement.

Bernice groaned as she pulled herself up out of the tub. The singing had stopped. She dried herself off and put on her nightdress. By the time she had finished in the bathroom, her daughters had already gone off to bed.

"Goodnight, you two," she said lovingly, as she crossed the darkness to her room.

"Night, Ma," the voices answered together.

"That was a good story you told tonight, Ma."

"Glad you liked it."

Bernice's bedroom resembled a hospital room in its starkness. The white walls had turned a dull yellow over the years. The color of the bedding and drapes had similarly aged. The wood floors, which were washed weekly with vinegar and water (to keep away the pests), still retained a hint of their original luster. All four walls were bare save for one plain wooden cross that hung above the headboard. An antique dresser and sewing machine stood in front of the single bed, a nightstand next to it. On the stand was a neat pile of library books—*Rebecca, Their Eyes Were Watching God,* and *Wide Sargasso Sea*—pushed up against a small lamp. A Bible that had once belonged to her mother sat on top of the heap.

"Dear God, thank you for another day. Please protect my girls and give me the strength that I need to make it through many more tomorrows. And I beg you, please help me forget all those things that are not worth remembering. Amen." She picked up the Bible and held it close.

"Good night, *Maman. Je t'aime.*" She kissed the Bible's flimsy cover, switched off the lamp, and attempted to sleep.

The stale air was stifling when she woke. The heat instilled a sense of foreboding. She wanted to go right back to sleep but resisted the urge. Too many things had to be done. She poured talcum powder into all of her many folds, creases, and crevasses and pulled on one of her dresses, grabbed her purse and bundle buggy, and left the apartment without stopping for a single bite.

The drone of televisions and the ventilation system filled the hallway as she made her way past crumbling walls, broken fixtures, and litter. The three-story building, constructed in 1900, the same year she was born, was nothing to look at but it was the only home she had known for the last fifty-four years.

Outside, the street was quiet and deserted save for a lone garbage collector. To get to her destination, she had to pass a rundown park and a number of derelict buildings.

In the bank there were more than thirty people queued up to cash their government checks and pay bills. Not being able to stand the thought of waiting, she feigned a limp as she walked to the back of the line. She then concocted the most desperate expression that she could and shot a look toward the business teller. The unoccupied worker waved her over to his wicket, paid her bills, and cashed her check. As she shoved the cash into her purse and trotted toward the exit, she paid no attention to the dirty looks that followed her.

At the pharmacy she picked up her blood pressure medication, and in the scantily stocked grocery store bought all the food her money would allow.

By the time she completed her errands, she was hungry, exhausted, and drenched in sweat. As she pulled herself and the buggy up the last creaky step, she was overcome by a fit of coughing.

While she stood there huffing, having what she would later describe to her daughters as a mini-stroke (since she was prone to exaggeration), one of her neighbors, a young woman of caramel complexion, came up behind her. The petite woman appeared overly distracted as she struggled with a bag of laundry in one hand and an infant in the other. When she finally noticed Bernice, she looked at her with the blankest of stares and asked in a quiet voice, "Are you okay?"

The woman's concern tickled Bernice. She enjoyed the way the young lady sounded as if she had sung the words instead of speaking them. The three words were the very first her new neighbor had spoken directly to her. The two had only nodded and waved at one another in the past.

Bernice took in the woman's mysterious gaze and breathed in her fresh scent—citrusy with only the slightest hint of perspiration. *She must be accustomed to the heat*, Bernice thought. The woman appeared to be in her twenties. She had a roundish, asymmetrical face, and a nose that was neither straight nor flat but somewhere in-between. Her black hair was neatly combed to one side and pinned up fashionably. Her large, brown, doe-like eyes were her most prominent feature.

"I'm fine. Peachy keen, thanks. Just catching my breath is all," Bernice puffed as she forced a smile.

"Are you sure?"

"Yes, I'm sure. No need to worry about me." Bernice noticed a fresh plum-colored bruise on the back of the young woman's arm as she walked away. This wasn't the first time that she had seen such a mark.

Another tenant exited from an apartment a few doors away. This tall woman wore a sleeveless dress that drooped off her emaciated shoulders. She also carried a small baby in her arms. Her auburn hair, which was cut in an uneven bob, looked as if she had chopped it off in a fit of anger. The bottom part of her face appeared masculine with its square jaw and cleft chin, but the rest was softened by her button nose and light-blue eyes. She looked as if she hadn't slept in days.

"Are you alright, Miss?" she asked in a strong European accent.

Bernice took a few seconds to breathe in the woman's floral scent before giving her the same reply she had given before. When the second neighbor vanished down the stairs, her strong rose-scented perfume still lingered in the hallway.

Catching her breath, Bernice collected her buggy and wobbled slowly to her apartment wearing a look of satisfaction. The brief encounters had made her happy. It felt like déjà vu. In her neighbors' empty stares she saw a reflection of herself and her mother and a glimpse of a fighting spirit. For the first time she recognized that they were not the victims that she had believed them to be. The signs of distress were less apparent close up. She was moved and inspired and knew right way that she had another story.

That afternoon, visions of her neighbors came to her while she napped. She saw the two walking hand in hand and smiling. They were in a state that she had never seen them in before. They were happy, and they were together.

After dinner, Bernice beamed as she sat between two loud, clunky fans in her cramped living room. The rickety tables shook as the machines oscillated back and forth. Neither the noise nor the persistent mugginess bothered her. She was too excited to let any of that affect her rare summer joy.

In front of her on the coffee table, neatly arranged on a silver tray, were a teapot, three teacups, two glasses of milk, a large plate of chocolate-covered cookies, a pound cake, and a bottle of vodka. A love seat was positioned on the other side of the table, in front of the window. The only other piece of furniture was a hutch where knick-knacks were kept. The overall muddy hue of the room was balanced by colorful afghans and homemade doilies.

The sound of splashing water and two squabbling adult female voices could be heard in the background.

"Move now, let me have my turn at the sink," one voice demanded.

"No, you already had your turn," the other replied.

"Chang and Eng, come on now. Hurry up!" Bernice called out playfully. She often referred to her middle-aged daughters, Eva and Ava, by the names of the famous Siamese twins, Chang and Eng Bunker, since they were always side by side, never more than a few inches apart.

"What's taking you two so long? What are you doing, taking a whore's bath or something? Just splash a little water on and come out already."

"We'll be there in a minute," Ava yelled. She and her sister were attempting to cool off.

"And stop calling us those crazy names," Eva added.

"Move a sec, now. You're hogging all the water," Ava said peevishly.

"I'm not hogging anything. You had plenty already. Just move your big fat ass."

"Stop fighting and get out here. I have a new story tonight," Bernice yelled.

"New!" the twins chorused.

"Did she say *new*?" Eva asked.

"Yes I said it—N.E.W."

The bickering and the sound of running water came to an abrupt halt. Heavy shuffling quickly followed as Eva and

Ava emerged. The women, who were blind and just as round as their mother, walked carefully, keeping their heads fixed on one rigid plane. Their pale eyes sparkled as they moved in perfect sync.

As mirror twins, each was the exact reflection of the other. Eva was left-handed while Ava was right-handed. Eva had a beauty mark on the left side of her nose while Ava's mole was found just to the right of her nose. Both accentuated their matching mustaches.

"A new story?" The twins squealed excitedly.

"What's it about?" Ava asked.

"It's something I dreamt."

"But I don't even remember the last time you had a new story."

"I know. That's why I was telling you to hurry. Sit down. Sit down. I poured your tea and milk for you already, and the cookies and cake are there too."

The twins squished together on their love seat across from Bernice. The three looked like a trio of seated Buddhas.

As they each reached for a cookie, Bernice sat up, cleared her throat, and recited, "I see the moon."

"And the moon sees me," the twins joined in.

"God bless the moon, and God bless me," the three concluded.

Once that brief ceremony was performed, Bernice poured herself a teacup full of vodka (her perfect cuppa), took a swig, then sat back and began her story.

"Not so very long ago, there was a big shake-up in the heavens. The problem was that there weren't enough souls to go around. So it was decided that they had to be divided and shared."

"Wait, now, wait. I thought you said this was a new story?" Eva interjected.

"Yeah, we know this one already," her sister agreed.

"Don't worry, the story starts the same, but it's not the same. Just hold your horses for a minute and listen, alright? So it was decided that one would become two in the heavens."

"When does the new part start?"

"Will you stop interrupting me? Just listen. So in the heavens that night there were many tiny explosions, and the stars popped like popcorn. One particularly brilliant star split in half and became two. Each then made its journey down to Earth. One traveled to a tropical location, the other to a colder place on the other side of the world. Each reached Earth at the exact same moment, and each became a beautiful little girl. One was called Violet. The other was Rose."

Eva and Ava concentrated on their mother's every word, while they continued to nibble their cookies and slurp their milk.

CHAPTER 2
The Story of Violet's Birth

AS THE SUN SHONE brilliant and gold over a tiny island, the painful cries of a woman rang out. She was giving birth. Neighbors stood vigil outside, waiting for the sound of a new life. Months earlier, they had heard something altogether different.

"What are we going to do with a blasted baby? How are we going to feed it when we don't have enough food for ourselves? How are we going to stretch the few pennies we have?" Babies need clothes and other things you know. Things we don't have. Did you think of any of this before?"

The pregnant wife held her tongue.

The baby inside the womb knew that she was the one the angry man meant. She had already felt his fists and hard-toed boots. The attacks had increased as the months flew by. To defend herself, she swished about. The cushion of the amniotic sack and her mother's reflexes provided additional protection. To show her sympathy, she tried to make her mother comfortable and chose a peaceful Sunday afternoon to be born.

"Push now, woman! Get on with it," the midwife bellowed. She was nine months pregnant herself and still had a long list of chores to do in addition to delivering her own child. The young mother couldn't understand the woman's irritation or her insistence on pushing. Her eyes were already falling out of their sockets from all the pushing.

"Just give me one more big one."

With one last heroic effort, the baby slid out. Its first sound was melodious and seemed more like a song than a cry. The midwife was too preoccupied to notice.

The young mother looked down in awe at her beautiful daughter and decided to name her Violet, after her favorite color.

When the baby was taken outside for the very first time, her mother held her up to show her the green lushness of their island and the turquoise sea that surrounded it.

"Look, my darling, this is your country, your home. Isn't it the most lovely place you've ever seen?"

Through her barely opened eyes, Violet looked around. When she saw that the ocean stretched in every direction, her first thought was, *I'm going to have to learn to swim.*

As Violet grew, she could not help but notice her father's lack of regard toward her. He took little interest in her and avoided all forms of physical contact. He left early every morning and returned late each night. His days were spent cutting cane, his nights in the rum shop. When he was home, the exaggerated, violent way in which he did things was apparent to anyone within earshot.

One evening when Violet was five years old, she was awakened by the loud sound of a dog's painful yelp. She knew right away that the poor mutt had crossed her drunken father's path.

"Where's my supper?" Violet's father roared the moment he thumped into the house. "I'm hungry. Where's my blasted food?"

Violet listened as her mother scurried from her bed where she had most likely been sleeping with her eyes open.

"And don't burn it up. You know I don't like burnt food."

"I know," Violet heard her mother reply.

"You better know."

A loud thud followed as her father took a seat.

Violet marveled at how this pint-size man could make himself sound so heavy.

"Come here, woman."

"But I'm heating up your food."

"I said come here, woman."

"But it'll burn if I don't watch it."

"Just leave the damn thing alone and come."

Violet counted backward from three, knowing that her mother would obey.

"Come let me taste you."

There were a few seconds of ruffling noises, then a loud clomp as someone fell to the floor.

Violet knew it was her mother.

"Why do you taste so damn sour, woman? What happened to that sweet taste of yours? You're not old enough to taste so nasty."

"I'll try to taste better next time," Violet's mother conceded. "Go see about the food, now."

A few minutes later, an enamel plate was placed on the table.

"Ahh!" Violet's father growled. The plate hit the floor. "Are you trying to kill me? The damn thing almost burnt the roof of my mouth off."

"I told you that I needed to watch the stove."

"You told me what?" He stood up and kicked the chair. "You told me what?"

"I said that I needed—"

Before Violet's mother could finish, a symphony of crashes, bumps, and cries rang out.

Violet waited for the racket to end before she crept out of her bed to collect a tin box from her chest. She found her mother kneeling on the floor cleaning up the pidgin peas, rice, and meat that had been spewed everywhere.

"Are you okay?" Violet asked with the concern of someone much older.

"I'm fine child. What are you doing out of bed at this hour?" She shielded her face from her daughter.

"I came to see about you."

Violet reached down and examined her mother's bloody chin. She had seen worse.

"Don't, don't…" Violet's mother moaned.

"Let me see what he did this time. I need to clean you up."

Violet took out a bottle of iodine and some gauze from the tin box. With the skill of a trained professional, she went about cleaning and dressing the wounds, while her mother sat still and emotionless.

The next afternoon as Violet walked from school, past a row of pastel-colored homes and tropical plants, she heard the sound of a familiar voice.

"*Hey! Ma-til-da; Ma-til-da; Ma-til-da, she take me honey and run away, yeah.*"

When she turned around, she saw her father smiling from ear to ear, carrying a mound of over-ripe mangoes in the folds of his arms.

"Look what I got for my girls," he announced happily. His crooked smiled looked awkward on his oblong face.

"I see," Violet said nonchalantly.

"I chose the best of them for you all. And in my pocket I got some of your favorite sweets from Mrs. Gumb's shop."

Violet felt excited and guilty all at once.

"I brought the peppermint ones and the chocolate ones."

"Oh," Violet replied, trying to sound indifferent.

"Come on now, I'll race you home."

"That's okay. You go ahead."

"Oh come on, have some fun. On your mark, get set, go!"

He nudged her. She tried to resist, but then her stringy legs betrayed her and carried her off behind him.

She watched as her father greeted her mother with a soft tender kiss to her bruised cheek. The look her mother gave him seemed to say "All is forgiven."

"You get all those mangoes from Mr. Highliger?" her mother asked.

"He told me that they would just go to the animals if I didn't take them."

"He has a way of putting things, doesn't he, that man," her mother replied.

"He sure does," her father agreed.

Her mother pushed a mango toward her.

"Here, child, go wash it."

Violet frowned and refused to take it. The fact that it had come from Mr. Highliger (via her father) was reason enough.

Mr. Highliger was Violet's father's boss. He was a short, bull-legged man who did everything with an air of superiority. While his workers toiled in the hot sun, cutting sugar cane for pennies, he stood in the shade sipping limeade and screaming orders.

"No time for resting now! Don't cut it so short—longer! Put more force into it. Rest on your own time!"

Sometimes he would run into the field and whip his men with branches from the tamarind tree. Violet's father, tired from a night of drinking, was often his victim. Not being able to retaliate, he kept his anger bottled up, only to release it at home. This was the gift that was brought home more regularly than the overripe fruit. It was the one Violet's mother had grown accustomed to.

"Let me hear what you learned at school today," Violet's mother coaxed while they sat on their stoop one evening.

Violet wasn't in the mood. Her mother pulled her onto her lap.

"Go ahead, now, you're always so good with the poems. Let me hear."

Violet paused, then held her head erect.

"A mouse found a beautiful piece of plum cake, the richest and sweetest that mortal could make; 'twas heavy with citron and fragrant with spice, and covered with sugar all sparkling as ice," she enunciated carefully.

As she finished the verse, her father stormed up to the

house, grabbed her mother by the arm, and dragged her inside. Violet watched from the doorway as her mother stood rigidly, accepting her husband's blows placidly.

"Why are you just standing there, woman? Do something," her father yelled.

Her mother looked as if her mind had drifted off somewhere far away. No matter how hard her husband hit her, she remained unmoved. With one last slap, he left.

"Why didn't you fight back, like he said?" Violet asked as she slid up beside her mother once her father had disappeared.

Violet's mother said nothing.

"Why didn't you fight back?"

"Because, I'm not supposed to."

"Why?"

"Don't you remember what I told you? I'm the woman. Women are not supposed to fight back. We're supposed to take whatever our husbands give us. We're supposed to support them and make them feel good when they're feeling low. We're supposed to make them feel like men. That's what my mother did. And that's what she told me I would have to do. Tears and lashes are all a part of married life. You're much too young to understand now. You'll understand it all when you're older."

"Maybe your mother was wrong."

"Mothers are never wrong."

That night, alone in bed, Violet prayed.

"Please Lord, please make me strong enough so one day I can hurt my father as much as he has hurt my mother. And please don't let mothers always be right."

• • •

"The moon must now sleep," Bernice said as she smiled and concluded the first part of her new story. Eva and Ava applauded.

"That was wonderful, Ma, just wonderful," Ava cheered.

"Yeah," Eva echoed.

Bernice stood up and curtsied. Her daughters normally praised her after each story, but they had never applauded before. Bernice was touched.

"I'm taking a little bow now," Bernice announced.

Eva and Ava applauded even louder.

CHAPTER 3

The Story of Rose's Birth

THE NEXT DAY the temperature had reached record highs.

"I don't want you two dropping like flies out there, so you better stay put," Bernice ordered after breakfast.

"Aw, it's not that bad, Ma," Eva insisted.

"What are you talking about? It's hotter than hell out there. The heat's got my head pounding like a hammer," Bernice replied. "That heat will be the death of you, you hear me? Mark my words. And if you two die, then what would I do?"

Not wanting to argue, Eva and Ava conceded.

While Bernice spent the day in bed, nursing her heat-induced headache, the twins busied themselves.

"We'll go bake something," Eva commanded, as she waddled toward the kitchen.

Ava followed behind.

The kitchen was a fair-sized room, large enough to hold

a small dining-room table and four sturdy chairs. The stained linoleum floor, porcelain sink, and lopsided drawers showed their age.

"Sugar cookies, that's what I feel like making."

"Why do you always get to decide, Eva?"

"Because you never have an opinion, Ava."

"Sure I do."

"Okay, then what do you want to make?"

"I don't know. It doesn't matter. I guess we can make sugar cookies."

"You see!" Eva exclaimed.

Their hands, noses, and tongues guided them as they gathered all the necessary items.

Measurements were gauged by fingers and all uncertainties were resolved by taste. They had been baking on their own for more than twenty years now. It would have been longer had it not been for their mother.

"What if you burn yourself or cause a fire. Just let me do it," Bernice had always insisted.

"How are we going to learn to do anything, if you always do it for us? We're blind, Ma, we're not crippled, you know," Eva had argued.

"I guess you're right about that. Your eyes may not work, but your hands and legs are just fine. Thank God for that."

After the dough was mixed, Eva rolled it out, while Ava used a glass dipped in flour to cut out perfect circles. The two hummed as they worked. It was Eva's job to grease the cookie sheets and place them into the oven. Once the cookies were baked, Eva removed the sheets from the oven and Ava scooped the cookies onto plates and into containers.

"Watch out, you clumsy ox. Those things don't grow on trees you know," Eva scolded when Ava dropped a cookie.

Ignoring her sister, Ava picked it up and popped it into her mouth.

"I hope it burns your tongue."

The twins made dozens of cookies and gobbled down a large number in the process.

"Now we'll listen to some music," Eva commanded.

Ava agreed without protest. Music always came after baking, the same way dessert always preceded story time. These routines were followed religiously, like steps to an endless waltz.

Eva and Ava's room resembled their mother's in its simplicity. There was a double bed, which they had shared since they were girls. Above the bed there was a picture of Jesus. A dresser stood against the wall. The battered record player sat on top. Beside it was their tiny, treasured collection of albums that had once belonged to their father. All were famous operatic performances, by Italian composers, each more tragic and melancholy than the next.

Eva went directly to the turntable. She felt each album's jacket and selected the one she wanted while Ava ate cookies on the bed.

"You know, we're not supposed to be eating in here," Ava said as she stuffed her face.

"Oh, pish posh—never mind that. We'll just clean up the crumbs afterward."

The second the needle touched down, a somber operatic voice filled the room. Ava smiled. Her sister had selected, *La Bohème*. It was her favorite.

Che gelida manina,
se la lasci riscaldar.
Cercar che giova?
Al buio non si trova.

The sisters knew all the arias by heart. They had never received any formal training, but both had exceptional voices and were perfect mimics. Their mother had told them that God had given them their talent to make up for their unattractiveness. The scratches and bumps of the overplayed records reassured them that they were not growing old alone.

The twins, reclined and sang along until they started to feel drowsy. When they drifted off the music was left to play.

That evening the twins were already squished together in their seat, anxiously waiting, when Bernice emerged from the kitchen with the dessert tray.

"You need some help with that, Ma?" Eva offered.

"No, no, I'm fine. I just got to take my time is all." She was thankful that her daughters couldn't see that her sweat was trickling onto the cookies.

"Are you going to tell us about the other girl tonight, Ma?" Ava asked eagerly.

"Yes."

"We're listening," Eva said, grinning.

Bernice was so eager to begin that she started telling the story right away, skipping the customary ceremony altogether. The twins took note of their mother's digression. If it didn't trouble her that she had just changed a more-than-fifty-year-old tradition, then it didn't bother them.

• • •

In a quaint Western European town, night had fallen and it had been threatening to rain. A scrawny little mouse of a woman was sitting, nervously embroidering. Her unborn child jutted out of her like a torpedo about to explode. The tightness across her abdomen told her that it wouldn't be long.

I don't think you should go to the track tonight. It wouldn't be a good idea with the rain coming and all. Why don't you stay in and read? You haven't read in so long and I know you really enjoy it. She rehearsed quietly as she prepared to face her husband who was almost four times her size. He had lost his job as a lawyer because of his gambling addiction, but he still hadn't stopped. His days were spent lumbering around the house barking orders and complaints to his wife.

"Why is this shirt so wrinkly? Iron it better."

"How come there's no meat in this stew? This cabbage is overcooked!"

His evenings were spent at the racetrack or the poetry society, where he gave the impression that he was the gentlest man alive. His young wife's shattered nerves and black-and-blue bruises told a different story. She had been forced to work as a maid to support the family.

"Are you looking for something in particular?" the wife asked as her husband rummaged through the closet.

"Where the hell is my lucky hat?"

"It's back there somewhere. Would you like me to find it for you?"

He stood up with the brown-feathered fedora on his head.

"Oh you found it," she said, trying to hide her disappointment.

He took his trench coat and flung it over his shoulders. "Why are you staring at me? Can I help you with something?"

She said nothing.

"What, cat got your tongue? Out with it."

She began to tremble.

"What the hell do you want?"

"Must…must you go tonight?"

"What do you mean must I go?"

"But…the baby might come tonight, and it's going to rain."

"Baby, smaby," he mocked. "That baby is not coming tonight. I guarantee you that. Don't you know anything? Babies are never born when it rains. You silly woman, you're just worrying yourself about nothing."

"I guess you're right," she said with a downward glance.

It was already very dark outside. A slight drizzle had just begun.

"You see! Here it comes." He stepped out of the house.

Inside the womb, the baby wriggled about. She had never liked how her mother always accepted her father's every word for the truth. So to remind her mother that she was neither silly nor stupid and to show her father that babies came any time they pleased, even when it rained, she decided to be born that very night.

A sharp clap of thunder startled the young wife. As she rushed about closing all of the windows in a panic, she began to feel her belly constrict more forcefully. She doubled over in pain with the next loud clash. It was clear that the contractions were increasing with the intensity of the downpour.

When tears started to well up in her eyes, she quickly wiped them away.

"No time for that now. Don't you do that, you hear me?" Taking in a deep breath, she calmed herself and grabbed the small suitcase that she had had the good sense to pack days earlier. With her raincoat and a sturdy umbrella in tow, she set out for the hospital on foot.

The storm had knocked out all the power and left the street dark and deserted. The only source of illumination was supplied by brief flashes of lightning. Heavy rain hammered the sidewalk, and strong winds blew all sorts of debris every which way. She cringed as a tiny kitten flew by and let out an agonizing meow. The wretched creature's misfortune mirrored her own.

The labor pains grew more unbearable with every step she took, but she soldiered on. Holding on tightly to the suitcase and the flapping umbrella, she prayed that the baby would wait.

"*You'll be fine. Don't worry, you'll make it,*" a tiny voice encouraged her from her abdomen. "*You'll be fine.*"

When her water broke, she took it for a rush of rain, but the growing pain in the small of her back told her otherwise. Just as she got a glimpse of the hospital, a flash of lightning felled a large tree in front of her, and a violent burst of wind carried away her umbrella. There was no choice but to climb over the tree trunk. When she didn't think she could move another inch, the voice returned.

"*Go ahead. Don't stop now. You're almost there.*"

At the hospital, looking as if she had just been spit out by the same whale that swallowed up poor Jonah, she mumbled with her last ounce of energy, "Help me," before collapsing to the floor.

A nurse and orderly ran to her side. Just as they were trying to revive her, a baby girl slid out. With her, the child brought the strong scent of roses. The fragrance revived the mother and floated through the hospital, making it smell like a rose garden in full bloom.

"Do you smell that, sister?" the orderly asked the nurse. "It smells like...like flowers...like roses."

"Don't smell anything but ether," replied the nurse, who lacked imagination. "Let's get this woman and her child off the floor."

The young mother believed that her daughter was the most beautiful creature she had ever seen. She thought about naming the child Rain, after the torrential conditions she had been born in, but decided instead on Rose, after the noticeable fragrance that had accompanied her into the world.

The new mother was concerned about her husband's absence, but baby Rose was pleased by it. One particular conversation months earlier had told her everything she needed to know about the man.

"Just get rid of the damn thing," he had hollered.

"How could you say such a thing?" her mother murmured back timidly.

"What did you say?"

"I...I just asked, 'with what money?'"

"Just sell that ring of yours," he snapped back.

"You want me to give up my wedding ring? I can't do that."

"Why, not? You might as well. I already got rid of mine."

"I just can't."

Rose knew that if her mother had not defied her husband that one time, she would have never been born.

Rose's mother took full advantage of her five-day stay in the hospital. In the crowded ward, among the cheerful cackling of new mothers and the cries of newborns, she was able to doze more soundly and peacefully than she had in a very long time. Baby Rose didn't give her any trouble. She just lay quietly and waited patiently to be fed, washed, and changed.

On their return home, Rose and her mother were greeted by an angry tirade.

"Do you know what I've eaten in the last five days?" Rose's father blurted out as he held up his five sausage-like fingers.

You could have eaten those fat fingers of yours, Rose's mother wanted to say. Knowing exactly what would follow, she rushed the baby into the next room and deposited her into the bassinet.

"Answer me! Do you know what I had to eat?"

"No, I'm sorry, I don't," she replied on her return.

"Stale bread and butter. Did you hear what I said? Mouldy bread and rancid butter. Now what kind of food is that? Am I in prison or something? How is a man my size supposed to survive on that rubbish? I'm sure those maggots in jail eat better than that."

"I'll go and pick something up and get some proper food into you, okay?" Rose's mother offered. "Ah, but maybe in the meantime, the baby...maybe you could go and take a look at her. She's so pretty. I think she looks a lot like your mother."

"Does she have any food to give me?"

"No, but..."

"Then I don't want to see her. If I was interested in seeing her, I would have gone to the hospital, now, wouldn't I? Don't you think? Use your God-forsaken brains for once."

"Well, I just thought, since she looked so much like your mother, you would want to see her. I…I named her Rose. Wasn't that your mother's middle name?"

"I really don't give a rat's ass what you named her. I just want some real food." He began to look around the living room as if he had misplaced something.

She followed his gaze until it stopped at the mantle.

"Where are the radio and that vase my grandmother gave me?" she asked, pointing to the empty spaces.

There was no reply.

"What happened to them?" she repeated.

"I needed them."

"You mean you gambled them away."

"I said I needed them!"

"But they weren't even worth anything. Why did you even bother?"

"Because it was a sure thing."

If it was so sure, you would have won, she wanted to say, but instead said, "I…I was thinking that maybe you could go back…go and ask your boss for your job back. Now that the baby's here, he might consider it."

"You were thinking what?" he asked as he approached her.

She stood frozen as she anticipated what he would do next.

"I just thought…"

"You need to stop thinking. You don't understand anything, do you?" He pushed his finger into her temple.

"I'm sorry." She cowered. "I didn't mean anything by it...." Her voice quivered.

"You don't have any idea how I feel, do you? How am I supposed to go in there holding my head up when my wife has been working as a maid for half the goddamn office? You tell me how. How am I supposed to do that? Tell me!" he shouted, directly in front of her.

"I don't know." She wiped his saliva from her face. "But I think—" Before she was able to continue he grabbed her shoulders.

"You don't think anything, you understand me? You've done enough thinking already. So just shut up—now. Just shut the hell up!"

He shoved her chest and sent her down with a thump. She looked up at him, dejected. Her eyes pleaded, *Please don't.* He responded with a kick.

In the next room, Rose was wide awake and upset. She had heard it all before and had had enough. She shook the bassinet with her minuscule body. Then, with all the power that her tiny, five-day-old lungs would allow her, she yelled, "Why don't you just stop!"

On the other side of the wall, no one heard. Her father was too busy throwing blows and her mother receiving them.

It wasn't until months later that Rose's father finally took the time to look at her. He was pleased by what he saw. Rose did remind him of his mother. From that moment onward, his heart began to soften toward her. Regular interactions where he spoke softly to her and read poetry followed.

One afternoon when Rose was five years old, she came home from kindergarten and was greeted by her father. He was wearing the most cheerful of expressions.

"Are you okay, Papa?"

"I'm great, darling," he said. "Look what I found." He held up a book with a frayed cover.

"What is it?"

"It's my Keats. I found it in the attic this morning. Shall I read you some?"

"You want to read it now? We haven't had supper yet."

"But I've been waiting the whole day to read it to you. Let's sit down and read it now, why don't we?"

Rose wasn't sure if her father's upbeat mood was something that she should welcome or fear.

"Where's Mama?"

"She's still at work. We can read a little before she gets back." He twitched with excitement. The giddiness did not suit someone of his size.

"Okay, I guess," Rose conceded.

By the time she had settled in her usual place on the rug in front of his desk, he had already taken his place behind the desk and begun.

> My heart aches, and a drowsy numbness pains
> My sense, as though of hemlock I had drunk,
> Or emptied some dull opiate to the drains
> One minute past, and Lethe-wards had sunk:
> 'Tis not through envy of thy happy lot,
> But being too happy in thine happiness.

"This was my favorite poem when I was a boy."

Rose had never once pictured her father as a boy. "What kind of boy were you, Papa?"

"A good one. A very good one."

"Were you good in school?"

"I was at the top of my class," he answered with a smile. "The teacher always called on me first. He used to say I was going to be a great orator one day."

He resumed reading.

The man behind the desk seemed so different when he read. He didn't appear to be same man who constantly berated and harmed his wife. The love-laced words of his books also didn't fit with the foul language he normally used. Rose could never reconcile his two opposing sides. She accepted and appreciated the lover of poetry and hated his violence. She had hoped that he would one day find it in his heart to share his gentler side with her mother, but he never did.

• • •

"My God, that one was a real bastard wasn't he?" Eva yelled just as Bernice finished.

"No need to swear or bring God into it," Bernice insisted. She wiped some sweat from her brow and got up to stretch. "He's no different from the rest of them." She placed her head directly in front of the fan. "Every single last one of them's the same." She grabbed a large piece of chocolate cake and shoved it down her throat.

"Was our father anything like that man?" Ava asked tentatively. She knew the subject was a sensitive one.

"What's that?" Bernice said, coughing up a piece of cake. "I hope you're not asking about that man again."

Ava didn't dare reply.

All she and her sister knew of their father was that he had

died when they were still toddlers. They didn't know what type of man he was or even what he looked like. Because of their mother's secrecy, they envisioned their own version of what he might have been like. The man of their imagination was a kind, sweet, older gentleman who wore flannel pajamas and read the daily newspaper while he smoked his pipe. He was a loving person who always greeted their mother with two kisses on her cheek and one on her forehead.

The twins' mission to find out about their father had much to do with their own sense of identity. They wanted to know where and what they had come from and what made them who they were. They wanted to understand where their talent for music had come from and why their temperaments were so different from their mother's. They wanted to know if twins or blindness ran in his family. Mostly, they were curious about what he had done to make their mother hate him so much.

The only actual details Bernice had shared had to do with the day of his death. She refused to tell them anything more. They had been told that he had woken up one cold December morning, repaired a leaky faucet, gone to the store to buy a bottle of milk, and had dropped dead on the sidewalk on his way home. This was all they knew.

The twins felt that if they kept bringing up the subject, eventually Bernice would give in. What they didn't know was that Bernice had every intention of taking all of her secrets to the grave with her. For their part, Eva and Ava never let up. They established a nightly ritual, right after story time when they would make their plea.

"Please tell us more about our father."

"Please tell us about him."

"Please tell us."

"Please."

This was followed by what seemed to be an endless assault of "Please, Mother. Come on, Mother."

Bernice's response would always be the same: "Look, Chang and Eng, he's dead. There's nothing more to tell so just stop pestering me, alright?"

After each night of petitioning, the twins would lie in their bed and pray that their wish would be granted. Along with this prayer, they also asked God to allow them to lose their virginity. As fifty-three-year-old virgins, this was equally as important to them.

Bernice, alone in her bed, would pray that her daughters would just let sleeping dogs lie.

CHAPTER 4

A Trip to the Park

ON THE THURSDAY after Bernice started her new story, a slight breeze provided a temporary reprieve from the excessive heat of the previous days. The twins were thrilled. Now their mother couldn't prevent them from going outside. They couldn't wait to feel the intensity of the so-called cancer rays that their mother was always warning them about. Summer may not have been Bernice's favorite time of year, but for them it was like two whole months of Christmas mornings.

Some time around mid-July each year, everyone in their small community came out of hiding, creating a sudden eruption of activity. The commotion made the sisters feel as if they were a part of something bigger, even though their lives remained unchanged. Sounds became sharper and aromas more intense. They were like children; the weather made them want to head to the park.

Once they were dressed in their matching pink muumuus,

which their mother had laid out for them, they took turns
pulling back each other's tangled gray locks into two tight
ponytails. The final touch was a sprinkle of baby powder
down the cleavage.

While they sat putting on their Chinese slippers, Bernice
shouted to them from her room.

"Don't stay out too long. That sun will fry you!"

"Yes mother," they chorused.

In the kitchen they grabbed a handful of salted crackers
and wobbled as quickly as they could out the front door.

By the time they reached downstairs, they had already
finished their snack and had decided to play the smell game;
a summer pastime that they had played since they were children. The rules of the game were simple. The first one to
properly identify a new scent scored a point.

"Dog piss," Ava yelled loudly the minute they stepped
outside the building. Her sister stopped and sniffed.

"That's not dog piss. It's old man's piss, Ava. It probably
belongs to that old wino who sleeps in the stairs sometimes."
She giggled.

The walk to the park was effortless because it was a
straight line. Since they had walked the same path hundreds
of times, their feet knew the way by heart. No one paid much
attention to them, since they were a regular fixture in the
community, no different from the abandoned cars.

Their ears were bombarded with the pounding footsteps
of children and lively conversations.

"Man, I told you not to touch my bike. How many times
do I have to tell you not to touch my things, fool?"

"Did you hear about what happened to Miss Munger
down the street? Found her dead, they did."

"Wait up, wait up will you? I said, wait up!"

"Ricky, get in this house right now. Did you hear me? Right now!"

The twins turned around when they heard the clicking of a lopsided gait accompanied by the smell of fresh cloves.

"Mrs. Misic," the twins said together.

The woman with the wooden leg lived in their building and had known them since they were babies.

"Hi, Mrs. Misic," Ava said.

"Hi," Mrs. Misic replied and then went on her way.

Even though their conversations rarely went beyond these monosyllabic greetings, they had always been curious about her false leg.

"How the crippled woman lost her leg is her own business, so just never mind," their mother had told them.

"Rat shit and sour milk," Eva shouted as they walked by a row of boarded-up buildings. The next block where a liquor store stood next to a vacant lot didn't give off any distinct smells apart from a general garbage odor.

"And the soup of the day is minestrone," Ava said sticking her head out toward the road to smell the deli across the street.

"And the cook boiled up some cabbage and baked some peanut butter cookies earlier on," her sister added. The restaurant smells had always been their favorite.

"Do you smell that? It's your boyfriend—the Stickman!" Eva teased.

Ava inhaled and coughed.

"Yeah, you're right. It's him, alright. We're already here." She adjusted her dress and smoothed back her hair.

The Stickman was a tall, skinny creature who looked like a praying mantis. He was the neighborhood drug dealer who could be found in the exact same location year-round. Of all the scents the twins knew by heart, his was the most pungent. It was a vile combination of body odor, and wet dog, with a slight hint of skunk. For years the twins had used his stench as a marker. They knew that the park was just two blocks away whenever they got a whiff of him.

"How you ladies doing today?" the Stickman asked in a deep baritone.

Eva spat and hurried off, while Ava slowed down and lingered.

"We're fine. How are you?" Ava replied, smiling brightly as she fantasized about being alone with him.

"It's not too hot for you, is it?" he asked.

"No, not at all. It's perfect. A perfect day," she stuttered.

"Nice pink dresses you two have on today. Show off your figures." He chuckled.

She missed the sarcasm in his voice. "Thank you."

Eva yanked her sister's arm.

"Well, you have a nice day, you hear?" Ava called.

"Same to you, honey," he replied.

Ava was elated. "Did you hear what he called me?" she beamed.

"Yeah, yeah, he called you honey. So what? That's what he calls anything that goes by in a dress."

The park was an unattractive mess of concrete. There were four green wooden benches—all missing one or more rungs— a dilapidated swing set, a short metal slide that turned into a frying pan in the summer heat, and one wobbly teeter-totter. There were no trees, shade, or flowers to speak of. A patch of dried, scraggly crab apple shrubs provided the only greenery.

The twins walked directly into the middle of a raucous balloon fight. Small groups of kids ran about with loads of water-filled balloons folded up in their stretched-out T-shirts.

"You better fucking watch out. I'm going to get you, you little piece of shit!"

"Fuck you."

"No, fuck you." They shouted back and forth.

One balloon flew toward Ava and struck her on her left thigh. A loud roar of laughter followed. Ava didn't notice; her head was still in the clouds. Eva reached down and touched her sister's dress. It was soaked.

"Why don't you go and take your goddamn game somewhere else. You see what you did, you little brats?"

"Shut your fucking hole, you big fat pig," one scrappy kid yelled back. He threw another balloon and ran away. The balloon broke on the ground directly in front of an elderly man who sat listening to a news report on his transistor radio.

"You better run," Eva jeered.

"Awful fuckers," the old man muttered. "No home training." He smelled of Old Spice and Craven A cigarettes.

Ava lifted the now-clingy garment from her leg.

"It's okay. It's not so bad. Don't worry, Eva. The sun will dry it up. Let's just go sit down. And you should really watch that mouth of yours. What would Ma say?"

"She's not here so she can't say anything."

The twins walked to their usual spot and turned their attention to the fuzzy sounds of the portable radio.

It is alleged that the suspect arrived home to find her husband in bed with their neighbor. She reportedly left the room and returned with one of her husband's collectible swords, then

proceeded to stab him. The witness said they heard some very
loud cries for help…

Eva and Ava were engrossed. Since Bernice had thrown
out their radio, the park was the only place where they could
still hear the news.

"War, war, war—all they talk about is war. I don't need
to hear anything more about any more wars and all that
noise. My goodness—that's not music. It's all just a bunch of
racket," Bernice had yelled before flinging the radio down the
garbage chute.

The sisters weren't at all pleased with their mother's
impulsive act. They could listen to endless broadcasts about
war or any other subject, for that matter. They were fascinated
by it all. The news bulletins reminded them that there was a
world beyond their five short blocks. It helped them feel less
isolated. And when they heard the soaring disco sounds of
Barry White or the infectious rhythms of the Bee Gees that
their mother so despised, their spirits were lifted. They felt as
if they could just get up and dance, but they never did.

As the twins took in the news, which competed with the
sounds of overexcited children and cheerful birds, something
else got their attention. It was the faint scent of roses. Their
heads turned simultaneously as slow footsteps brought the
fragrance closer. It reminded them of their mother's story
from the night before. They listened as the person took a seat
beside them. The babbling baby confirmed that it was their
neighbor.

The mother was repeating the baby's gurgling sounds
back to him. It sounded as if they were consoling one another.

The twins were captivated—they could have listened to
the jabbering all day.

CHAPTER 5
The Story of Bernice's Gift

WHILE THE TWINS were out, Bernice took the opportunity to clean. A full week hadn't passed since she last cleaned, but it didn't deter her.

"Cleanliness is next to Godliness and only God can help me keep those filthy pests away," she would say about the roaches and rodents that infested the building. She collected some old rags, the broom, mop, and a bucket of water spiked with vinegar and began in the twins' room.

"Why does it always smell so musty, stale, and lonely in here," she said on entering the room. She went directly to the window, which wasn't a part of her regular clean up. When she saw the amount of dirt that had accumulated, she shook her head.

"Filthy, just filthy."

The rag blackened with debris as she took periodic glances outside. The cloudless sky reminded her of the ocean.

When she lifted the covers off the bed, crumbs fell to the floor.

"How many times do I have to tell them."

As she stripped the sheets, she thought about the many tales she had told her daughters and how they had sometimes questioned their origins.

I told you two, I don't make up the stories I tell you. They all come from my dreams.

All of them?

Every single last one of them.

To settle the argument, Bernice told them one of the few stories about herself.

• • •

The summer when I was about six years old, I decided I was going to do something that I'd seen my older brother Charles do a thousand times before. I was going to climb the biggest tallest tree I could find in the woods. When I found it, I shook my fist at it and said, "You big lug, you better watch out because I'm going to clobber you."

The tree, which wasn't accustomed to people speaking to him like that (especially bony little girls like me), replied, "I'd like to see you try."

"Okay, just watch me," I jeered as I started up the tree.

"You better be careful little girl, you're going to hurt yourself."

The tree continued to mock me the whole way, but I didn't listen to a word of it. When I reached the highest branch, I realized two things. I was afraid of heights and I had no idea how I was going to get down.

I panicked and closed my eyes and tried to stay as still as possible. When my eyes were opened again, I looked down, and my head started spinning. The dizziness intensified, then I blacked out and fell. My brother found me an hour later.

While I lay unconscious in the hospital, I heard my mother's, the nurses', and my brother's prayers. Charles's were my favorite. They made me chuckle.

"Oh heavenly Father, please don't let my little sister die," he said. "Please let her live. If you let her live, I promise that I won't touch or interfere with myself for a whole year."

While I remained in a coma I had the most vivid dreams I had ever had. Most of them were from the past. I saw my parents being born and growing up. I saw how happy they were when they first met and how quickly that happiness slipped away. I also saw the lives of people in far-off lands. Their births, deaths, and all of the mundane activities in between were displayed for me. This was the most confusing part. I didn't know why I was being shown these things.

When I woke up, I remembered every single detail of those dreams. From that time onward, I continued to have the same type of visions. Every night I was taken somewhere and shown another day in some else's life.

• • •

By the time Bernice had finished cleaning her daughters' room, she was so pooped that she decided to leave the rest of the cleaning for another day and took a nap instead.

After dinner that evening, she rested in her room. The cooler temperatures that had allowed the twins to venture outdoors had not provided her with much relief. While sitting on the foot of her bed, she exhaled and examined her wrinkles in the mirror. Stretching back the loose skin, she tried to recall a time when the lines didn't exist. The attempt only made her look like a fish. As she ran her fingers through her gray split ends, she thought about the inevitable. She had been thinking about it with more and more regularity. At her age she knew that death could arrive unexpectedly at any time. It had a way of doing that. Her own mother had died very young—too young. She worried about her girls and what would become of them when she was gone. She wondered if she had done right by them and if her coddling had been too much. *What benefit,* she thought, *would it be to be so isolated and so dependent on her? What benefit was there to being all alone in the world?* The telling of the new story was liberating for her. It was a way of getting closer to all that she had been avoiding.

"What's taking you? We're waiting, Ma. Come on. You said that you would be right out," Ava yelled from the living room.

"Hold your horses, I'll be right there," Bernice shouted back. She paused to take in a deep breath and got up.

"It's about time. It took you long enough. What were you doing in there all that time?" Eva asked. The twins had been busy munching on some pumpkin pie.

"So, who was eating in bed?" Bernice asked as she took a seat.

"No one," the twins answered together.

"Whoever did, make sure you don't do it again. Otherwise you're just inviting those pests to sleep with you."

The twins could tell that Bernice wasn't feeling like her usual self.

"What were you doing in there so long?" Eva asked.

"It doesn't matter what I was doing. Just let me get to the story." She sighed, and took a swig of vodka. Once her whistle was wet, she wiped her mouth and began.

• • •

One day when Violet was seven, she was in her room having a pretend tea party, when she was overcome with a sudden feeling of anger. The feeling confused her. The next day, as she hid and watched her father beating her mother in the front yard, she felt a strange surge of gladness. Again she was baffled.

What she didn't know was that her mixed-up feelings belonged to another little girl who was a thousand miles, a hemisphere, and a whole ocean away. By some miracle these emotions were sent through the heavens to her.

The anger Rose felt when her father showed his cruel side traveled across the sky and became Violet's anger. The transmission also went the other way. Violet's emotions also became Rose's. Each girl came up with her own theory to explain what was happening.

Rose was in the tub gazing up at the pregnant moon in the night sky, when she suddenly felt an unexpected jolt of guilt. Right there, she decided that the source of all her odd feelings was a little girl in the moon.

After that night, she spent many hours peering up at the moon, hoping to get a glimpse of her little friend. But she never did.

"Are you there, Letty?" she would whisper and place her

hands on the window pane. She had given her imaginary friend the name Violet, but called her Letty for short.

"Can you hear me? I know you're sad. Sometimes I get sad too. But it's okay. You don't have to worry. I'm here. I'll always be here."

Violet came to her own conclusion as she sat outside Mrs. Gump's shop sucking on some cherry-flavored shaved ice one afternoon. As the red syrup dripped down her hand, she imagined that she had a twin sister who had been lost and was trying to find her way back home. At night, she whispered to her invisible twin as she touched a spot next to her pillow.

"Can I tell you something? You promise not to get mad? Sometimes you make me feel like a puppet or something— like you're a ghost inside of me. Why do you do that? Like right now I'm feeling like something terrible just happened but I don't even know what it is. Why are you making me feel these things?"

At that very moment Rose had just found her father sprawled out on the kitchen floor. It looked as if he wasn't breathing.

"Mama, Mama, come quick!" Rose yelled in a panic.

When her mother saw her father, she gasped. She stepped cautiously toward the body, knelt down, and placed her hand in front of his mouth. Then she picked up his wrist. It was limp. There was no pulse. She nudged his shoulder. Still no response. She jumped up and started darting around the room. Her eyes remained glued to the body.

"Don't just lie there. Get up, you stupid ape," she yelled.

Rose watched on in terror.

"He's not getting up, Rosie."

"Is he dead, Mama?"

"I think so."

A sinister look came over her mother's face. She marched toward the lifeless body and kicked it and kicked and kicked it some more. When she had exhausted herself, she climbed over her dead husband's engorged stomach and stood there proudly, looking as if she had just harpooned Moby Dick.

She smiled, then the smile became a giggle. Soon she was laughing uncontrollably. Rose was transfixed. Her mother's behavior both frightened and thrilled her.

• • •

Ava sat forward in her seat, "Did she do it? Did she kill him?"

"Hush now, let me continue," Bernice replied.

"Just tell us."

"No, she didn't kill him. He died from untreated liver disease, okay? Can I go on now?"

• • •

The morning after Rose's father died, Violet found her mother sitting on the ground outside with fresh wounds.

"What happened this time?" Violet asked. The terrifying feelings of the night before were still with her.

"All I said was good morning, darling."

"Where is he now?"

"Long gone."

"Where?"

"Work I guess, or maybe down by the—"

Not waiting to hear the rest, Violet took off, leaving a trail of dust behind her.

"Where are you going in your night clothes child? You didn't even wash your mouth," her mother yelled after her.

"I'm going to get him," Violet hollered back.

She walked in a huff down a lane, across a dirt road and up a hill to the cane field.

"You see my father? Is he here?" Violet asked Mr. Highliger, who stood idly eating an apple.

He scrutinized Violet with his beady eyes. "I guess you forget your manners with your clothes. Where's the 'good morning' little girl?"

"Is he here or not?"

"Today's his day off."

"You know where he is?"

"Can't say that I do, but you could always check down by the rum shop. He could also—"

Violet was off again.

She caught a glimpse of her father through the window as she approached the lime green shack. He sat propped up by his elbows, with an empty glass in front of him, staring at nothing in particular. The sight of him boiled her blood. She clenched her fist, readied herself like a bull about to charge, and stampeded toward him. Tiny puffs of smoke came out of her ears and her nostrils as she got closer.

Her father and the owner of the shop, looked at her with expressions that said "What are you doing here child? A rum shop is no place for a little girl."

Violet shot back a look that could have killed Goliath and charmed Medusa. The owner was mesmerized. Her father was unable to speak or move and was having difficulty breathing. The longer she stared at him, the more constricted his air passage became. He felt as if her hands were wedged around his neck. But her toothpick-like arms were still dangling by her side.

Grabbing his chest, Violet's father gasped for air. The owner stood by and did nothing. He had seen his customer in far worse states.

As Violet stood staring down at her father, she wished him dead. But just as it appeared that he was about to pass out, a fly landed on her eyelid, disturbing her concentration. When she raised her hand to shoo it away, her father took this chance to catch his breath.

Seeing her father breathe normally again disappointed Violet. Had she been able to will his heart to stop she would have done just that, but to her dismay, it continued to beat.

• • •

"That Violet was one tough cookie," Eva said.

"Yeah, she wasn't afraid of anything. I wish I was more like her," Ava commented.

"You can be brave when you want to be, Ava. You remember that time you, you…" Eva said encouragingly, waiting for her mother to jump in.

Bernice remained silent.

"What time? What did I do?" Ava asked anxiously.

Eva didn't know what to make of their mother's silence.

"Oh yeah, the time you cornered that mouse in the bathroom and killed it. You alright, Ma?"

"Of course, I'm alright. What could be the matter with me?"

"Are you thinking about something, Ma? You seem extra quiet," Ava added.

"I'm not thinking about a thing. I'm just a little tired is all. It's way past my bedtime, anyway. I think, I'll just go to bed."

The twins listened as Bernice shuffled slowly to her room and closed the door.

"I think there's something wrong with her," Eva whispered.

"How do you know?"

"Because she didn't eat a single one of our cookies," Eva said.

"You're right, she didn't. I wonder what's bothering her. She usually cleans off the plate."

"You two should go to bed too. Remember, we have to get up early tomorrow," Bernice yelled from her room.

"Okay, Ma."

"We're just going to tidy a little first."

"Okay, alright, good night and sweet dreams," Bernice yelled.

"You too, Ma."

CHAPTER 6
The Story of Eva and Ava's Birth

THE NEXT DAY was laundry day. While Bernice did her regular laundry once a week, she insisted on washing the blankets, cushions, pillows, curtains and anything else that could be crammed into a washing machines, once a month. This made for many loads and a long day in the laundry room. At six-thirty a.m., one hour earlier than their usual waking time, Bernice tapped on her daughters' bedroom door to remind them that they had to get up.

They sorted, and jammed everything into nine large garbage bags. When they left the apartment, they looked like a set of drowsy Santa Clauses parading with their shiny sacks flung over their shoulders.

The basement was dark and smelt of funky feet. Most of the area was taken up by storage cages that looked like medieval dungeons. The laundry room was bright and cheerful in contrast. Two rows of machines were separated by a long counter that was used mainly for folding.

Bernice went right to work. She filled the coin slots with four dimes and set the temperature. Then went down the row pouring soap powder and arranging the garbage bags.

"Here, Ava, put these in here," Eva ordered.

"These are whites, right, Ma?" Ava asked Bernice, as she began stuffing the clothes into a machine.

"No, no, no, they're not white. They're colored," Bernice wobbled over and snatched the bag.

"Eva, told me to put them in there."

"Do you always have to listen to everything she says? All you do is follow her along. You've been doing that since birth, you know. Always second, always behind her."

"Yes, we know the story, Ma," Ava said.

"We've heard it millions of times," Eva added.

The story always came to mind when they were in the basement, since they were almost born there. They had been told the story for the very first time just minutes after their birth in their mother's still-trembling arms.

● ● ●

It was October 17, 1917 and me and my big belly were downstairs fumbling through the storage locker, looking for God knows what, when low and behold, there was water all over my leather shoes. All I could think was, why here, why now? I didn't want to give birth in that awful place. So I rushed up the stairs out onto the street, and hailed the first taxi I saw without bothering to tell your father. I didn't have a penny on me so I was hoping that the driver would take pity. I pretended to be in more pain than I actually was, and the poor bugger brought it hook, line, and sinker.

"I'm here to deliver my twins," I announced when I saw my doctor. The pock-marked doctor and his nurses gawked at me like I was crazy.

"Mrs. Archer, we've been over this so many times before. You're having one baby, not two," the doctor insisted. You see he had mistaken your synchronized heart beats for one.

"Oh ye of little faith, watch and see," I said to myself.

In the labor room, I grunted, pushed, and grunted some more and then there you were, Eva. You were the first. You had your work cut out for you making your way through the dark mysterious tunnel. By the time you saw the light, you were bushed. The doctor held you by your feet and said, "Mrs. Archer, you are the proud mother of a baby girl."

"Wait Doctor, the other one is about to come out."

"I told you Mrs. Archer—" He stopped and felt my abdomen.

"Wait a second, there *is* another one there." He realized I wasn't crazy after all.

So while they cleaned and checked Eva to make sure she had all her digits and no tail, Ava made her descent. Since Eva had cleared the path already, all Ava had to do was glide right out. She arrived exactly fifteen minutes after Eva, with a wide-eyed, all-knowing expression that said, "How could you not know that there were two of us?"

• • •

"What are you daydreaming about?" Bernice asked Ava.

"Oh, nothing."

"Whatever it is. It's making you move slower than molasses in winter," Bernice joked. She took over and pushed the last items into the machine. Then she arranged three of the heavy metal chairs in one neat row.

"Come sit down, you two. The chairs are over here," she announced.

Right away, Bernice began to tap idly on the arm of the chair.

"Maybe you should have brought along your knitting," Eva suggested.

"I know, but it's too late for that now."

"What part of the story were you going to tell us tonight?" Ava asked.

"Does Rose meet the moon girl, and does Violet talk with her twin again?" Eva asked.

Bernice shook her head and smiled coyly.

"Better."

"Better?"

"How better? What do you mean, better?"

"Romance," Bernice replied.

"Romance!" Ava repeated enthusiastically. She immediately thought of the Stickman in a bathtub full of bubbles.

"But they're still kids, Ma," Eva said.

"They're much older in the next part of the story. Adolescents."

"Ah, adolescents," Ava repeated.

Eva shushed her sister. "How old?" she asked.

"Seventeen."

"Seventeen. That's a good age," Ava said.

"Yes it is," Eva agreed.

The twins were excited because their mother hardly ever broached the subject of love.

"So, you're really going to talk about IT?" Ava asked.

"Yes, can you two handle that?"

"Oh, of course we can handle it. It's just all so new and different."

"I can definitely handle it, Ma," Ava added eagerly.

"Do you want to hear it now?" Bernice offered.

"You mean right this minute?"

"Right here, in the laundry room, Ma? We don't have to wait until tonight?"

"No, you don't have to wait, unless you want to."

"No, no," Eva and Ava shouted together.

"I see the moon," Ava began.

"Oh we don't need to do all of that anymore. I'll just begin," Bernice interrupted.

"No problem, Ma."

The twins forced their fleshy backs into the chairs and gave Bernice their full attention.

CHAPTER 7
Violet and Rose Blossom

A FEW WEEKS AFTER the incident in the rum shop, Violet had been listening to the pelts of rain on the tin roof as she watched her father's shadow moving about frantically in the bedroom. When he finally emerged, he was carrying a large burlap bag over his shoulder.

"Well, I'm off," he said, leaving the house. Violet was mystified.

On her mother's return, Violet relayed all of her father's unusual behavior. Her mother was just as confused.

They found the bedroom stripped bare of all of his belongings.

"He's gone? Just like that!" Violet's mother moaned. She was grief stricken.

"Don't worry, Mama. Everything will be alright." Violet tried her best to comfort her mother.

The following Sunday in church, Violet and her mother

sat behind and eavesdropped on two of their nosey neighbors.

"Did you see when that little piece of man marched out with his whole house on his back?" the first neighbor began.

"Yes, my dear. Do you know where he went?" the second asked. She cocked her head for the reply.

"Well, they say he found some fresh meat on the other side of the island over by Cleverly Way."

"Why, after all those years?"

"They say he was looking for more of a challenge."

"A challenge, how so?"

"Someone who fights back and doesn't sit still when he beats her."

"That man is a damn fool." The gossip sucked her teeth.

When Violet saw her mother's tears, she pulled out a handkerchief and tried to wipe her sadness away.

As a result of Violet's father's desertion and Rose's father's death, both girls entered their adolescence fatherless, living in homes free of violence. By that time, curves had replaced their boyish straight lines, and the two had transformed into beauties who attracted a string of admirers.

Douglas Weiss was the most tenacious of Rose's admirers. In the library, where she spent all of her spare time escaping the ordinariness of her life, he spied on her from behind the bookcases and traced her path, making sure to touch all the books that she had handled. He even went as far as following her home.

It took the shy guy almost a whole year, however, before he made his move.

"Hello, I'm Douglas Weiss," he said as he greeted her one day at the entrance of the library.

His hand trembled as he held it out to her.

She stared at him blankly.

"How do you do?" he stuttered.

She didn't know what to make of the puny, pock-marked man in front of her. His thinning hair and feminine shoulders weren't the least bit attractive.

As she tried to manoeuver her way around him, he kept shifting from side to side.

"Hello," she finally said.

He offered his hand once again, but she refused it.

"Nice to know you, Rose." He grinned.

"Do I know you?"

"Oh, kind of, I guess. I've seen you here in the library."

"How do you know my name?"

"I asked the librarian."

"Oh?"

"Of course, she didn't tell me right away. I had to ask more than once."

Rose was growing impatient. "Do you mind? Can I get by please?"

"Sure, sure, I just wanted to introduce myself and perhaps ask you for a coffee or tea or whatever you prefer."

"Sorry, I don't drink coffee or tea."

"Then milk. We can drink milk."

She tried to get pass him again.

"May I call on you this Sunday?"

It was exasperating. She began to feel like one of the Billy Goats Gruff.

"Sure, sure, you can call on me this Sunday. Do as you like," she finally conceded, believing he had no idea where she lived.

"That's wonderful, that's great. I'll be there three p.m. sharp." He was pleased with himself.

At three p.m. sharp the following Sunday, there was a faint knock on Rose's front door. Reading upstairs in her room, she sat up to listen.

"Oh, for me? How lovely!" she heard her mother exclaim.

"Rose, Rose! Can you please come down? There is someone here to see you."

"Who is it?"

"It's Douglas, Douglas Weiss. He says that you are expecting him."

Rose was dumbfounded. She couldn't believe that the troll had actually found her.

"Rose, come now, don't keep your guest waiting."

Rose had to pry herself out of bed.

Downstairs, she was greeted with the bizarre sight of the red-faced man dressed in a white suit. He stood awkwardly holding a large bouquet of yellow roses. Her mother held an identical bunch.

"Look at the beautiful flowers the young man brought," her mother said, smiling from ear to ear. "I've invited him for coffee."

"Oh, I'll be more than happy to drink milk," Douglas interjected.

"Milk? No, no, don't be silly. We'll drink coffee. We always have our coffee now. You've arrived at the perfect time."

Douglas handed Rose the flowers and Rose handed them off to her mother.

"Douglas tells me that he's studying to become a doctor, and his father is one of the biggest patrons of the university."

Rose's eyes were glued to the top of the staircase where she longed to escape.

"I guess I have to find some vases to put these gorgeous flowers in. Don't they smell heavenly, Rose? Take a seat, Douglas, I'll be right back with the coffee."

In her mother's absence, Rose did everything she could to avoid eye contact with Douglas. The situation was unbearable.

"Please, help yourself," Rose's mother said as she returned with the coffee and some sweets.

Douglas didn't waste a beat. He sat down and dug right in. Rose watched him as he gobbled down all of the treats she had been looking forward to enjoying later. Neither said a word. Rose's mother filled the uncomfortable silence with idle chatter about the weather, her corns, and her nagging ulcer.

When the ordeal was over, Rose observed as Douglas waddled like an old lady to the door.

Every Sunday that followed, Douglas arrived at three p.m. sharp, bearing gifts for both mother and daughter.

As time went on Rose's mother grew fond of Douglas. She appreciated that he came from a good family, was polite and generous, and didn't gamble. What pleased her most of all was that he was much smaller than Rose. His nonthreatening girlish demeanor was also reassuring.

Rose disliked Douglas because they were opposites in every way. While she was tall, studious, and an avid reader, he was short, a bad student, and didn't read much. She attributed his poor communication skills to this last shortcoming.

Douglas wasn't at all discouraged by Rose's lack of interest. He believed that with much effort, Rose would grow to love him in time. He began by diligently reading and studying all of her favorite books and paying close attention to everything that was dear to her. When he compared himself to the unfortunate Akaky Akakievich of Gogol's *The Overcoat,* one afternoon, Rose was tickled.

"You do remind me of him a little," she said with a smile.

From that day onward, Douglas entertained Rose with his knowledge of all her best-loved characters and treated her to all of her favorite things. Over time she became more open to their friendship and began to look forward their meetings. There was, however, no development of any romantic feelings, since she viewed him much in the way she would a girlfriend.

Regardless of Rose's feelings, Douglas remained hopeful. He was thrilled to be around her and was always happy to be seen in public with what he believed to be his prized beauty. The spring dance at the university was no exception.

The auditorium was large and dimly lit. There were many people enjoying themselves on the dance floor. Rose and Douglas found a place against the wall.

"Do you...do you...would you like to dance?" Douglas stuttered.

Rose shook her head.

"Are you sure? I saw you tapping your foot; you must want to dance."

"Not now. Maybe a little later," she lied. Past experience had taught her that Douglas was a terrible dancer. His preoccupation with rubbing her bra strap whenever they were close didn't help.

While she surveyed the room, he kept a watchful eye on her feet. It wasn't long before Rose's eyes came to rest on one spot on the dance floor where a muscular young man was dancing alone. He stood out from the crowd not only because of his smooth dark skin, but also because of the way he was moving so freely.

She wondered who he was, what his name was, what his voice sounded like, where he was from, and what it would be like to dance or be alone with him. Never once had she felt so drawn to anyone.

When Douglas announced, "I'm going to get something for us to drink. I'll be right back," she was overjoyed. It was just the opportunity she had hoped for. Right away, she turned and tapped a young blonde woman standing next to her on the shoulder.

"Excuse me, do you know who that is over there?"

"You mean Sam?" The woman asked coyly.

"Is that his name?"

"Yeah. It's Sam Ansah. He's a med student. He transferred here last semester. He's African. They say his whole village raised money to send him here. Isn't he delicious?"

Rose nodded in agreement.

"Sam Ansah?" Rose asked.

"Yeah, that's it."

"Sam Ansah, Sam Ansah," Rose whispered to herself. She was still whispering the name when Douglas returned with the drinks.

"Oh, it was all my pleasure, Rosie," he replied, mistaking one of her murmurs for a "Thank you." She was too preoccupied to notice.

Sam Ansah stopped dancing and went to stand against the wall on the other side of the room. Rose watched him carefully as she sipped her drink. Douglas missed everything.

From across the room, Sam Ansah could feel Rose's eyes on him. He had noticed them when he was still on the dance floor and had deliberately swayed extra vigorously. Her regard was unlike the suspicious or unfriendly stares that he had grown so accustomed to. Hers was much warmer and interesting. He looked directly at her and smiled.

She blushed and responded with an embarrassed grin. "I'll be back in a flash. Nature is calling," Douglas said before trotting off.

Thank God for his weak bladder, she thought to herself.

Once alone, she felt a force moving her in the direction of Sam Ansah. She felt so impulsive. In the seconds that it took her to cross the floor, she lived out a fantasy. It involved falling in love, getting married, and running away to Africa.

Face to face with the dark stranger's prominent nose and wide jaw, she lost her ability to speak. It was if as she was under some sort of magical spell. The stranger had been equally afflicted. When she finally snapped out of it, the only thing that she could think of doing was to offer her hand. The instant her fingers grazed his, she felt a form of energy, as if the rays of the sun had been taken from the sky and placed between their palms.

Without saying anything, he led her to the middle of the dance floor as the first slow song of the evening began to play. He pulled her close to him and they danced in silence. She felt as if she were floating.

Douglas spotted Rose and Sam right away. Feelings of indignation percolated within him as he charged toward them. In the fury, he felt his body shifting and transforming. His back straightened and his legs moved closer together. Suddenly, he was no longer walking with the hunched waddle of an old lady. He was standing tall and strutting like a man. This was a first for him.

His new posture and gait immediately caught Rose's attention. She had never seen him look so masculine. Knowing that her bliss was about to end, she quickly whispered something into Sam's ear. The rays of sunlight shone once again. Just as she spoke the last syllable, Douglas grabbed her arm and shoved Sam, who he now recognized as his classmate, to the floor.

Looking up from the floor, Sam wondered what he had gotten himself into. Douglas, now even more furious, wanted to kick him, but he feared the glare of the crowd. Instead, he seized Rose by her wrist and dragged her out of the hall. Everyone watched in amusement. Putting up no resistance, she kept her gaze fixed on Sam as if she were in some sort of trance.

Outside on the road, Douglas finally released his grip. The second he did, his manly prowess and posture disappeared.

"What was that about?" Douglas demanded, out of breath.

Rose looked down at him and rubbed her forearm. The sudden aggression had taken her by surprise.

"Say something, please," Douglas huffed. The episode and his transformation had taken its toll.

Feeling no obligation to reply, Rose rushed off.

Douglas took some deep breaths, then set off at a jog behind her.

• • •

Both Eva and Ava were now on the edge of their seats.

"Wow, Ma!" Ava exclaimed.

"Does Douglas catch up with her? What did she whisper in Sam's ear?"

"You'll just have to wait for the next part to find out." Bernice got up and took some clothes from a pile on the counter and shoved them into a dryer.

"Can you just give us a hint?" Ava begged.

"No, you'll just have to—"

Bernice watched as a young freckle-faced teenager entered the laundry room. The heavy-chested girl, who was scantily dressed in a pink terry halter-top and short cut-off jeans, carried a small basket in one hand and a cigarette in the other. She sauntered over to the first washer and opened up the lid.

"Is this your fucking shit in here?" she said to no one in particular.

Eva and Ava recognized the shrill voice and the mild smell of egg shampoo as belonging to the youngest Sullivan sister. She was the wildest of the bunch according to their mother. Bernice had described them as no-good, sleazy tramps.

"They're mine. I'll take them out in a second," Bernice replied.

The young girl stomped down the row of washers, opening all of them.

"Is all this fucking stuff yours?"

"Yes, just hold on a minute. I'll empty them out for you," Bernice insisted trying to control her temper.

"Fuck that, I'll take it out myself." She put out her cigarette and started yanking the things from one of the machines.

The twins knew it was best not to intervene. Eva had already been punched by one of the older Sullivan sisters some years ago when she had stepped in to defend her mother.

"I said I was going to empty them out myself. Don't you dare touch my things," Bernice forced herself between the girl and the machine.

"You see, all you had to do was wait," Bernice scowled.

"Yeah, yeah, whatever." The girl lit another cigarette and turned her attention toward the twins.

"Hey, Thing One and Thing Two, you want a smoke or something?"

"No thanks, we don't smoke," Eva and Ava said together.

"Oh, my gosh, you guys are good—like a pair of fucking parrots." She pulled a plastic bag filled with bingo chips out of her front pocket, placed four into the slots on the machine, threw in her clothes with some soap and left.

Bernice shook her head and bellowed, "Good for nothing cheat!"

"The same to you, bitch," the girl yelled back.

"Our mother is not a bitch. You are," Ava added softly, knowing full well that the Sullivan sister was out of earshot.

"Not everyone can be proper girls like Rose and Violet," Bernice said.

"I guess not," the twins agreed.

CHAPTER 8
Another Summer Remembrance

BERNICE WOKE UP feeling not at all like herself the next morning. The churning feeling in her stomach told her that it was much more than her summer blues. When she tried to get out of bed, she felt a sharp pain in the left side of her abdomen.

"Must be some of those old-lady aches and pains," she said out loud.

After resting for a few seconds, she tried to get up again, but this time the pain jabbed her in the right side.

"Look, I don't appreciate this, okay. So let me be," she moaned. "All I want to do is get out of this bed and get some things done."

When she tried a third time to struggle out of bed, a spasm shot across her chest and forced her to lie down. As she lay there stiff as a corpse, it felt like one morning in the summer of 1917, all over again.

That day she had woken up caked in sweat in the empty farm-house. A letter lay discarded on the bed next to her. It read:

Dear Bernice,

It is with great sorrow that I write this letter to tell you that your dear brother and my dear friend, Charles, is no longer among us. I was hoping that he would recover and that I would have better news for you, but there is no news but sad news. Last month our artillery was bombarded with an attack of mustard gas. Many of our men were hit, but Charles got the worst of it. I was not in the field at the time, so I was spared. When they brought Charles back from the field, I could hardly recognize him. His body was covered with yellowish blis-ters, he could barely speak, and his eyes looked like they had been welded shut. For four whole weeks he suffered, unable to recline or sleep for fear of choking. On his last night, when I went to visit him, he gestured for me to move closer. When I put my head next to his mouth, he forced out these words in a painful whisper: "Tell Bernie that I love her." He was dead within the hour. I know this is the worst possible news that I could bring to you, but please take solace in the fact that your brother loved you very much.

You have my most humble condolences.

Yours most sincerely,
Jonathan Ford

She couldn't even find the strength to cry anymore. She and Charles had not parted on good terms the summer before.

The day before he shipped off, she had gotten a glimpse of him with his sweetheart, Carmen, at a distance on the dirt road. It appeared as if they were arguing.

"Stop it," Bernice yelled out and ran crying into the house. "Just stop it." She had seen similar episodes many times before with her parents.

Charles didn't appear at all roused or upset, when he entered the house a short while later. Bernice was crying on the couch.

"What's wrong, Bernie? Why are you crying again? I told you that I won't be gone long. I'll be back before you know it. I promise." He was trying to sound upbeat for the sake of his sister.

"How could you?"

"How could I what? You've known that I had to leave for a long time now."

"I'm not talking about that."

"Then what are you talking about?"

"You know exactly what I'm talking about."

Bernice ran upstairs.

Charles was confounded.

In the morning, he stood outside her bedroom dressed in his uniform with his duffle bag at his feet. He tapped softly on the door.

"Bernie, are you up? I have to leave now. Are you going to come out and give your brother a good-bye hug and kiss?"

There was no response. Charles tried opening the door, but it was locked.

"Bernie, come on. Whatever you think I did, I'm sorry, okay? Come on and say good-bye. I have to go."

There was some rustling sound on the other side of the door.

"I hear you, Bernie. Come on now. I really wish I didn't have to leave you, Bernie, but I do. I wish I could stay right here with you and forget all about this war." He started to tear up.

It was quiet on the other side of the door again.

"Say something, why don't you, Bernie. It may be the… Bernice, come on, please don't let me leave like this. Let me see you before I go. Please come out."

There were more rustling sounds in the room again, then the door opened. Her eyes were bloodshot and her hair matted. She looked as if she had been crying the whole night. The sight of her brother's uniform set off more tears.

Charles wrapped his arms tightly around her. "You'll be alright, Bernie, I won't be gone long. You'll see. I'll be back in a flash. And I'll write. I'll write as much as I can. I promise. And you can write me, too. You'll see. You'll be fine, and Carmen said she would come and check in on you."

Bernice nodded and continued to sob. He let go and kissed her forehead. Taking up his bag, he kissed her once more and ran down the stairs.

"I love you, Charles," she said in a tiny whisper. "I love you."

That evening, when Carmen dropped by, Bernice was lying in bed motionless.

"Bernice, are you alright?"

"He's gone," Bernice whimpered.

"I know. I saw him off at the bus station this morning. He said you were upset at him for some reason."

Bernice nodded.

"What is it Bernice?"

"I saw yesterday."

"What did you see?"

"You were arguing."

"Arguing?"

"You were on the road."

"You mean down there in front of the house? Oh my goodness." Carmen covered her mouth.

"Why did he do that?"

"Bernice you've got it all wrong. We were just acting out a scene from *Othello*. I'm going to audition for it."

"You were acting?"

"Yes, your brother would never fight like that with me. He's a saint, a great guy."

Bernice nodded again and burst into tears. Carmen comforted her.

Bernice shook her head in disbelief, as she remained unable to move in her bed. "I didn't want to remember any of that," she moaned.

"Could you two please come here? I need some help," Bernice hollered toward the door.

Within seconds, Eva was at her door. Ava followed close behind.

"Ma, you okay? What's wrong?" Ava said, sounding concerned. She was not accustomed to her mother asking for help.

"Oh, I'm fine. It's just these old bones of mine."

"Are you sure? It doesn't sound like your bones," Eva said sternly.

"Yeah, yeah. I'm just going to rest it out. It'll be fine. I need you two to take the garbage out and sweep the kitchen floor. I was just about to do that before these darn bones acted up."

"You swept that floor last night. It's fine. What about breakfast? Do you want us to get you some?"

"Don't feel much like eating."

The twins looked worried.

"You don't feel like eating?"

"You don't want to eat, Ma? That doesn't sound good."

Ava moved closer to Bernice, reached down and found her forehead.

"You do feel a little warm. Maybe something is wrong."

"Of course, I'm warm. It's 150 degrees outside!"

"I know, but you don't feel or sound like yourself."

"Maybe we should take her to the doctor," Eva suggested.

"I'll be fine. I just need to lie down a bit longer. And what's that quack going to tell me—that I'm old? I already know that. And besides, I already have an appointment to see him next week for my annual checkup."

"Maybe I can call to change your appointment for today then, Ma," Eva said.

"You don't feel like eating, Ma. That's serious. You always feel like eating," Ava added.

"Oh don't bother. I'll be fine."

"Well, better safe than sorry. Don't you always say that, Ma? I'm going to call."

Eva located the push button phone at its regular spot on the wall next to the front door. She knew the number by heart.

"Hello, yes, this is Eva Archer calling. My mother is Bernice Archer. She has an appointment with the doctor next week, but we were wondering if you had any time available today…yes…okay…11:30…okay. Yes, we'll be there. Thank you." She hung up the phone.

"We can go today at 11:30, Ma. Ava, help Ma get dressed. I'm going to take the garbage out," Eva yelled.

"Alright!" Ava yelled back.

"Don't forget to take the one from the bathroom," Bernice reminded her.

Eva left the front door ajar as she made her way down the hallway. Using the varying degrees of creaks and squeaks of the weather-beaten floor, she found the small room at the end of the hallway that contained the chute. She paused to listen to the voices of a man and a woman having a heated discussion. It was a familiar sound.

"Where else am I supposed to take her?" a female voice pleaded.

"Just find somewhere else. That place is nasty and so are the people who go there," the male voice answered.

"It's the same people who live in this building."

"Exactly. I don't want my child around those scallywags."

"Oh, she's your child now?"

"She always been my child, so you better keep her out of that dirty park. You hear me? I'm gone."

Eva stood as still as she could and waited for the faint scent of tobacco that accompanied the heavy footsteps to pass.

"Howdy to you, too," Eva said mockingly under her breath.

When she exited the garbage room, she almost jumped out of her skin. Someone was in front of her.

"Sorry, did I scare you?" a melodic female voice asked.

It was the woman who had just been arguing.

"No, not at all," Eva lied.

"I'm in my stocking feet. I guess that's why you didn't hear me."

"Oh, I guess."

"You're not with your sister today."

"No, she's in the apartment."

"You two are usually together."

"Yes, I guess." Eva was thrilled to have the young woman's attention all to herself.

"I hear you two singing sometimes. It's very nice. I like it."

"Thank you. I'm glad you like it."

"Oh, I'm so sorry. I'm in your way, aren't I?"

"Oh, that's perfectly alright. No problem at all," Eva said, sounding sweeter than usual. The young woman moved out of Eva's way. "Well, nice talking to you." The door to the garbage chute opened.

"Same to you. Have a nice day." Eva smiled.

Back in the apartment, Bernice was dressed and propped up in the chair. Ava was standing next to her.

"She likes our singing!" Eva exclaimed.

"Who?" Ava and Bernice asked together.

"The young woman down the hall."

"Which one?"

"You know, the one who sounds like she's singing when she talks, the one from the islands. Wait, is she Violet from the story, Ma?"

A moan escaped from Bernice. "Oh my word, now the pain is in my back. Shouldn't we get going?"

Eva checked the dials of her open-faced watch. "We'll be too early."

"Then, we'll just get there early. Come help me up."

"But…"

"But nothing. Let's go. You don't want me dying on you, do you? And besides, we have a long bus ride ahead of us."

Ava helped her mother up.

"It's going to be too uncomfortable for you to take the bus, so we should just take a cab," Eva suggested.

"Cabs cost money."

"We can use your just-in-case money," Ava interjected.

"So what happens when something happens?" Bernice asked.

"One is happening now, Ma. Come on."

"Okay, okay, walk me over there."

Ava led her mother to the glass cabinet. Bernie took some cash from a small bear-shaped cookie jar and shoved it into her knee-highs. "Okay, let's boogie."

"You didn't answer my question, Ma."

"Which one was that?"

"About Violet in your story."

"Can't you see I'm suffering here? Leave me alone for a second, why don't you."

"Yeah, leave her alone, Eva. She's not well."

"Fine, but I know what the answer is."

In the cab Bernice rested in the front, while Eva and Ava enjoyed the passing smells and sounds from the back seat. When they passed the boundary of their neighborhood, the sound of the traffic became more aggressive, the smells less pungent and more perfumed. As the buildings grew taller, the air became more congested.

At the end of the ride, Bernice paid the driver with the cash that had been moistened by the sweat of her hairy legs. She had hoped that he would refuse the bills, but he didn't.

On the sidewalk, Eva and Ava felt immediately disoriented.

"About how many steps are we away from the building again, Ma?" Ava asked.

"About twenty-five, if I remember correctly."

"Twenty-six, if you count the step up to the door," Eva corrected.

"You don't have to bother counting, just hold on to me." Bernice squeezed between her daughters, laced her arms around theirs, and led the way.

Two men in gray suits stared at them as they made their way toward the building.

Why don't you take a picture? It would last longer. You've never seen three fat women before? Normally Bernice would say these thing out loud, but she just wasn't up to it at the moment.

The doctor's office was on the third floor of the high rise. When they got there, they found it locked, with a note taped to the door.

"Office will re-open today at 11:30," Bernice read.

"You see, Ma, I told you we were going to be early," Eva said.

"What are we going to do for the next hour?" Ava asked.

"Let's just go back home, I'm feeling fine now. That little bit of walking did me some good."

"We can't go back home now, Ma," Ava insisted.

"Why not?"

"Then we'll be wasting your just-in-case stash."

"Oh, never mind that."

"Ava is right. Don't you remember what you always say about wasting money?"

"What do I say?"

"Wasting good money is as stupid as wearing a sun dress in January," Ava chimed in.

"You also said that 'Thou should not waste money' should have been one of the commandments."

"So I said those things. What about it?" Bernice leaned against the wall.

"So that means we shouldn't go back home. You should really see the doctor anyway, Ma. Let's just go and wait in that lobby. You remember where we waited last time."

"Yeah, sure okay, whatever."

The lobby was deserted, save for a derelict who looked as if he would have been more at home in Bernice's neck of the woods. He slept upright with his eyes wide open.

"He looks like old Frederick," Bernice said.

"Smells like him too," Eva added covering her nose.

The three settled into a row of faux leather seats.

"It's nice and cool in here, but this place gives me the creeps. There is no life down here. Where are all the people?" Bernice rambled.

The twins sat in silence.

"Who died? Why are you two so quiet?"

"We're just taking it all in, Ma."

"Taking all of what in?"

"Everything."

"So, what are we going to do so that I don't feel like I'm at funeral or something."

"You could take a nap, Ma," Eva offered.

"I don't feel like napping now, and how am I supposed to nap on this hard thing?"

"You could continue the story, Ma. That's if you're feeling up to it," Ava suggested.

"I'm feeling just fine now. Whatever it was seems to have passed."

"Are you sure?"

"Sure as I'm sitting here."

"Well then, can you answer my question and tell me if the woman down the hall is Violet?"

"And the one who smells of roses, she must be Rose," Ava added.

"I'll get to that after. Just let me continue the story." Bernice shifted around trying to get more comfortable.

CHAPTER 9
Romance Blooms

SAM ANSAH STOOD shivering on the bank of the river, just as the sun was beginning to rise. Shoving his hands deep into his pockets, he wondered again what he had gotten himself into. The tingling sensation from the night before may have had something to do with it, he thought. He didn't even know the name of his dancing partner, yet he had followed her instructions. Only six minutes had passed since his arrival, but the frigid air made it feel more like thirty. Just as he made his mind up to leave, she appeared. The girl in front of him looked even more beautiful than he remembered under the glow of the early morning sun.

When Rose had whispered her request into his ear the night before, she wasn't sure if he would come, so she smiled tenderly to show her gratitude.

When they sat down together the effects of the sun came once again between their shoulders. Not knowing what to say, each glanced quietly into the river. Rose had never been happier.

After several more minutes of awkward silence, they spoke simultaneously.

"My name is Rose."

"I was afraid that you weren't going to show up." Sam spoke with a heavy African accent. Their answers also overlapped.

"I'm so sorry that I was late."

"Rose. That's a pretty name."

Another short pause followed. Then, as if they were two marionettes controlled by the same hand, the two turned to face each other. She stared at his still-quivering full lips. He saw the sparkle in her eyes.

"Would it be okay if I kiss you?" she asked. Her brashness surprised even her.

He seemed uncomfortable. She giggled, then she leaned forward and placed her lips on his mouth. He relaxed and reciprocated. Her heart smiled as she relished the soft warmth of her first kiss. It was more dazzling than she could ever have imagined. There was no need for words.

In the weeks that followed, the two, like mice, sought out dark isolated spots, on rooftops, stairwells, and abandoned buildings where they could share time alone without being discovered. In those moments they clung to one another as if their lives depended on it.

Sam studied Rose's anatomy, chemistry, and physics as he suckled her pink nipples and used his fingers to test her succulence. During this time, she learned all about love. It was gentle, caring, warm, and constant. It smelled of a fresh spring day, tasted of joy, and felt like peace. It had arrived and given her another life, one that she had only previously read about.

Rose found herself scribbling Sam's name anywhere and everywhere. She would have written it across her forehead and her chest, but she knew the relationship was better kept secret.

"Who's Sam Ansah?" Rose's mother asked her as she stepped out of the shower. "Do you know who that is?"

Rose swallowed hard.

"No, I don't know."

"Then why is his name all over the newspaper? You were the last one to read it."

"No, no I wasn't. I think the boarder had it last."

"Well it looks like your handwriting." Her mother held up the paper.

"It looks like that new boarder's handwriting to me."

"I don't think that woman knows anyone by the name of Sam Ansah, and besides, look. It says Rose Ansah right here in the corner." She pointed to the spot.

"I was just doodling. It doesn't mean anything. Just silliness really."

"So who is this Sam Ansah fellow, then?"

"Oh...he's just the name of a character in one of the books that I'm reading. It's by an African novelist, about a guy who goes abroad to study, but then his father dies and he has to go back home."

"I see. Why didn't you just tell me that in the first place?"

"I just thought that you would think it was silly."

"No, it's not silly at all, Rose. How's Douglas doing? I haven't seen him in a long time."

"Oh, he's great. We're meeting today after school."

"It sounds like you two are getting serious. Tell him he's welcome to drop by anytime."

"Ah...he's very busy these days with school and all."

"Well that's okay, as long as you two are enjoying yourselves. That's what being young should be all about."

Rose adjusted her towel. "I should go get dressed."

"Yeah, yeah, go ahead. Oh, I'd like to read that book of yours when you're done with it."

"Sure." Rose sighed.

After school, Rose rushed all the way past the train tracks to the edge of town to an abandoned warehouse. At the back, she tapped four times gently, then entered.

Sam was already seated in the corner studying by the light of the window. He placed his book down the moment he saw Rose and smiled with an infectious grin.

"There you are, my sweet. Who have you selected for us today?"

"Emerson." She kissed his forehead.

"Good choice. Which one?" He caressed her calf.

"Give all to love." She pulled out a blanket from her school bag.

"Excellent. I love that one. *Give all to love...*"

"*Obey thy heart.*" She cleared away some debris and spread the blanket before sitting down.

"*Friends, kindred, days...*come."

He joined her.

"*Estate, good fame,* mmm, you smell good." He kissed her neck.

"*Plan's credit and the muse.*" She undid the buttons of her blouse.

"Nothing refused." He cupped her breast, then peeled back her bra.

"Nothing refused." She reached down into his trousers.

"Tis a brave master. Let it have scope." He quickly undid his belt, and slipped his trousers off.

"Follow it utterly." She grinned and pulled him on top of her.

"Hope beyond hope." He caressed and kissed her.

"High and more high." She moaned and stroked his uncircumcised penis.

"It dives into noon. With wing unspent. Untold intent," he groaned, slipped on a condom and entered her.

"Untold intent," she sang out in ecstasy.

• • •

Eva and Ava sat forward. Their mouths were wide open.

"Ma, you do know that this is a public place," Eva said.

Ava hit her sister.

"Just let her continue. No one's listening to her but us."

"And besides, it's almost time for your appointment," Eva continued.

"I guess it's too much for you, huh?"

"It's not too much for me, Ma, and we still have plenty of time." Ava was annoyed with her sister.

"Okay then, I'll finish this part of the story."

"Yeah, go ahead, Ma. Finish it," Ava insisted.

Eva remained silent. The homeless man on the other side of the lobby was now wide-awake and salivating.

"Yeah, go ahead," he mumbled under his breath, as he spread some newspaper over his bulging crotch.

• • •

At the height of lovemaking, Emerson was abandoned and replaced with animal grunts.

"Oh, Mommy," Sam screamed as he climaxed. He rolled off of Rose.

"The gods arrive," he cried out, exhausted.

"They most certainly have," she agreed.

At that exact moment across the ocean, Violet was replacing some scattered hymn books in church when she felt a strange gratifying sensation radiate throughout her body. It wasn't the first time she had felt such things, so she let it pass.

She had already been to church earlier that day and had planned on attending the evening song and prayer. The building had become her sanctuary away from her mother.

Since she had been abandoned, Violet's mother had become the personification of misery. With her wrinkled brow, twisted sour mouth, and the smell of malt vinegar seeping from her pores, she was now always argumentative, blaming Violet for everything.

"You see what you did now, you made the sun so blasted hot. Who told you to let it rain so," she would say.

All Violet could do was apologize. To keep the peace, she made sure to stay as silent as possible, knowing that it took two to quarrel.

Just as Violet was finishing with the hymnbooks, a round-faced boy appeared out of nowhere. He had a white envelope in his hand.

"This is for you Miss Violet." He smirked and handed it to her.

Violet was written beautifully in red letters. Her heart started to flutter.

"Who gave you this?" She looked around at the now-empty church.

"Sorry, I'm not supposed to say." The boy giggled and ran off.

She sniffed and examined the note, trying to find any clue she could. She took another look around, then stuck her finger in the corner of the envelope to open it.

"Thanks for tidying up, Miss Violet," the pastor boomed from the altar. Violet almost jumped out of her skin.

"No problem at all, Pastor Brown." She discretely slipped the envelope into her purse.

"We need more young ladies like you in the church," he added.

"Thank you, pastor. See you this evening." She waved and left the church.

Violet focused on the treasure in her purse as she hurried home. She envisioned all of the words of admiration, love, and longing that she would find. So absorbed in her fantasy was she that she didn't even notice the crowd that followed a machete-wielding old man chasing after his wife and her young lover.

At home, she went directly to her mother's room to make sure she was sleeping, then snuck quietly to her own room, not bothering to eat. Love before sustenance, she thought.

She had waited her whole life for something extraordinary to happen to her, and now it had. After taking a few seconds to caress and smell the envelope once more, she ripped it open. A stiff piece of paper neatly folded in four was found inside. It read, *I like you.* Violet was disappointed. She

had hoped for flowery, love-filled words, but got unimagina-
tive and unromantic prose in its place. Had it not been for
the penmanship, she would have believed that the note was
from the little delivery boy himself.

In the weeks that followed, Violet's admirer redeemed
himself. He sent more notes by way of the boy. Each one was
more elaborately worded and passionate than the one before,
each ending with borrowed verses of poetry. This pleased her
very much.

She tried on many occasions to coax out information
from the boy, but his reply was always the same, "Sorry, I
can't tell you, Miss Violet. I need the money and I don't want
any licks."

Exactly twelve weeks after the arrival of the first envelope, the mystery was revealed. Her admirer appeared after
the service with the last envelope in his hand. Violet panicked when she saw him. Her eyes moved from the masculine
hand up the broad chest to an angular face. His luminous,
light-brown eyes were striking. She had never seen such radi-
ant eyes. Looking at them was like staring into the sun. The
handsome man was well-dressed, gangly, and about ten years
older than she was.

He stepped up gallantly, placed the envelope in her hand,
and receited:

> *"A mouse found a beautiful piece of plum cake,*
> *the richest and sweetest that mortal could make;*
> *Twas heavy with citron and fragrant with spice,*
> *and covered with sugar all sparkling as ice.*
> *My Stars! cried the mouse, while his eye beamed with glee,*
> *Here's a treasure I've found; what a feast it will be."*

Then he bowed his head, grinned and offered her his hand.

"Hello, I'm Robert Black, pleased to finally meet you."

Her hand trembled in his. She smiled bashfully, marveling at how charming he was and how he had made the rhyme sound so romantic. She was certain that she was the plum cake and he the mouse.

"Pleased to finally meet you," she beamed, no longer mindful of the other parishioners.

The next day as they strolled along the bayfront in the capital, she was in ecstasy listening to the hum of his sweet voice. It made her forget everything.

"Look how beautiful you are. You're a star." He stared intensely at her.

"You know, I saw you for the first time right over there." He pointed in the direction of some pink colonial buildings.

"You were the loveliest little thing I'd ever seen. It looked like you were daydreaming or something, with your mind somewhere in the clouds. I asked some people around if they knew who you were and found out all about you in a matter of minutes. You know how small this place is. Everyone knows everyone else's business."

"When was this?"

"Oh, months ago, when I just got back from St. Thomas."

"Why didn't you talk to me then?"

"I couldn't do that with a girl like you. I knew I had to do something special."

"The letters?"

"I knew they would work."

"They did."

"You see, I'm the type of guy who always gets his way. I even talked my way into this job I have now. I didn't have the right qualifications, but I convinced them that I was a quick learner."

"I see."

"My mother said when I was born she knew that I would do good things. She said she saw a wisdom in my eyes from the very beginning. That's why she busted her ass to send me to that private school. I was the only one she sent. All the rest of my brothers ended up cutting cane."

Violet was in awe.

The following Sunday, in the place of church, Robert took Violet back to his small rented room above a bakery. Within a few minutes of arriving, he had taken off all his clothes and was posing in front of Violet as if he were Michelangelo's David. Violet was stunned. She didn't know what to make of the raw looking organ that dangled between his legs.

"Would you like to touch it?" He smiled broadly.

She looked at it with a mixture of trepidation and disgust.

"I promise the snake doesn't come with teeth. It won't bite." He took her hand and placed it on him.

"It feels like a cow teat," she squirmed and jumped back.

"It's okay. We don't have to do anything you don't want to. We can wait."

She was relieved.

The following week Robert kept his clothes on and spoke about poetry and his dreams for the future, making sure not to attempt any overt movements or gestures. The week after he took just his shirt off and encouraged Violet to caress his chest without laying a finger on her.

"You're not like him at all, are you?"

"Him?" Robert looked puzzled.

"My father."

"No, not at all. We're two different species altogether."

On the third Sunday, Violet was no longer able to contain her curiosity.

"I think I'm ready now," she said, pointing coyly to the fold in Robert's crotch.

He smiled, led her to his single bed, and undressed her. After only a few thrusts, tiny pulsations began to radiate through her pelvis. The vibration spread quickly down her legs and up to the rest of her body. At the height of the experience, her whole body shook as if she were having a seizure. Had the sensation not been so enjoyable, she would have believed that she was about to die. The shaking amazed and fascinated him as well, so much so that he shed a tiny tear. What he didn't know was that he had not been responsible for the eruption.

At that exact same moment, on the other side of the ocean, Rose and Sam were taking part in similar activities. The instant Violet reached her climax, Rose also reached hers. This was the very first time the young women experienced something in tandem. This unified experience intensified the outcome for both couples.

From that Sunday onward, Violet took part in a different kind of ceremony in Robert's rented room. There, the congregation consisted of just two: Violet and her new pastor, Robert Henry Black. By default, Machiavelli's *The Prince* became their Bible, since it was the only book that he owned. In his sermons, he preached about the acquisition, preservation, and protection of love.

"It would be best to be both loved and feared," he would yell when he climaxed. She wasn't certain what he actually meant, but she embraced her newfound religion whole-heartedly.

● ● ●

The twins' startled expressions spoke for themselves. Neither knew what to say.

"I guess it's time to go back upstairs now," Bernice said.

Ava and Eva nodded and got up.

The derelict quickly removed his hand from underneath the newspaper when the three women walked by.

CHAPTER 10
A Warning for Bernice

AFTER MORE THAN an hour-long wait, Bernice was called in to see the doctor. The twins insisted on going in with her because they wanted to hear the information straight from the horse's mouth.

The doctor, an exceptionally hairy man, was in an upbeat mood.

"Hello, ladies, I see you couldn't wait another week to see my handsome face," he said with a Persian accent.

The three women giggled.

"What brings you here today?"

"Well, Ma was all stiff this morning," Eva started.

"And she didn't feel like eating," Ava continued.

"Sounds serious." The doctor smiled and glanced down at the file on his desk. His expression changed. "Well, if what I suspect is true, it's probably diabetes. You've been on the borderline for some time now. You probably have to be put on insulin."

"You mean I'll have to stick a needle in me every day?" Bernice groaned.

"Yes, most likely."

"We'll help you, Ma."

"Yeah, Ma. We'll take care of you," Eva added.

"And who's going to take care of the two of you?"

"We'll take care of ourselves. We're fifty-three years old."

"I know how old you are."

The doctor looked at the three women with concern.

Relief from the heat came in the form of rain. When Bernice stepped out of bed, she heard the welcome downpour. Her appetite had returned, so she snuck quietly to the kitchen.

"I just need a little pick-me-up," she murmured to herself. Rummaging through the pantry, she found only a tin of salted crackers.

"Where are all the cookies and cakes?" Bernice hollered.

The twins appeared, looking very serious.

"We threw them down the chute," Eva announced.

"You did what?"

"We ate some first, and then we threw the rest down the chute," Ava clarified.

"I heard what you said. I just don't believe that you would do that. The doctor said I had to cut back, not go cold turkey."

"Ma, just eat some crackers and come to the bedroom for your shot."

The twins wobbled off together.

Bernice shoved some crackers in her mouth.

"They taste like sawdust!"

The twins stood waiting like two officials by Bernice's bed.

"Sit down and check your sugar level first, Ma."

After a few seconds the machine beeped.

"What does it say, Ma?" Eva asked. "And tell us the right number."

"It says that I'm still alive. Just give me the shot already." She lifted her dress up.

Eva searched around for a good spot on her mother's stomach.

"Stop that. You're tickling me!" Bernice chuckled.

"Sorry, Ma."

"I can't find her belly button."

"What do you take me for, some sort of beached whale?" Bernice lifted Eva's hand up and placed it down again. It's around there somewhere. I haven't seen that thing in years."

"I'm going to jab you now. You need to stay still, okay? No jerking around, you understand?"

"Alright already, why does it have to take so damn long?" Bernice squeezed her eyes shut and took a deep breath.

"Are you ready?"

"Ready as I'm ever going to be."

Eva plunged the needle into her mother's abdomen.

"There. I'm done."

"Good." Bernice opened her eyes. "I don't know how people can do this by themselves. It's a good thing I have you two."

"Yes, it is," Eva agreed.

"I'm just going to lie here for a bit."

"Okay, we'll leave you alone, then."

"If you want, I can continue the story now."

"Are you sure, Ma? Are you up to it?"

"You don't have to if you don't want to, Ma. Remember the doctor said you should rest," Ava offered.

"Yeah, yeah, sure, sure. I've had enough rest. All this nonsense has gotten in the way long enough. Go grab some chairs."

The twins rushed out and quickly returned with a couple of kitchen chairs. Both were out of breath.

"Okay, we're ready."

Bernice fluffed up her pillow.

"Okay, so am I."

CHAPTER 11
Love Sours

VIOLET'S MOTHER HADN'T found out about the letters, but it was impossible for her not to discover Violet's new Sunday activity. The gossip started in the church, as it normally does, and spread swiftly from there.

When she heard the news, she greeted Violet that night with a hard smack to the face. The moment Violet felt the sting of the slap, she knew that she had been found out. All she could do was rub her throbbing cheek while her mother called her every single vile un-Christian name under the sun.

"Ah," Rose said as she felt her cheek. She lay naked with Sam in the abandoned warehouse.

"What is it?" Sam sprang up.

"I think maybe an ant or something bit my cheek. Is it red?"

He examined her face.

"I don't see anything." He moved behind her and began to massage her back.

She moaned and forgot all about the sting. "Say something in your language for me, Sam."

"Why?"

"Because I want to hear what it sounds like. Just give me a little sample. Please?"

"Okay. *Fun hii yote ni kunizuia kazi yangu.*" His voice sounded deeper.

"What did you say?"

"I said, all this fun is keeping me from my work."

"Hmm, I like the way that sounded."

"Good, I'm glad."

"So will you go right back home when you finish with school, or will you stay for a little while?"

"I'll go home most likely. I want to open up a clinic eventually."

"In your village?"

"There or close by."

"Would you take me with you when you go back? I'd love to see where you came from."

He pulled his hands off of her shoulders and hesitated. "Ah, there's no place for someone like you back there."

She was puzzled.

"My turn now." He tapped his neck.

She took her place behind him without any further discussion.

When Rose woke up a few weeks later feeling extremely nauseated, she knew right away that she was pregnant, and she knew exactly when it had happened. The only time that they had not taken any precautions was the day after the extraordinary climax. They had wanted to reproduce the experience, but the experiment had failed.

When she met Sam a few days later by the river, she felt completely drained.

"What happened to you? You look terrible," he said as he kissed her hello.

"I haven't slept a wink in a few days."

"Are you sick?" He checked the lymph nodes on her neck. "Let Doctor Ansah see what's wrong with my beautiful patient."

"You're not going to find out what's wrong with me there, Sam." She moved his hands to her stomach.

He sprang backward. "What!" His face contorted. "Are you sure? Did you see a doctor?"

Rose nodded.

"This is not possible, we used...!" he screamed with a shrill voice.

"There was that one time, you remember? And why are you yelling like that?"

"I'm yelling because I'm upset. Don't you understand? I don't want to be a father. I can't be a father now."

"Well you are. I mean you will be..."

"Don't even say it."

"Well you will be."

"I hope you don't think I'm going to marry you now. I have to finish school and—"

"I never said you had to marry me." A large lump was now in her throat.

"And if you want me to be perfectly honest, I don't even love you!"

"But you said—"

"I never said that I love you. I don't know what you assumed, but I never said those words."

"But I love you," she whimpered.

"You're too young to know what love is. You're only seventeen. Lust and love aren't the same thing, you know."

"So what are we going to do about this?" She placed her hand on her abdomen.

"*We* are not going to do anything. I told you I can't be a father. Not now, not for a long time." His voice boomed.

"What does that mean?" Her lips started to quiver.

"It means what you think it means. Look, I need to get out of here." He grabbed his bag, flung it over his shoulder, and jogged off.

She watched him leave in disbelief. When he stopped and turned around, she felt a tiny sliver of hope.

"Look, I know this may come off sounding crass, but I don't think we should see each other anymore. I think that would be for the best." He turned back and continued on his path.

She remained completely motionless. A part of her wanted to yell after him and chastise him for being such a selfish, uncaring, disgraceful, heartless bastard but she couldn't find the strength to open her mouth. All she could do was plop down on the riverbank and cry.

After night had fallen, she was past the point of exhaustion and was no longer able to produce tears. With the help of a nearby tree, she was able to straighten her stiff joints, and stand up.

Putting one foot in front of the other, she staggered away from the water and made her way through the woods. When she reached a pathway, she noticed a dark figure at a distance. As the form shuffled from side to side, she realized who it was. Douglas. The off-balance nature of his walk suggested that he had been drinking.

Since Douglas had committed to memory Rose's walk, the contours of her body, and everything about her, he recognised her right away. Seeing her had a sobering effect on him. The twenty beers and shots of whiskey now seemed like water. His plans of jumping in the river and ending it all were also quelled.

As he got closer, she adjusted herself to appear as normal as possible, but he saw right through the façade.

"Rose?" he slurred. He wanted to ask her what she was doing out so late in the woods, but he didn't dare. Rose had ended their friendship a few days after the spring dance, and she had refused to speak to him ever since. It had been months, and he still was feeling the devastation.

"Douglas? What...what are you...?" Engulfed by a flood of emotions, she broke into sobs.

This confused him even more. He moved closer and patted her awkwardly on her shoulder. "Ah, there, there. You'll be okay."

Her sobs intensified.

"What...what happened? Why all those tears?" he stammered.

She hung her head.

"You can tell me. I want to help. What's bothering you, Rose?"

She didn't budge.

"Please stop crying, Rose. I hate seeing you like this. If you tell me what's wrong, maybe I can fix it and make you happy again. I want you to be happy, Rose."

She lifted her head and looked directly at him for the first time. "I don't know what I'm going to do," she heard herself say.

"Do about what?"

"I'm pregnant."

"Pregnant!"

"I met someone and…we…and here I…I just found out. Nobody knows yet except me and him."

"Pregnant!?" he repeated again, somewhat stunned. "What about this man, the father?" His words scorched his throat.

"He doesn't want anything to do with me now."

"He told you that?"

"Yes. Just now. Right after I told him."

"That's horrible, you poor thing. No wonder you're look-ing so awful." He slipped his arm around her. "What will you do?"

"I don't know."

"Wait, I know what you should do. You should get married."

"But he doesn't want anything to do with me."

"No, no. I mean, we should get married."

"What?"

"If we get married, then I can look after you and the child."

"You want to marry me? What about school and your parents?"

"Being married is not going to stop me from finishing school. And my parents, well, I guess they'll be glad to be rid of me. I don't think they ever really liked me. I'm nothing like my brother, their perfect son."

"But this baby, it's not yours…it's not your responsibility."

"If marrying you will help you, then I'll do it. I want to do this for you, Rose."

"I can't do that to you. Thanks for offering, but just I can't." Rose shook her head and walked off. Douglas watched her leave.

The next day, Douglas visited her at her home. Rose was surprised to see him.

He spoke to her in hushed tones in the kitchen, as her mother napped upstairs.

"Do you know what I was going to do last night?" he asked.

"No."

"I was going to jump in the river."

Rose was taken aback. "Why would you do that?"

"What reason did I have to live? You deserted me and—"

"I didn't mean to…"

"Well, you know why I didn't go through with it after you left last night?"

"No, why?"

"Because you need me. I know you need me. I want to marry you, Rose. I'm not drunk now. I really mean it."

He took Rose's hand in his.

Rose looked down.

"Look at me. I want to do this for you."

"Do you know what this means? Are you sure?"

"As sure as Akaky needed a new overcoat."

Rose smiled and nodded. "Okay, I accept. Okay."

Douglas was overjoyed.

As for Rose, she knew that marriage wasn't something

that one should jump into hastily, but she felt she had no other option.

• • •

"Their decision was made with the best of intentions." Bernice let out a big yawn. The rhythmic pitter-patter of the rain was making her sleepy.

"Do you mind if I continue later? I feel like resting my eyes."

"Sure, Ma. No problem."

"You should rest. You've been through a lot in the last little while."

The twins collected the chairs.

"Is soup okay for later?" Eva asked.

"Soup will be fine." Bernice was already half asleep. "Just fine."

"Sweet dreams, Ma."

As soon as the twins left, Bernice opened her eyes and lay awake staring at the ceiling.

"I know what would cheer Ma up," Eva said as she shuffled with the chair into the kitchen.

"What?"

"A trip to the island. That always cheers her up."

"That might be too tiring for her."

"Well, let's let her rest a few more days, and I'm sure she'll be up to it by Sunday,"

"We can make egg-salad sandwiches," Eva suggested.

"Yeah, we could do that."

"Should we start the soup now?" Ava asked.

"Yeah, I guess."

On Saturday morning, Ava brought a tray packed with pancakes, sausage, toast, a glass of orange juice, and a cup of tea into her mother's room.

"I got your breakfast for you, Ma."

Bernice took a little while to open her eyes. "Hah! Do I smell apple pancakes? Am I dreaming?" Bernice asked groggily.

"No, Ma. You're not dreaming. We made them for you."

"Oh my, I can get used to all of this special treatment. You two have been really spoiling me." She sat up in bed.

"Do you want to eat it now, or do you want to—"

"Hand it right over here. I hope you put syrup on it. I haven't had anything sweet to eat in days."

"We'll put some jam on it instead, Ma. You shouldn't eat syrup. The jam tastes just as good. Try it, you'll see."

"I'll be the judge of that." She cut a piece of the pancake covered in strawberry jam, and placed it in her mouth.

"Mmm, not bad. Not bad at all."

"I told you. So then, it looks like you'll be fine to go to the island tomorrow?"

"Oh, I'm fit as a fiddle. I've been feeling fine for two days now, just taking advantage of the royal treatment that you two have been giving me is all." She grinned playfully.

"We sort of suspected that, but we didn't mind taking care of you. It was fun doing it for a change."

"So what are we taking with us tomorrow?"

"Well, Eva and I were going to make some sandwiches, but there's no more bread, so we have to go to the store to get that and some fruits too."

"What store? You two can't go to the grocery store. You won't be able to find your way around there."

"We were just going to go to Mr. Wong's. He always gets the stuff for us."

"Yeah, but don't you remember how you were cheated that one time, and that other time he touched my bottom."

"He never touched you, Ma."

"He sure did. His hand grazed right there." She pointed to a spot on her behind.

"He never touched you, Ma. I'm sure you just imagined it or it was some sort of accident. Mr. Wong is not that type of guy."

"Okay, but just don't get too close to him."

"Alright, Ma, we're going to go now. We'll make the sandwiches when we get back."

"These pancakes are delicious," Bernice said again with a full mouth. "Almost as good as mine."

Eva was already waiting for her sister by the front door.

"She thinks Mr. Wong is going to fondle us and cheat us."

"Mr. Wong wouldn't do that."

"Yeah, I know."

The corner store was located in the opposite direction from the park. There seemed to be less commotion on that side of the street. The twins had to travel only two short blocks, past a dry cleaner and a fish-and-chip shop to get there. The jingle of the bell that hung on the door and the smell of pine cleaner told them that they had arrived.

When they entered the store, Ava stopped dead in her tracks. The Stickman was there.

From the strength of his stench, she could tell that he was directly in front of her, close enough to touch.

"Is that all you want?" Mr. Wong asked.

"Yeah, that will do for now," the Stickman replied.

When the Stickman passed by Ava, he brushed her arm accidently. She was elated even though he left the store without acknowledging her.

"What can I do for you ladies today?" Mr. Wong asked.

"We need a loaf of bread, three apples, a half dozen eggs, and a package of Tang," Eva replied.

"Oh, Mr. Wong, that was the Stickman who just left, right?" Ava interrupted.

"Yeah. What a stinker!" He laughed.

"What did he buy?"

"What he always buys."

"What's that?"

"Why do you need to know what he bought?" Eva nudged her sister. "Never mind her, Mr. Wong."

"Oh, it's quite alright. He got some pop, chips, and some of that sponge candy that the kids eat." Mr. Wong started moving around the store, collecting items for the twins. "Don't tell me you like that smelly fellow. He's no good."

"She knows that Mr. Wong. Everyone knows that."

"There could be a good person under there, Eva. You never know."

"No, no. That one is good for nothing." Mr. Wong laughed again. "What kind of apples do you want, the red, green, or yellow ones?"

"The red ones," the twins answered together.

Mr. Wong made his way back to the front counter.

"You would be better off with one of those geezers who sit around all day doing nothing. At least they don't do any illegal things." He rang up the groceries.

"You're absolutely right, Mr. Wong. She would be better off with anyone else."

"That'll be one dollar and eighty cents, please." He carefully placed the bag of groceries into Eva's hand.

"Thank you. Here you go." She gave him the money.

"I owe you twenty cents change. Here it is." He dropped the coins into Eva's palm.

Eva handed the coins to her sister, who examined them.

"Don't worry, I give you the right change."

"Thank you."

Outside, Eva turned to her sister.

"Is it all there?"

"Yep, four nickels. Twenty cents. It's all there."

"Good."

The two continued on their way home.

CHAPTER 12
An Excursion to the Island

THE NEXT DAY was a perfect day for a picnic. It was only moderately hot, and a slight breeze blew. Bernice insisted that they all wear their matching tie-dye dresses and sun hats for the occasion.

To get to the island, they had to take a bus, the subway, another bus, and a ferry. Moving from one mode of transportation to the next, the three women had to remain as close as possible. They walked at times with their arms interwoven like a set of chorus girls. Bernie guided from the center, while the twins carried all the bags.

"Okay, let's get up. The next stop is ours," Bernice said loudly from the back of the packed bus. She took Eva's hand and Eva in turn took her sister's. When the bus came to a complete stop, there was an eruption of noise and activity.

Bernice and her daughters felt right at home amid all the commotion.

The walk to the ferry docks wasn't a long one. The line to buy tickets moved fast. "Three seniors, please," Bernice said to the women behind the glass. She had been passing the twins off as seniors long before their fortieth birthday.

The woman gave the tickets with no questions asked.

The ferry was just arriving as they pushed their way through the turnstile. A stampede broke out when the gate was opened. Bernice waited for things to settle before she boarded.

"Can we sit upstairs?" Ava asked eagerly.

"It may be too packed up there to find a seat," Bernice replied.

"Let's just go see," Ava insisted.

"Yeah, you get the best ride up there," Eva added.

"Alright, hold on then. The stairs are directly ahead."

When they got to the upper deck, Bernice looked around.

"You see, all the seats are taken. Nowhere for us old folks to sit," she said loudly and with a sense of purpose.

"You can sit here," a young mother said. She pulled her two children up from the seats.

"Why do we have to get up for them?" the little boy protested. The mother hushed him and yanked him away.

"Thank you, Miss. Very kind of you," Bernice grinned from ear to ear.

"Thank you," the twins echoed.

Seeing the three women wouldn't fit on the bench, a young couple gave up their spot.

"Oh, how nice of you," Bernice said.

"Thank you," the twins repeated.

"The air feels and smells better already," Bernice said as she sat and closed her eyes.

While Bernice napped, the twins enjoyed the breeze and listened to the splashing of the waves, the squawking of the seagulls, and the hum of the boat's motor. A familiar clicking sound caught them off guard.

"Mrs. Misic?" Ava turned her head.

"Good day for the island," Mrs. Misic sang out. Her clove scent was not so strong in the middle of the lake.

"We're lucky to have such perfect weather," Mr. Misic joined in.

"Yes, beautiful," the twins chorused.

Bernice pried her eyes open.

"My Jovanna just loves the island." He placed his arm around his wife and kissed her cheek.

"And what my Jovanna wants, my Jovanna gets." He gave her another peck to the cheek.

Bernice grimaced.

"Let's go to the front, honey. We can see better there," Mrs. Misic said.

"Enjoy your day, ladies." She limped away with her husband.

"Thank you. You too," the twins replied together.

"That man is always slobbering all over that woman. I don't know how she can stand it." Bernice whined.

Eva and Ava smiled.

"Is that the way Papa used to slobber over you?" Ava asked timidly.

Bernice looked out over the water.

"He was like that in the beginning."

The twins were stunned that Bernice had not changed the subject as she normally did.

"Did you ever go with him to the island?" Eva asked, not expecting an answer.

"Only once or twice, after we moved here," Bernice replied without hesitation.

"Was he like Mr. Misic is with his wife?" Ava asked.

"Would you like to hear a story about it?"

The sisters nodded their heads emphatically. They couldn't believe their luck.

"Okay, I'll tell you after we eat lunch." Bernice closed her eyes and became quiet again.

"Are you okay, Ma?" Ava asked.

"I'm fine, just resting my eyes is all."

After the ferry docked, the women walked past the crowd and the general craziness and made their way toward a quiet part of the island. Bernice chose a spot under a large oak tree. The beach lay in front of them, and a rose garden to their left.

"Roses," Eva sighed.

"Yeah, you should see them. They have almost every color in the rainbow. The nicest ones are the miniature pink ones." Bernice pulled the blanket out and spread it.

"What about yellow ones? Those are the most romantic. Do they have yellow ones?" Ava asked.

"Of course they have yellow ones," Eva insisted. "She said every color in the rainbow."

"Yeah, there's great big yellow ones."

"Did you make sure that there were no ants, Ma?" Eva asked.

"Remember I got bitten by one of those nasty things last time?"

"No ants," Bernice replied.

"What about dog poo?" Ava sniffed about.

"None of that either. You two can sit down now."

Eva and Ava plopped down and took off their shoes.

"Here you go." Bernice handed each of her daughters a sandwich, then poured some Tang from a plastic jug into Styrofoam cups.

"Ma, you need to have your shot after you eat, okay?" Eva reminded her.

"Yeah, yeah. I know." Bernice chomped down on her sandwich.

"I don't know how those people could go in that water."

"I know. It must be freezing."

"Your father swam in there once."

The twins turned toward their mother.

"Are you going to tell us that story now?" Ava asked.

"I guess, I have to, since I promised. Let me finish my sandwich first."

The twins listened as their mother chewed slowly. They could tell that she was stalling. "Okay, are you done?" Ava asked after several minutes.

"Yeah, just let me wet my whistle a little more." Bernice poured another cup of Tang for herself. "Well, I guess I never told you that I met your father for the first time when I was only a few days old," Bernice began.

The sisters were all ears.

• • •

Back home, your father's family, the Archers, were our closest neighbors. They lived only a stone's throw away from us. Our mothers were best friends. Your father and me were born only a few months apart. He was convinced that he loved me from the very first time he laid eyes on me. I was fresh out of the oven, and he wasn't even three months old when his mother held him up to see me. At that time he had no control of his wobbly head, but he said his heart knew right away. He stared at me drooling and gurgling. His mother understood everything.

"Look, I think my son is smitten with your daughter," she said.

"Ah, that's just gas." My mother giggled.

Your father claimed that from that day onward his love grew with each passing day. Even after his family moved to the other side of town when we were five. On my eighth birthday he proposed to me for the very first time.

"Bernice, will you do me the most supreme honor of giving me your hand in marriage?" He knelt down in front of me and acted as if he were King Arthur or something.

"I don't think kids in elementary school have any business talking like that and asking such questions," I replied. But that didn't deter him. He just kept on asking the same question in the same way every year on my birthday. The last time he asked was on my seventeenth birthday.

It was an Indian summer day and I was sitting in my favorite spot under the apple tree. He came up on his bike and handed me a cake of soap that had been carved to look like a smiling sun.

"Happy Birthday, Bernice. What do you think of your present?" He sat down next to me.

"It looks like all of your other crazy inventions."

"So you like it?"

"How can I not?"

"So, how you doing? Are you still thinking about Charles?"

"Of course. All the time."

"Would it help if I sang to you?"

He always sang to cheer me up, especially after Charles died.

• • •

"Is that where we get our singing from?" Ava interjected.

"Yes, yes, of course. I thought I already told you that."

"Never!" the twins said together.

"Well, now you know. Let me get back to the story." She brushed some crumbs off the blanket.

• • •

"Not now, maybe later," I answered in regard to the song.

He jumped to his feet and began pacing around with his hand in his pocket. "I was thinking, it being your birthday and all…" he started.

I sat there waiting for him to slip into his usual Knights of the Round Table spiel, but he pulled out a velvety box from his pocket and handed it to me. I was expecting a flower stem or electrical wire, but it was a real store-bought ring with a small diamond and all.

"Will you?" he asked with the most fearful look in his eyes.

I paused. He held his breath.

"Yes, I will." I figured I had made him wait long enough.

We were engaged. The poor guy started crying.

Some weeks later, I suggested he spend the night because it was pouring buckets outside, and he only had his bike. We started off sleeping in different rooms, but around midnight, he came to my room. When he slipped under the covers, I was naked as a jaybird. He was so embarrassed, he turned his body away.

"You don't have to be afraid." I reached over and pulled him closer to me and kissed him.

That one kiss led to another, and then another. Once it was over, he was bawling like a baby, and I was convinced that I was in love.

However, some months later, on our wedding night, I lay next to him not feeling a thing—no epiphany, no connection, no affection, not even any real happiness—only maybe some gratitude. It was only in that moment that I realized I didn't love Ben like a husband. He was more like my brother or a very good friend. But I couldn't bear to tell him. It was too late, the vows had been said, the presents unwrapped, and he had already found a job and an apartment in the city. I felt a sense of doom because I knew that love could slowly turn into appreciation, but gratitude could never become true love.

• • •

The twins waited for Bernice to continue the story but she said nothing more. She lay back on the blanket and closed her eyes.

"I'm going to take a little cat nap now. You can give me my shot after," she announced.

"But what about the rest of it?" Ava asked, confused.

"The rest of what?" Bernice yawned.

"The rest of the story, Ma."

"Let's leave the rest for another time, why don't we? I don't have anything left in me right now."

The twins, although puzzled by the abrupt ending, were quite satisfied with what they had heard. Their mother's new openness thrilled them.

For many days that followed, the twins discussed the details of that one story in their bed at night.

"He doesn't sound like that bad a guy, does he?" Ava began as she clung to her side of the bed.

"Not at all," Eva replied.

"Then why do you think she was refusing to talk about him all this time?" Ava asked.

"It must be something that happened after they married."

"You think he hit her?"

"Maybe. Anything could be possible."

"You think he hit us?"

"We were only babies when he died. He doesn't sound like the kind of man who would hurt a child."

"No he doesn't. He sounds sweet just like the Stickman."

"How many times do I have to tell you? That man is the farthest that you can get from sweet. He's not even sour. He's downright rotten."

Ava swung her pillow at her sister.

"You're just jealous."

"Jealous of what?" Eva swung back.

"That I have a boyfriend and you don't."

"You don't have a boyfriend."

"Yes I do."

"No you don't."

"Keep it down in there. I'm trying to sleep here," Bernice yelled from her room.

The bickering stopped.

On the way to the park the next day, Ava insisted on taking a detour to Mr. Wong's to buy some sponge candy.

"I don't know why you're wasting ten whole cents on that guy," Eva scolded.

"It's just a small token of my affection."

"He's not even going to care, and Ma is not going to like it either."

Ava ignored her sister.

As they approached the café, they could hear a large commotion up ahead. People were yelling and screaming. It sounded as if most of the neighborhood was there. The idling engines told them that the police had already arrived.

"You don't know what the fuck you're talking about. I was right here when it all started. That guy there came out and pulled a knife," said one loud voice.

"What the fuck have you been smoking, you fucking four-eyed monkey. The guy was only trying to defend himself," another voice answered.

"Okay, so let me get this straight now…" a calmer voice, most likely a police officer's, interrupted.

The twins could feel the anxious energy all around them. The crowd parted like the Red Sea as they pushed their way through. They had no interest in lingering since their mother had always told them to stay clear of trouble.

"I have something for you today, Mr. Stickman," Ava said as she reached his corner.

"Nice, nice. How did you know that was my favorite?" He grabbed the sponge candy from Ava and rammed it into his mouth. "You're a nice lady," he said as he leaned over.

Ava felt something brush past her right breast. It was the Stickman's hand. She froze. She didn't know what to do.

"Are the fuzz still busy up that way?" he asked.

Ava said nothing.

He repeated the question.

"Yeah, they were talking to some people."

"Good, good. Thanks. Now you have yourself a good day, lady."

"Same to you."

Ava was still stuck on the touch. She lingered a bit before rushing to catch up to her sister.

"He…he touched me!" she exclaimed. "The Stickman touched my boob."

"That's what you get for throwing yourself at him. He thinks you're easy now."

"I wasn't throwing myself at him."

"Yes you were. What do you call getting that candy for him? I hate to tell you this, Ava, but he doesn't like you. He's just trying to be nice to you because he feels sorry for you."

"Why would he feel sorry for me?"

"Because you're an old, blind, fat virgin," Eva sneered.

"Well, so are you."

"But my faults are not as obvious as yours."

"What's that supposed to mean?"

"If you don't know, I'm not going to tell you. How did it feel, anyway, you know, when he touched you?"

"It felt normal. Nothing special. Just a little tap. You're not going to tell Ma, are you?"

"Why would I do that? Ma doesn't need to know every little thing that happens," Eva replied as she hustled ahead of her sister.

The park was quieter than usual. As the twins found their spot, they heard the squeaking of the two rickety swings and the coos of two excited kids.

"They really seem to like it," a woman with a thick European accent said.

"I'm sure they could do it all day if we let them," another voice replied.

The twins recognized their neighbor's voice right away.

"Wouldn't it be nice to be a baby again?" the first woman continued.

"Yes. Simple. No care in the world. That's the way it should be."

The two women snickered politely.

"You live in my building don't you?" one of them said.

"Yes. I've seen you too."

"My name is Rosalie. Rose for short."

"Hi, Rose. I'm Violet—Let, for short," she joked.

The twins felt for each other's hands. They couldn't believe their ears.

"We knew it. Rose and Violet are real people," Ava squawked, barging into the living room.

Bernice was sitting quietly reading in her armchair. "Of course, they're real people," she replied without looking up. "I told you I dreamt about them."

"Didn't I ask you if that woman was Rose a while ago?"

"I know you had your suspicions." Bernice looked up.

"But we didn't know for sure. Now we do." Ava sat across from her mother.

"What do you take me for—some crazy old lady with no wits about her?" Bernice folded her page and placed the book on the armrest. "I told you how those dreams of mine came about."

"But we always assumed most of your stories were made up," Eva said.

"Oh ye of little faith. Don't you know your mother has many talents, more than the average person. So tell me what happened to bring on this sudden realization of yours."

"The two women were in the park and they said their names were Rose and Violet," Ava blurted.

"They didn't say it to you, did they?"

"No, they introduced themselves to each other."

"Their kids were on the swings, right?"

"Yeah, how did you know?"

"That's what I dreamt last night."

"So you dream something one night, and the next day it comes true?"

"That's the way it usually works. I'm never able to see too far into the future in my dreams. I can see the past, but never the future for some strange reason. And sometimes things don't happen chronologically."

"So when did you first start dreaming about Rose and Violet?"

"Years ago, when they were first born."

"So how come you never told us their story until recently?"

"All the stories about little girls with shared souls were about them."

"But what about the parts that you're telling us now?"

"Those parts, I only started dreaming about after I saw them, one after the other, one day some time ago. That's when I made the realization."

"What realization?"

"That they were the people from my dreams."

"Have you ever seen people from your dreams before?" Ava asked.

"No, never."

"How did you know their names?"

"I dreamt them, of course."

"You sure you didn't overhear them somewhere? Like we did?"

"I'm positive."

"So you must have seen when they came here in your dreams."

"Yes, of course. That's the next part of my story."

"Can we hear it?"

"When—now?"

"Why not?" the twins asked together.

"Let me go to the toilet first. I gotta pee something fierce." She tottered to the bathroom. "Are you two hungry? The roast is almost done."

"No," the twins replied. They sat quietly and waited for their mother. When Bernice got back she made herself comfortable, burped, and continued the story.

CHAPTER 13
A Long Desire Fulfilled

SEVERAL MONTHS AFTER the impromptu proposal, Rose and Douglas were married. There were only four people present in the church that day: Rose, Douglas, Rose's mother, and the priest. Douglas's parents had declined the invitation since they didn't approve of the bride.

"What an embarrassment. What are people going to think? Since you insist on marrying her, take this and never come back," Douglas's mother said coldly to him. Then she handed him an envelope that contained a check and two plane tickets.

"You must know, we have a reputation to maintain," she added. Had she known the true paternity of Rose's child, she would have been even more appalled.

"So you're just going to ship me into exile like some criminal?" Douglas whimpered.

The reply was a scornful sneer.

In the church, almost everyone was happy. Rose's mother glowed. She couldn't believe Rose's luck. It didn't even bother her that Douglas's family wasn't there.

"It's a shame that they won't be able to make it. They must be very busy people," she had commented.

The priest was pleased to marry anyone who already had a bulging baby bump, and Douglas was overjoyed to be finally fulfilling his dream. Rose, however, didn't share any of these sentiments. She wanted to enjoy the day, but she couldn't. She was sad. She sobbed so inconsolably throughout the ceremony that anyone would have believed there was a funeral that day and not a wedding.

"Are you okay, sweetheart?" Rose's mother whispered as the priest read a passage from the Bible.

"I'm fine. It's just that everything seems to be happening all at once," Rose replied between sobs.

"Don't worry, you'll be just fine. Just fine." The apprehension in Rose's mother's voice betrayed her.

"By the power vested in me, I now pronounce you man and wife. You may kiss the bride."

Rose's body stiffened as Douglas pressed his lips to hers. The respectful kiss was their first. The ceremony had not ended the awkwardness between them.

Rose and Douglas reached their new home in America just as the weather was turning cold. The first thing Rose noticed about the place was its starkness, everything from the buildings to the sky was a sea of gray. She searched into the distance for a hint of color but only saw a dark stick-like figure billowing in the wind.

There were no signs of life in the dingy hallway on the

second floor, only hushed TV sounds behind closed doors. Douglas put down the luggage in front of apartment 202 and opened the door.

"Ladies first." He gestured for Rose to enter.

She entered reluctantly. The interior was just as drab as the exterior. Everything seemed to be in a state of disrepair. Garbage had been left everywhere.

"Nice place, eh?" Douglas declared. In his elated state, he could see only a fresh start and possibilities.

Rose kicked away a pop bottle and maneuvered herself down to the floor. She sat silently staring at nothing in particular, slipping easily into a melancholy trance.

"I hope you don't think I'm going to marry you now. I have to finish my schooling. I don't want to be a father. I don't even love you!" Sam's voice echoed through her head. She tried her best to ignore it, but it wouldn't go away.

While Douglas cleaned and repaired everything in the following days, Rose sat dazed and disengaged, only moving when it was absolutely necessary. Sorrow infused her veins and weighed her down. The only thing that brought her any sort of pleasure during this time was the sound of two female voices singing close by.

Douglas assumed that Rose's depression was just homesickness, so he allowed her to be as glum as she wanted for as long as she wished. He knew nothing of the angry voice that haunted her.

"I found the library today," he announced one day when he returned home.

She was in the same spot where he had left her.

"Look what I signed out for you." He handed her a copy of *Dead Souls*.

She looked at it and laughed. He was heartened to hear this.

"That's exactly what I've been behaving like, haven't I?"

"Yes, I guess."

"I'm so sorry. Will you forgive me?" she asked.

"Yes, of course I will." He smiled and kissed her forehead.

From that day onward Rose tried hard to be more communicative and helpful, but the cloud of sadness seemed to be forever present.

Once the apartment was spic and span, Douglas purchased all the necessary items needed to create a comfortable home. He bought a crib and all the other essential things for the baby-to-be. He selected items of the highest quality because that's what he was accustomed to. Wanting to make sure that Rose stayed healthy, he prepared nutritous meals and encouraged her to take daily walks.

"You must eat all of this good soup," he would say as he sat on the floor next to her, feeding her and wiping her chin. She hardly had an appetite.

"I can feed myself, you know."

"Yes, I know, I just want you to be good and strong."

"Thank you."

"You're more than welcome."

As the weather grew colder and drearier outside, Rose slipped slowly back into her depressed cocoon. In her quiet corner, hours turned into days, days into weeks and weeks into months. All the while her abdomen grew at a steady pace.

One afternoon after Douglas had finished feeding her, she looked down and saw that she was sitting in a pool of water.

"Really now! All you had to do was get up and go to the bathroom," he said with a trace of anger in his voice. He hadn't showed any signs of it before, but he was growing weary of Rose's almost vegetative state.

"It's my water. My water broke," she said, suddenly sounding alive. "We have to go to the hospital now."

"Oh, my goodness. Oh!" he squealed, then got up and quickly prepared to leave.

Rose labored for more than ten hours. As the baby emerged, she felt her sadness slowly dissipating, as if the child were expelling it. Douglas watched on with equal amounts of elation and squeamishness at the newborn's arrival.

"It's a boy," the doctor announced.

Douglas puffed up his chest proudly.

"Would you like to cut the cord?" the doctor asked.

"Of course, of course," Douglas replied. His hands trembled as he took the scissors.

"Is that the way they're supposed to look…with that stuff all over them?" he asked.

"That's vernix. It's perfectly normal," the doctor reassured.

"We'll wash it all off in a minute," the nurse added.

Douglas began to look even more uneasy. The doctor, patted Douglas's shoulder and retrieved the scissors.

"Not to worry, young man. Most fathers feel the same way. I'll do the honors. We don't want to hurt the little rascal, now do we?" The doctor quickly cut the umbilical cord and handed the child over to the nurse.

"You should be proud. You have a healthy son there." He placed his hand on Rose's abdomen.

Rose was exhausted.

Douglas quickly turned his head at the first sight of the afterbirth.

After the baby was weighed, cleaned, and swaddled, the nurse put him in Rose's arms.

"Here you go, Mom. Here's your little man."

"Thank you," Rose replied.

She gazed down at her handsome new son and the last remnants of her sadness dissolved.

"Is the baby supposed to be this color?" Douglas took a few cautious steps closer. "And the lips, why are they so…and the nose so…? Why is…Rose?" He groaned and fell to the floor. The nurse looked down at him in amusement.

"Are you okay there, Sir?" she asked, trying to hold back her giggles.

Rose looked down. "What happened?"

"Just a simple case of a fainting husband. It happens all the time, but usually during the birth." The nurse slapped Douglas as hard as she could in the face. He snapped out of it.

An ugly scowl came across his face the moment he was back on his feet.

"Who is the father of this child?" he demanded in his mother tongue.

Rose had never seen him so angry before.

"Why are you only asking now? You never wanted to know before." Her sadness had returned.

The nurse pretended not to listen as she cleaned up.

"All this time you were carrying the child of that guy, and you never thought once to tell me?"

"Well, who else's did you think it was? You knew it wasn't yours when you asked me to marry you."

The nurse's interest piqued.

"Well, all this time, you could have said something."

"I would have told you if you'd asked."

"How could you have told me? You've hardly said two words since we've been here. I feel like I've been living with a deaf mute."

"I'm sorry. I just haven't felt much like speaking...but I...I really appreciated all that you've been doing."

"Now all of that has been a big waste of time, hasn't it? A big fucking waste of time."

"What do you mean by that?"

He stormed out.

"Do you need anything before I go? Someone will be along shortly to take you and the baby to your room," the nurse said sympathetically.

"No, I'm fine," Rose replied, knowing that her statement couldn't have been any farther from the truth.

You're pregnant. You're pregnant. You're pregnant. The sound of the doctor's raspy voice echoed in Violet's head as she trudged home. She had gone to the clinic that afternoon not knowing what to expect. *I'm not ready for this...I'm too young...Maybe I can give Robert the son he always wanted...I'm not going to be able to finish school...Doesn't every man want a son? What about Ma?*

Her mother was cooking when she arrived home. "Ma, I

have something to tell you." She was eager to get the ordeal over and done with.

Her mother turned and glared her.

"I know what you have to tell me. You're pregnant."

"You know?" She was shocked and relieved at the same time.

"Your face has been getting rounder. You went to the clinic?"

Violet nodded her head and held her breath.

"I see," her mother said softly.

Violet shifted her body to a defensive stance and prepared for the onslaught, but it never came. Her mother just bowed her head and began to weep.

She wanted to embrace her mother as she had done when she was a child, but her mother was no longer that same vulnerable person. She had become much more unapproachable and difficult since her husband had abandoned her. So much so that Violet couldn't discern if the strong feeling that she felt toward her was love or hate. If it was hatred, she thought, it would have had to be the kind reserved only for those we love the most.

"I'm sorry, Ma. So sorry." Tears began to well up, as she caressed her mother's forearm. Her mother turned to embrace her. The two held each other and cried a puddle.

When Robert was given the news, he touched Violet's stomach and said, "A ship under sail and a big-bellied woman, are the handsomest two things that can be seen."

Violet was confused. "So you're happy?"

"Of course, I'm happy. Now you really are mine."

"I've always been yours."

"But now it's official."

"Not exactly, my mother said..." Before she could finish what she was saying, Robert was on his knee.

"Violet James, will you marry me?"

"Yes, of course, I will marry you, Mr. Black." She was ecstatic.

"I promise I'll take care of you, put you first, and do everything in my power to make you happy," he said.

Violet couldn't have been any more pleased.

Three short weeks later, Violet and Robert stood at the altar. Dressed in black, Violet's mother frowned throughout the entire service. She felt that her daughter was making the biggest mistake of her life. The majority of the parishioners agreed. They believed that Violet was too young and innocent and Robert too shrewd. Regardless of this, they all cheered happily as the couple walked down the aisle as husband and wife.

"I've decided that it would be best if I traveled to America to make a better life for our family. I spoke to my brother already, and he's sending me a ticket and said that he would help get me settled. And when I'm settled, I can send for you," Robert announced one evening just before bed.

"America?" Violet sat up in bed.

"Yes, America, the land of promised opportunities, where those proverbial cases of milk and honey can be found."

"But we just got married, and the baby is coming..."

"That's why I have to go, so I can give the two of you more. Do you want to spend your whole life in this small place?"

"But we just started—"

"We'll have a better life up there. I can make more money and—"

"But what am I going to do without you?"

"You have your mother."

"But she's not my husband. You are."

"We won't be apart for long, and I'll send for you when I get things organized."

"Organized? And how long is that going to take?"

"Maybe a couple of months or—"

"You don't even know how long, do you?"

"I'm not a future teller. I don't know how long it's going to take, but it can't be all that long."

"So what am I supposed to do?"

"When I start making money, I'll start sending some for you."

"What about the baby? What if you miss the birth?"

"I'll…I will—"

"What if things don't work out for you up there?"

"Of course they'll work out for me, Violet. Don't you know I was the youngest public health inspector in the history of the Eastern Caribbean, and I graduated at the top of my class? I'm unstoppable. Those people up there won't be able to touch me."

"So when do you leave?"

"As soon as I get the ticket."

"Will you write?"

"Of course I'll write."

"How often?"

"As often as I can."

The next day Violet shared Robert's news with her mother.

"What do you mean he's leaving?" Violet's mother hollered. She was through feeling sorry for her daughter.

"He said that he would send for me as soon as he could."

"I'm sure he would," her mother responded sarcastically. "What kind of man leaves his pregnant wife after only a few weeks of marriage? I knew he was rotten from the first time I saw him. You see what I told you? I knew it! Those too-perfect, pointy, over-polished shoes told me everything I needed to know about that scoundrel. What kind of man puts that kind of care into something he's going to use to walk in the gutters? A selfish man—that's the kind of man who would do something like that. A scallywag, that's who!"

"He said it would be for the best."

"The best for who? The best for him."

"The best for us."

"You're a damn fool if you believe it's for the best."

"I believe him, Ma."

"If you believe him, then you're a bigger ass than I thought you were. I told you that man was no good. Now, who's going to look after you and that big belly of yours?"

"He said that's what mothers are for."

"Me? I can't even look after myself. I'm washing my hands of this damn nonsense." She rubbed her hands together.

"But you're my mother."

"Yes, I'm your mother, but you're a married woman now. You're no longer my responsibility. You think I could go back crying to my mother after I married your father and he was beating my backside? No."

"But I'm going to need—"

Before Violet could finish her sentence, her mother got up and walked into her bedroom.

"You're on your own, child. You made your bed, now you have to lie in it, no matter how messy that thing is. I don't want any part of it. That's what you get for getting involved with that type of man."

All Violet could do was collect her purse and leave.

In Robert's tomb-like rented room, where there was no way of knowing if it was day or night, Violet quickly discovered how unprepared she was for independence. She hadn't learned to cook properly and had no idea what was happening to her changing body.

Each day, she stared at a reflection she no longer recognized. The protruding belly and broad face with its exaggerated features seemed to belong to someone else.

Her mornings were spent sewing odd scraps of material that her mother had given her before the misunderstanding. Afternoons, she wandered the streets of the capital, picking up small amounts of fruits, vegetables, cornmeal, tinned milk, and rice when she needed them. Occasionally, she would go to the bayfront to dip her feet in the water, or to the library to look up books on pregnancy.

Her mind wandered during the endless hours she spent alone, her only comfort being the smell of fresh bread from the bakery below and Robert's letters, which she read over and over.

One stormy evening as she sat listening to the pattering of the rain outside, she closed her eyes and focused all her attention on the feelings that had been overpowering her. It didn't take her long to pinpoint the exact location of her sadness. It was on the right side of her belly just below her rib cage, very close to her womb. Her anger was a few inches above.

Without any difficulty or effort, she was able to move from her first trimester to the third. But this all changed one Friday afternoon when she started to feel pain in the small of her back. She realized in that moment that childbirth was one thing that was best not done alone.

"Ma, oh Ma! Please Ma!" she cried in agony as the pain intensified.

Downstairs, one of the bakery employees, who also happened to be a midwife, heard her moans and came to her aid.

"Come and sit on the edge of the bed," the woman instructed. "I've been watching that belly of yours grow. I knew that your time was coming soon."

"God bless you," Violet sighed.

After a few hours, a baby girl was born intact and healthy. When Violet saw that the baby had Robert's eyes, a part of her wanted to scoop them out; another part wanted to bathe them in kisses. She did neither. She only continued to stare at her new baby in wonderment.

News of the little one's arrival brought Violet's mother to her bedside that very night.

"What do we have here?"

"Your granddaughter." Violet was overjoyed to see her mother. "I'm going to name her Clara, after the girl from *Heidi*."

"Let me see the little scamp." She took the child up in her arms.

"You, my sweet child, you are all your father. But don't

worry, I won't hold that against you," she cooed. Her pungent vinegar scent now smelt oddly of the sea.

As Violet watched her mother with her daughter, she realized that the confused emotion she felt for her had been love all along.

In the following days, the new grandmother took care of everything and showed Violet all that she need to know, with more patience and kindness than Violet thought her capable of.

Robert kept his promise of writing. The new letters that arrived in blue and white airmail envelopes were always very wordy and in many ways similar to the ones that had first won her over. But in the place of "My dearest Violet" or "My beautiful sweet Violet" he wrote instead "Dear wife," or "Dear Mrs. Black." A litany of facts about his new home, his job search, and a small amount of cash were always enclosed. He concluded each letter with a famous quote about love and longing. Violet's favorite was "O that I were a glove upon that hand, That I might touch that cheek!" from *Romeo and Juliet*. He used this one repeatedly.

Shortly after the birth of her daughter, Violet received a letter that contained a money order, two one-way tickets, and a note that instructed her to get a passport, and to purchase warm clothing. She was overjoyed.

CHAPTER 14

The Beginning of the Troubles

"VIOLET AND HER HUSBAND were finally going to be reunited." Bernice stood up and stretched.

"So they arrived one after the other then?" Ava asked.

"Yes, Rose first, then Violet after her. Just like you and your sister."

"Maybe Ma should go lie down for a little bit," Eva suggested.

"I was just thinking the same thing myself." Bernice went to her room.

"You know what we should do, Eva?" Ava whispered.

"Why are you whispering?"

"Cause I don't want Ma to hear. I know how lightly she sleeps."

"Why can't Ma hear what you have to say to me?" Eva asked.

"Because I want to surprise her."

"Surprise her with what?"

"Sh. Keep your voice down. You're going to ruin the surprise."

"What surprise?" Eva was becoming annoyed.

"What if we could get Rose, Violet, and Ma all together so they could get to know each other better?"

"But Ma already knows them, doesn't she?"

"She doesn't know the real people. She only knows the ones in her dreams and imagination."

"I'm listening."

"Well, if we get them all together, then we can see what part of the story Ma made up."

"Most of it, Ava. Don't you know that already?"

"Well maybe there is some truth to her story. We can find it out by getting it straight from them."

"So how are we going to get them here?"

"We can have a tea party. The kind Ma and Violet had with their imaginary friends when they were small."

"Oh, how are we going to manage that? We've never had a party here before, let alone a tea party!"

"All we have to do is ask them to come to our place for some tea."

"But they don't even know us."

"Yeah, but they know we're their neighbors. It's not like we're complete strangers, and remember Violet said she liked our singing the other day in the hallway. We can tell them we'll sing and—"

"So we're just going to go and knock on their doors and ask them?"

"Why not?"

"What if they don't feel comfortable accepting our invitation, or what if they just don't want to come?"

"I have a feeling that they would come."

"Me too," Bernice yelled from her bedroom.

"Ma? You heard all of that?" Ava covered her mouth.

"Every single last word. You two have to wake up early to keep anything from me. I hear in my sleep."

"So you think they'll come?"

"Of course they'll come. I suspect that they would like to spend more time together," Bernice replied.

"Sure."

"Listen, since you two woke me up with your whispering, I might as well continue the story." Bernice shuffled from her bedroom.

"No, Ma, go back to sleep. We promise we'll be completely silent," Eva insisted.

"Never mind that. I'm already up." Bernice dropped back down into her armchair.

"Don't you need your rest, Ma?"

"You know what I'm going to say to that."

"You'll have plenty of rest when you're dead," Eva and Ava said together.

"Bingo." Bernice wiped some sweat from her brow and lay back in her seat. "Where did I leave off in Rose's part of the story again?" Bernice asked.

"Douglas had just fainted when he saw that Rose's baby wasn't white," Eva reminded her mother.

"Right, that's exactly right," Bernice put her head back.

• • •

As Douglas stormed away from the maternity ward, many furious thoughts raged inside him. He considered abandoning Rose, or giving the child up for adoption. He even pictured himself plucking the child from Rose's arms and throwing it out of the closest window. But he knew he could never do such a thing.

A few days later, Rose was forced to walk across town for almost a whole hour in the cold with the baby snuggled close to her. The scene was somewhat reminiscent of her mother's trek through the storm to deliver her.

Douglas decided that he would no longer wait on Rose hand and foot. He didn't want any form of contact with her or her child. He brought food, put it away, cooked his own meals, and slept on the couch. Rose raised no objections, but she fretted as she struggled to take care of the baby on her own.

Each day while the baby napped, Rose would lie beside him and study his serene expression and the rapid palpitations of his chest, contemplating the perplexity that had become her life.

What's going to happen to me and you now, baby? What can I say to Douglas to reassure him? Will he ever accept you? What have I done? Why didn't I say anything before? I didn't mean to deceive him. How else was he supposed to react?

A part of her truly felt sorry for Douglas. She knew deep down her reasons for marrying him were wrong. She had only conceded to save face. She had worried about how her mother and the town would react to her mixed-raced child. She feared that they would react the same way Douglas had.

"Can you just say something to me, please," Rose pleaded with Douglas after suffering twelve days of silence.

Douglas shut himself up in the bathroom.

"Why are you doing this?" Rose added. "Okay, I'm sorry I didn't tell you who the baby's father was. Is that what you want to hear?"

Douglas responded with a flush.

After Rose had given up hope of Douglas ever speaking to her again, on the twenty-fourth day, he tiptoed into the bedroom where she was nursing the baby, looked down nervously, and mumbled an unintelligible sentence. It was clear that his speaking skills were rusty.

"What?…Sorry, I didn't get that," Rose replied.

"I said, what should we name him?" he repeated more clearly.

"You want to name the baby?" She was thrilled and encouraged that he had used the inclusive 'we.'

"I haven't even thought about that."

"I know. You've been calling him 'baby' or 'little man'."

"I didn't realize I was doing that."

"I could tell."

"Oh?"

"Everybody should have a name. Any name is better than 'baby' or 'boy,'" Douglas continued.

"Someone used to call you 'boy'?" She asked sympathetically.

"They did almost my whole childhood."

"Who?" She realized that there was so much she still didn't know about him.

"My parents, but never mind that. Let's give this child a name."

"What do think? Do you have one in mind?"

"Yes, Thomas. That was the name of my good friend

when I was a boy. He never teased me and always called me by my name."

"Thomas, I like it. It's a strong name."

"Maybe he'll grow up to be a great inventor like Thomas Edison." He giggled nervously and gently touched the baby's curled-up fingers.

She was so relieved and tickled by his gesture that she mimicked his giggle.

On the other side of the ocean, Violet didn't know if she was doing the right thing by following Robert's instructions and ignoring her mother's warnings.

"You'd be much better off putting that money away and staying right here where you belong," her mother had lectured as she changed the baby's diaper. "And why is he sending for you now at the coldest time of the year? Does he want to freeze you and my grandchild to death?" She grimaced at the child.

"Don't worry, Ma. I'm sure he'll look after us."

"We'll see about that."

"He will. I know he will," Violet said. She was convinced.

"He better, for you and this child's sake." She scooped up the baby and handed her to Violet. "He better."

Violet rushed about getting everything together for her trip. She bought an assortment of long-sleeved shirts and long pants and applied for an emergency passport, although there was no emergency. As she ran these errands, her mind drifted to her mother and their looming separation. Ever since she had established that what she felt for her mother was not hate but indeed love, she couldn't imagine a place where the cantankerous woman didn't exist. She knew that she would miss all the small things about her: her new sea scent that at times still had hints of vinegar, the soft supple skin of her wrinkle-less face, the taste of her food, her course voice, and how she sometimes chuckled like an old hen. Violet secretly wished that she could stay on her island with her mother forever. She found it strangely ironic that she hadn't yet learned to swim but was leaving all the same.

On the day of her flight, Violet waited in the crowded departures lounge of the small airport, trying her best to con-tain her feelings. Her mother, dressed in her purple Easter dress, was doing the same. Neither of them paid attention to the loud clamor of excited voices around them. The baby, Clara, lay fast asleep in Violet's lap. She was already wrapped up, prepared for the frigid temperature.

Violet's mother loosened the blanket around her grand-daughter. She had rehearsed a speech, but at that moment she couldn't bring herself to repeat it.

When Violet looked over at her mother, she saw the dread in her eyes. It mirrored her own. She wanted to find some words that would quell her mother's fears, but none came. She wished that she could assure her mother that she would return to visit or send for her, but she didn't want to make any false promises.

A loud crackling sound came over the loudspeakers.

The flight announcement caught Violet and her mother off guard. They looked at each other and nodded. Violet lifted herself slowly out of the seat and stood, not sure of what to do next. Her mother remained seated with her eyes fixed outside.

"No, Violet. I don't want this." Violet's mother shook her head and began to weep.

Violet touched her mother's shoulder. Sobs started quietly in her throat, then they progressed to her chest. When her mother was finally on her feet, Violet wrapped her arms tightly around her. Their bodies trembled. High-pitched wails soon followed. Their laments, which could have easily been mistaken for the uproar after a horrible accident, drew the attention of not only those in the lounge, but also everyone in the surrounding area.

As Violet and her mother stood in what seemed to be their final embrace, the baby sweltered between them. Wanting to give her mother and her grandmother the time they needed, she offered no protest or complaint.

"You know I love you, Violet." Her mother's voice quivered.

"Yes, I know, Ma."

In the plane, Violet's chest was still heaving. She had no memory of how she had gotten out of her mother's arms and into her seat. She had forgotten how an airline employee had pried her from her mother's grip, and ushered her all the way from the departure lounge to the tarmac. She couldn't remember because she couldn't bear to.

At cruising altitude, she could still hear her mother's sobs. They sounded like tiny whispers in her ear. The wonder of being in an airplane for the very first time, high above the clouds and close to heaven had zero effect. Her only thoughts were of her mother.

• • •

In the kitchen after dinner the twins decided to start planning for the tea party. They thought it would brighten their mother's mood. They were both bubbling with excitement as they sat down at the table in the kitchen with her.

"So first of all, we should make up some invitations," Eva ordered.

"Good idea," Bernice said.

"Oh, should we invite Mrs. Misic and her husband too?" Ava asked.

"What do they have to do with this?" Bernice snapped.

"Yeah, it's for Rose and Violet," Eva agreed.

"I just thought we could make it into a real party and invite more people. You know, the more the merrier."

"Don't tell me you were thinking of inviting that smelly man of yours too?" Eva teased.

"What smelly man of hers?" Bernice asked. "Since when does she have a man that belongs to her?"

"She's talking about the Stickman, Ma."

"I know exactly who she's talking about. Didn't I tell you that guy was a no-good criminal?"

"I know what you said, but he has some good qualities," Ava responded in defense of her sweetheart.

"Name one."

"Well, he's always paying us compliments."

"That skinny stink-bomb compliments anything in a dress."

"I told her the same thing, Ma. You know she brought candy for him the other day."

"She what?! He's not even worth those pennies."

"You see, Ava? I told you that too."

"You two just hate men. It doesn't matter who it is."

"Not all, just the mean and smelly ones," Eva mocked.

"Especially the smelly ones," Bernice chuckled.

"You don't need to make fun of him. I'm sure he has a perfectly good reason for smelling the way he does. Maybe it's genetic."

"Maybe he just has a fear of soap and water." Eva laughed.

"And deodorant," Bernice added with a snort.

"Ha, ha. So funny I forget to laugh," Ava retorted.

"Okay, okay, enough of this silliness. Let's get these invitations done," Eva said trying to control her laughter. "Ma, can you get some paper and a few colored pencils? You're going to have to write them up for us."

"My, my, so bossy all of sudden. Who died and made you the king?" Bernice walked over to a drawer on the far side of the kitchen.

"All of a sudden? That's how she's with me all the time," Ava said. "She thinks she's some kind of dictator or something."

"At least dictators get things done," Eva replied in her own defense.

"Yeah, but all those things are bad."

"Well I can't be a dictator anyway. You ever heard of a woman dictator? All of those crazies are men."

"There you go again with that men stuff."

"I'm just telling you facts, Ava. That's all it is."

The twins continued to bicker as Bernice finished the invitations.

"Okay, here they are." She handed one each to Eva and Ava.

"Yours is for Violet," she said to Ava. "And yours is for Rose," she said to Eva.

"Okay," the twins said together.

In the hallway, they counted their steps to make sure that they got the right door. Rose's apartment was only two doors away. Eva pushed the invitation into Rose's mail slot and went back inside. Ava walked farther down the corridor to Violet's place. After she delivered the invitation, she heard someone come up from the stairwell behind her.

The pungent smell was unmistakable. It was the Stickman.

"Psst...hey you. Come here a second," he whispered.

He opened the garbage-room door.

Ava followed him willingly. Her heart was beating outside her chest.

Once the door was closed, he grabbed both of her breasts. She swallowed hard.

"You ever been fucked before?" he asked.

She shook her head and gulped for air.

"I didn't think so. Well, would you like me to do you the favor?" His hand began inching down her belly. "I can do it right here, right now, if you like," he continued.

Ava started feeling a bit tipsy. Feeling the Stickman's hand on her upper thigh, she finally came to her senses.

"Sorry, I'm not that easy," she declared proudly and yanked the Stickman's hand off her leg and left the room.

"Whatever," the Stickman responded unfazed. He walked back into the stairwell as if nothing had happened.

Ava had to calm herself before entering the apartment.

Bernice had a glass of milk waiting for her. She took it and joined her sister on the loveseat.

"There's something missing," Eva grimaced, referring to the milk.

Ava said nothing.

"Something sweet to go with it, perhaps?" Bernice asked.

"That's it," Eva said.

"But we don't have anything sweet, thanks to the two of you."

"Oh yes we do." Eva got up and went to her bedroom. "We're going to have to make some more for the party," she said, returning with a circular tin.

"I hope you haven't been eating those things in there," Bernice warned.

"No, just hiding them."

"I'll continue the story now if you share one of those with me," Bernice offered with a hint of desperation in her voice.

"Three sessions in one day, Ma? Are you sure you're up to it?"

"Sure, why not—if you give me one." Bernice began to salivate.

"You don't even know what's inside, Ma."

"I don't care. I know it's something sweet."

Eva drew the container closer to her chest. "What do you think Ava, should we give her one?"

"Why not?" Ava, replied, preoccupied. "She promised to continue the story, so give her one."

Eva took out a sugar cookie and handed it to her mother. Bernice quickly pushed it in her mouth and closed her eyes. "Mmm," she cooed in ecstasy. "That's good!"

"Okay, so here we go. I forgot to tell you one part so I'll go back a little."

CHAPTER 15

The First Encounter

ROSE AND HER MOTHER'S good-bye couldn't have been any more different than that of Violet and her mother. At the airport the day of Rose's departure, her mother tried her best to appear cheerful.

"How lucky you are to be off on such a great adventure," Rose's mother said as she forced the corners of her mouth up.

After the boarding call was made, they all stood stiffly.

"I'm sure you'll be very happy in your new home," Rose's mother embraced her daughter and shook Douglas's hand.

"Bye, Mama," Rose sobbed softly before dragging herself to the check-in counter.

"Bye, Rose, be well." She feigned another smile.

After the departure, Rose's mother continued to wear her mask of gladness.

She went about her days as if nothing had changed, but

in reality her world had been turned upside down. The sadness lingered in her heart and festered like an open sore. The situation reached its boiling point when she received a package from Rose one morning. As she held the small box, she felt her body seize and her windpipe constrict. In a matter of seconds, she lay unconscious on the floor. A few minutes later, her aching heart stopped beating all together, and she was dead.

Had she remained alive long enough, her spirits might had been lifted by the contents of the package. Inside were souvenirs, a picture of her newborn grandson, and a tiny lock of his curly hair.

Rose and Douglas sat in their bedroom at opposite ends of the bed, looking very sullen. Baby Thomas lay asleep between them. Rose's eyes were red and swollen from crying. Douglas's were dry and dull.

"I can't believe she's gone," Rose intoned.

Douglas looked distracted.

"I can't believe I'll never see her again," she added. "I can't believe…"

"Well, believe it. You can't do anything about it anyway, so just be quiet and let me think."

Rose was stunned by Douglas's insensitivity. Things had been going well with them since the baby was named. They spoke to each warmly, and Douglas had even gone so far as to shower her with lavish gifts.

"What's the matter, Douglas?" She feared that he was beginning to have doubts about the baby again.

He didn't answer.

"What's bothering you?"

Douglas picked at his finger.

"Our money is almost all gone."

"What do you mean, almost all gone? Aren't your parents sending you an allowance?"

"No, right before we got married, my parents, rather my mother, gave me a check and told me to go as far away as possible."

"Why did she do that?"

"Because she didn't want me to marry you and she hates me."

"Is that why she didn't come to the wedding?"

"Yes, neither of us lives up to her standards, I guess."

"So what about the money then?"

"It was supposed to last for a good year or so until we got on our feet, but I guess I wasn't careful with it."

"How much is left?"

"I counted this morning, and I only have enough to last another month or so."

"That's okay, we'll manage."

"How on earth are we going to manage?"

"Well, maybe you can get a job?"

"A job? What kind of job could I get? I never worked a day in my life, and my degree—I spoiled all of that."

"Well maybe you can go back to school here."

"With what money?"

"What about asking your parents for some more?"

"I can't do that," he screamed.

The baby jumped in his sleep.

"Why not? They're your parents. I'm sure they would be happy to help."

"No they won't." He was getting more and more agitated.

"Sh, you're going to wake the baby," she said softly. "Why won't they?"

"Because of that." He pointed to Thomas.

Her cheeks flushed with heat. "What did you just say?"

"I said if *that* didn't exist maybe I could go back to them, but now I can't, can I?"

"Are you now calling my son, our son, the one you named, *that*? Is that what you're calling him?" She was no longer able to suppress her anger.

"Yes, that's what I called him because that's what he should be called."

"That…" She got up and perched herself over Douglas. "That is a flesh and blood human being who should never be referred to like that. He's not an animal or some sort of object—he's an innocent child of God."

"That so-called child of God is going to ruin us, you hear me," he snapped.

"How could a helpless baby ruin anyone? If anything is going to ruin us, it's going to be your irresponsibility," she barked back.

"Just mark my words."

"What words?"

"Things would have been perfect for us if it wasn't for that child!"

"Well, I'm sorry you feel that way, but that child is not going anywhere."

"We'll see about that," he mumbled under his breath.

"What did you say?" she demanded.

He remained tight-lipped.

"I don't understand where all of this is coming from, Douglas. If it's the money you're worried about, you could always find a job that doesn't need a lot of skills or experience, and we could live on that. We don't need a lot." She tried her best to sound conciliatory.

"I'm not going to do that."

"Why?"

"I just won't, and that's that."

"Then what are we going to do? How are we going to live?"

"You should have thought about that before you went and got yourself pregnant by that fucking African." He stormed out of the apartment. The bang of the heavy door woke Thomas.

Seething with anger, Rose picked up her crying son, soothed him, and then hurried to the door.

Violet's flight had arrived early that morning. Her body shivered. The layers of long-sleeved shirts and pants felt to her as if they were lace. In all of her life, she had never experienced such discomfort. She sat waiting patiently for Robert to collect her, but he never appeared.

Hours later, she paced—her bundled baby in one hand and her small suitcase in the other—still hoping that she hadn't been forgotten. Just as tears were beginning to form in the corner of her eyes, she remembered that she had Robert's address.

As she made her way through the arrival lounge, she prayed that the money she had would be enough.

"Can you take me to this address?" She showed the airmail envelope to a short cab driver.

"Sure," he said, after a quick glance.

"How much?"

"Ah, for that address, about twenty."

"Twenty dollars?" she repeated. "I only have eighteen."

"The fare is twenty dollars, Ma'am."

"But I don't have that." Desperation was plastered all over her tired face.

"Okay, okay. Give me the money. Let's go."

"Thank you. God bless you."

She handed him all the money she had in the world.

"Where is the rest of your baggage?"

"There's no more. Just this." She shook the small traveling case in her hand.

"Let me have it." He took the bag and placed it in the back seat.

She sank into the car with the baby. "Thank you."

"No problem, Ma'am."

It wasn't long before she and Clara were fast asleep.

When the rattling of engine stopped, the driver reached back and gently nudged her. "We're here, Ma'am."

She sat up, rubbed her eyes and looked around. It was a gray, dismal sight. She wondered what happened to the sun and if she would ever see blue skies again.

"Are you sure this is the right place?"

"Yes, Ma'am, it's the address from the envelope."

"Is it possible that there is another street with that name?"

"No, there's only one."

"Are you sure?"

"I'm positive, Ma'am."

As she stepped out of the vehicle, a man with a funny wobble whizzed by causing her to stumble.

The driver rushed to her aid.

"Thank you. People can be so rude."

"You'll have to get used to the crazies. The city is filled with them." He handed Violet her bag and drove off.

She felt a sense of foreboding as she made her way toward the low-rise building. Something in her told her to turn around and go back to the airport but she knew what was done was done.

The stairwell was dark and smelled of urine. The steps creaked under her feet.

Realizing that she had forgotten the apartment number, she stopped. Crouching down, she placed the baby on her lap and rummaged through her purse. As she did this, a tall, pale woman with a tan baby stepped out of her apartment. From Violet's perspective, she looked like a giant.

The woman was startled to see Violet stooping in front of her. The two women stared curiously at each other for a very long time. Then Violet showed her the address on the back of the airmail envelope. The woman looked at it and pointed toward the other end of the corridor.

Violet nodded and continued to stare at the woman. As she did so, she was overcome by an oddly strange, almost peaceful, sensation. There was something weirdly familiar about her face. The recognition seemed to be mutual. As Violet struggled to get back to her feet, the woman stepped forward and offered her hand. When their palms touched, the eerie feeling they were both experiencing intensified. This puzzled them both.

When they were no longer connected, they pretended nothing out of the ordinary had just happened. Violet nodded her thanks and gathered her belongings while her eyes remained on the woman. She felt compelled to turn around and take one last look as she moved away, but she didn't dare.

Apartment 208 was tucked neatly in the corner. Violet found the door slightly ajar. She entered without knocking. Inside was dark. There were no apparent signs of Robert. Just as she was about to creep out, she noticed a dim light at the end of a narrow passageway. She tiptoed quietly toward it. The closer she got, the more certain she was that she was in the right place. She heard something that sounded oddly like Robert's voice, speaking in low, moan-like whispers. A female voice cooed back. Violet knew exactly what the sounds were. When she pushed open the door, her suspicions were confirmed. The man's back was turned away from the door, but she was certain it was Robert.

"I hope you are enjoying my husband's service!" Violet blurted out as she snuck up behind the couple.

The naked woman let out a high-pitched screech. Robert froze right where he was, while his lover scrambled about for her clothes. She hurried past Violet with her head hung down.

Violet watched as Robert turned around, conspicuously covering his penis. Her eyes burned through him as he shifted from side to side. He had put on a few pounds, and his posture was now more slouched and unsure. His face seemed to belong to a stranger. The once luminous eyes were now glazed and bloodshot.

The smell of sex still lingered. They both remained mute. Violet wondered what had caused him to change so noticeably. His blank expression offered no answers.

"How could you?" Violet heard herself say in a voice that didn't belong to her. "I wondered why you weren't at the airport to meet us. We waited and waited, but you never came because you were here doing your business with that woman." She began to unwrap the baby.

"This is your daughter. Her name is Clara. Here, take her. I'm exhausted. I need to sit down."

She handed the baby over to him.

He held the child at arm's length.

"The child needs to be changed," he said.

"Then change her." Violet dropped the suitcase and left the room.

In the living room, she searched the wall for a switch. The light was dim. The room contained only one battered couch, a lopsided coffee table, and a lamp without a shade. Newspapers and other garbage littered the floor. It was clear that Robert had not prepared for her arrival.

After brushing off some crumbs and retracting a broken spring she sat down. Her anger peeked as her body settled. A mouse scurried in front of her along the wall. She stamped her feet. "Goddamn you!"

She regretted not listening to her mother's advice. As she wiped away her tears, she heard the sound of two female voices singing. The melody was very soothing. It felt as if the song was just for her. Her mind drifted to her mother, then to the woman in the hallway, then to what she had just witnessed in the bedroom. All these thoughts swirled about in her head until she fell asleep.

• • •

"Do you want some tea, Ma?" Eva asked.

"Some tea would be wonderful," Bernice replied with a smile in her voice.

"I'll go and make some then."

Ava followed her sister.

"Do you think Ma was right about men and bowel movements, about them making you feel better than any man
can?" Ava sat down at the kitchen table.

"What are you talking about that now? Why are you
bringing that up?" Eva filled the kettle.

"In her stories, all the men start off all nice and all, but
then they turn into creeps."

"You don't have to worry about that, Ava. The Stickman
is already a creep." Eva chuckled.

"You don't have to laugh at me," Ava sulked.

"I'm not laughing at you."

"Yes you are."

"Do you really think that Stickman is a decent person?"

Ava was dying to blab about what had happened to
her in the garbage room, but she didn't want to give up the
Stickman. She also liked the idea of having a secret of her
very own for the first time in her life. "No, but he's really the
only man I know."

"How about Mr. Misic and Mr. Wong." Eva joined her
sister at the table.

"Those men don't count."

"Why?"

Ava hesitated. "They just don't, and our father wasn't like
that."

"How do you know?"

"Well, I don't know. Only Ma knows that for sure."

"And she won't tell us."

"Don't you remember, she started to tell us?"

"You know what we should do?" Eva got up.

"What? Make cookies?"

"No. We should ask Ma to tell us more."

Ava remained seated.

"Are you coming or not?"

"Yeah, of course, I'm coming." Ava sprang to her feet.

Bernice was snoring. Eva nudged her.

"Ma," Eva yelled. "Ma, wake up."

Bernice woke with a start.

"What…what is it? Can't you see that I was sleeping," Bernice snapped.

"We need you to continue telling us about our father."

"Wasn't that story enough for you?" Bernice asked.

"No, Ma. You didn't even scratch the surface."

Bernice stirred uncomfortably in her chair.

"Well, Ma?"

"Okay, bring me my bottle and I will tell you more, but you can only ask one question between the two of you."

Eva went to retrieve the bottle of vodka and handed it to her mother.

"So, what's the question?" Bernice asked.

"Did our father love us? Was he happy when we were born?" Ava blurted out without waiting for her sister.

Bernice shifted uncomfortably, opened the bottle, and took a short swig.

"Ma, did you hear me?"

"I heard you just fine. There's nothing wrong with my ears." She guzzled down some more.

"Are you sure you should be drinking so much?" Eva asked. "I don't think that's such a good idea with your condition and all."

"What about my question?" Ava interjected.

"Technically, you asked two questions. I said you could

ask only one. And I'm only having a little sip so you don't
have to worry."

"Okay, I'll change it to one. Did our father love us?" Ava
asked.

Bernice sighed and murmured something to herself.

"What was that? What did you say?" Ava asked.

"I didn't say anything."

"But we heard you," Eva insisted.

"I said, I didn't say a thing."

"I hope you're not planning on drinking that whole bottle," Eva scolded.

"Like I said, I'm only having a sip," Bernice snapped back.

"Ma, what's wrong, with you? You were fine just a few
minutes ago."

"I'm still fine. So you want to know if your father loved
you, right? I'll tell you all about it. Every stinking detail."

Neither Eva or Ava knew what to make of their mother's
flare-up.

Bernice settled into her seat. "You know the story of your
birth, right?" she started.

Eva and Ava nodded their heads.

"Well I never told you the whole story."

"How surprising," Eva said sarcastically.

"If you two are going to be rude, I'm going to stop right
now."

"I didn't say anything. Why do you always have to include
me when it's always her."

"Sorry Ma. You can go on now," Eva apologized.

"Yeah, she's sorry for her rude interruption, please continue Ma," Ava added.

"Well, what I didn't tell you about the day of your birth

was that your father wasn't there. He actually didn't show up until some time later."

The twins held their breath in anticipation.

"That day in the hospital while I labored, I had so many worries. The biggest was your father." Bernice continued.

"Wait, wait—that sounds familiar," Eva interrupted.

"It sounds like the story of Rose's birth," Ava agreed.

"It's nothing like that, just listen, okay?" Bernice barked.

The twins obeyed and listened.

CHAPTER 16

Ben Archer's Love

SO WHILE I TRIED my best to look after you two, your father was off gallivanting, God knows where. When he came back weeks later, he was in a terrible state, looking like a certified loon. His hair and clothes were unkempt and he smelled like he had been sleeping in the sewers. He started spilling his guts the moment he stepped in the door.

"Bernice, first let me apologize for running away the way I did. It was uncalled for."

I had to step back some from him. The sewer stench was deadly.

"Bernice, you know that I love you and that I've loved you since I was a little babe in my mother's arms. But loving someone, or two other someones the way that I love you scares the hell out of me. You remember when you found out that you were pregnant that I didn't know if I had enough love in my heart to share—well Bernice, I still don't know.

I thought I would have figured it out in the nine months of pregnancy, but I didn't. I tried, I really tried, but I just couldn't do it. You don't know how many sleepless nights I had. I lay in the bed watching you sleep and seeing your tiny body growing and being taken over. I prayed that they weren't hurting you. I prayed that they wouldn't kill you when they came out. I know women die in childbirth all the time with just one baby. I figured two would be twice as dangerous. That's why I ran. I couldn't stand to watch that happen to you. I couldn't stand watching them kill you. I'm glad they didn't. I walked around trying to get a grip on my emotions and getting the courage to come back and face you. For days I wondered how you were doing and wanted to be next to you. I prayed for an answer, but then I came to a very important realization."

"What was that?" I asked covering my nose.

"I realized that if you loved those babies then I should be able to love them too, because I love you."

"And?"

"And what? That's it."

"It took you two weeks to figure that out?"

"It was hard to come by."

"Well I'm glad you're back. Mrs. Misic was a great help, but she can't be here all the time."

"It's good that you had some help. I'm sure you needed it."

"I would have gone crazy without her."

"I'm going to wash myself, then I'll have a look at those babies. What are they boys or girls?"

"Two girls."

"Have you given them names already?"

"Yes Evaline and Avaline."

"Good choices. I like that—little birds."

After Ben had left a serious ring around the tub, he went into the bedroom and took a good look at you two.

"By gosh, they look just like my ugly uncle Ned. Why are their faces so mashed up?"

"All newborns look like that," I insisted.

"Not you. You were a beautiful baby. I was hoping that they would look like you."

"How do you remember what I looked like when I was a baby? I don't even think I have one baby photo of me."

"I don't need a photo. I see it in my mind whenever I want to. Well let's hope those faces get less squishy."

"Do you want to hold them?" I asked.

"Not right now. I think I really should sleep," he said.

Your father did pick you up. He also changed, fed, bathed, put you to sleep, and helped anyway he could whenever he wasn't working. I think he believed that if you were taken care of and out of the way, then he would have more time to spend alone with me. But after several months of doing this, he realized that instead of getting more time to spend with me, he was getting less.

When you were about two years old, he came home from work, and stood in the exact same spot where he delivered his homecoming speech and began wringing his hands. I could tell that I was about to hear some long-winded mumbo jumbo.

"What is it now, Ben?" I asked, impatiently.

"It just that, just that…" he blubbered.

"What, Ben, what is it? Out with it!"

"We'll it's just that I don't think I can help you with those babies any more. They're just too much work. We never seem to have a moment's peace, and I don't think we ever will have as long as they're here. So I wanted to propose something..." he began.

"And what would that be?" I was rather annoyed.

"From now on, I want to sleep in the room that we were planning on putting the babies in."

I shrugged my shoulders.

"If that's what you want, Ben."

"Yes, that's what I want."

So from that day on, that's how it was. Your father was in one room keeping to himself and the three of us were in the other. He kept himself busy by making model airplanes, and later he started to make his own moonshine. During that time he hardly said "boo."

• • •

"So he didn't love us. He resented us," Ava said, dejectedly. "Ma, is there something more you want to say?" She sensed her mother was ill at ease.

"No, nothing." Bernice sounded choked up.

"Ma!" The twins said together.

"I'm fine." Bernice began to hyperventilate.

"No, you're not," Ava went to her. Eva followed.

"Ma, what's wrong? Why are you breathing so hard?"

"I'm not," Bernice said trying to catch her breath.

"Of course you are, Ma."

"It's just my heat allergies is all."

"But you don't have heat allergies, Ma."

"Yes I do."

Bernice's breathing became more pronounced. When she started gasping for air, the twins panicked.

"Ma! What's going on? What's wrong?" they chorused.

Bernice tried to form some words, but the wheezing prevented her.

"I'm going to call an ambulance. Ava, go get Ma some water."

"Shouldn't one of us stay with her?"

"Okay, you stay then." Eva rushed to the phone.

"Can you please send an ambulance to 274 Sackville Street. Apartment 204. Yes. It's my mother. I think she may be having some sort of a heart attack or something. Yeah, she's short of breath. Okay, I'll do that. Okay, okay. Thank you."

"Ava, go get an aspirin and some water," Eva barked as she rushed to her mother.

Ava ran to the bathroom. Bernice continued to pant uncontrollably. Eva rubbed her back. "Don't worry Ma, you'll be all right. Everything is going to be fine. They're on their way now."

When the ambulance attendants barged through the door, Bernice got the fright of her life and fell unconscious.

"Ma, Ma, Ma," the twins chorused as the paramedics went to work on her.

In the hospital Bernice slept, while the twins stood on either side of her.

"How much longer do you think she's going to sleep?" Ava asked.

Bernice began to stir. Within a few seconds her eyes were

wide open. She looked around puzzled. "What is this place?" she muttered weakly.

"Ma! You're awake."

"Did I die? Am I dead?" she asked.

"Of course you're not dead, Ma."

"What happened to me? What was it? Is it my heart?"

"They said it wasn't your heart," Eva answered.

"The diabetes, then?" Bernice swung her head back and forth between her daughters.

"No, not the diabetes either," Ava said.

"Then what?" She grunted as she tried to lift herself up on her elbows.

"Ma, what are you doing?"

"Be careful."

"Then what?" Bernice repeated.

"They said it was most likely just anxiety," Eva said.

"Since when does anxiety put people in hospitals?"

"Don't know, but it did it to you."

"So how long do I have to stay in this place, since I'm not dying?"

"They said you can go home in a few hours."

"That soon?" Bernice tried to lift herself up again.

"Well, there's nothing really wrong with you, Ma."

Eva moved closer to help her mother.

"So what do we have to wait for then?"

"The doctor has to come and sign your chart or something like that so that you can be discharged."

"So what are we supposed to do in the meantime? Sit here and twiddle our thumbs?" Bernice was sounding more like herself.

"Well, why don't you eat some of the food that they left

for you?" Eva felt for the portable table and moved it closer to her mother.

"Do you want to continue Rose and Violet's story?" Ava asked. She knew it was best not to mention her father again.

Bernice lifted the covers off the tray of food. It was pureed meat, mashed potato, pudding, and a dinner roll.

"Just what I thought, mush. Don't these people know I have teeth?" She shoved the dinner roll into her mouth. "Okay, why don't you two sit down."

When the twins were seated, they signalled their mother to start.

• • •

Violet woke up disoriented, her daughter sprawled out on top of her. Both were soaked with the baby's pee. The room looked even more unwelcoming in daylight. She got up slowly and carefully began to take off the infant's things. Just as she was doing this, someone unlocked and opened the front door. Robert entered dressed in a bulky overcoat, looking exhausted. He carried a bouquet of flowers and an armful of take-out food. Violet inspected his face as he put down his offerings. Regardless of the changes, he was still as handsome as ever. She watched with confused longing as he shed his winter layers down to an industrial jump suit. He grimaced uncomfortably and cleared his throat.

"Look, what can I say but...but I'm sorry, Violet."

She said nothing.

"I said I was sorry. Are you just going to give me the silent treatment now?"

The sickened look on her face said it all.

"Say something, why don't you?" he pleaded.

Violet picked up the baby, walked to the washroom, and slammed the door. That was his answer.

In the days that followed, she only spoke to him by way of banging doors and venomous glares. She hoped that her silence would drive him to give some sort of explanation for his behavior and change of appearance, but he offered none.

Instead, she was treated to his nonstop self-pitying: "I can't believe that I've come all this way just to scrub up someone else's shit. You know that they don't pay me enough for what I do," or "You know you're still so beautiful, even with those few extra pounds of yours." And "My boss is a real asshole; can't stand the man. It's harder in this place then I thought it would be. They don't give breaks to people like me. I have to work harder and longer just to keep up. Back home I had a lot more respect, a lot more opportunity, a lot more of everything." And again, "Did you hear what I said about you still being beautiful? You're still my star, my beautiful piece of plum cake, the richest and sweetest that mortals could make."

After seven days of listening to Robert's monologues, Violet began to miss the sound of her own voice.

"It's too bad that they don't pay you enough," she heard herself say in place of an angry interrogation. She really wanted to know if he was in love with the woman from the first night and if he still had any room in his heart for his wife, but she was too afraid of what the answers to those questions might be, so she never asked them.

"Yes, it just awful how they treat people here," was Robert's reply as he embraced Violet. He was relieved.

Feeling Robert's body next to hers, Violet sighed and quietly surrendered.

Douglas waited until he was down to his last few dollars before he decided to do something about his dilemma. Late one blustery day, he pulled on his sheepskin coat, and left the apartment. He found the Stickman pacing in his usual spot.

"Ah, do…do you have anything that can calm my nerves?" Douglas asked in a hushed voice, even though they were the only two people on the street.

The Stickman gave him a suspicious sideways glance, then pulled out a tiny plastic sack containing ten small red-and-white capsules. "Here, this is just what you need, man. It's some of my best shit."

Douglas ogled the pills. "How much?"

"A two bill will do."

Douglas took his last two-dollar bill and handed it to the Stickman without the slightest bit of hesitation.

"You won't regret it, believe me." He placed the tiny package in Douglas's palm and sneered as he watched him hobble away.

Douglas shoved the first pill into his mouth only steps away from the Stickman's corner. As he climbed the steps back to his apartment, he began to get more agitated than usual, and his worries seem all the more overwhelming. This confused him since he had hoped to feel the opposite.

Rose was in the process of preparing to bathe the baby in the kitchen sink. The warmth of the water made her think of the stranger from the hallway for some reason. She could not help but feel that there was something special about the woman, something more than met the eye. The front door opened just as she was placing the baby in the sink. Douglas's steps sounded more frantic than usual. Uncertain of his state of mind, she quickly washed Thomas, then plucked him out of the water. She dried him as she walked from the kitchen to the bedroom.

Douglas looked extremely irate.

"You're back," she said, hurrying into the bedroom.

He shook his head with a crazy glare in his eyes.

"Can I get you some herbal tea or something?" she offered, trying her best to prevent another argument.

"I don't want any tea." He darted around the apartment, opening and closing doors and drawers as if he had misplaced something.

"What are you looking for?"

"I'm not looking for anything," he snapped back.

"If you're still worried about the money, I had a suggestion that might work," she offered as she moved closer to him.

"What kind of suggestion?" He stopped for a brief moment.

"What if I went out to work instead? I can do clerical or kitchen work."

"You...you want to go out and work and be the bread-winner in this family?" Douglas stuttered and began to move about again.

Rose nodded her head. "Sure. Hard work isn't a problem for me."

"Are you insinuating that it is for me?" he asked, raising his voice. His nostrils flared.

"No, not at all. I'm not insinuating anything of the sort."

"Then what are you insinuating—that I'm lazy?" He charged toward her. She prepared to defend herself.

"No, not at all. Never."

"You think because I don't want to work that you can go out and do it instead? You want to take my place as the man of the house? Is that what you want to do?" He was becoming uglier by the second.

She began to feel fearful of him for the very first time.

"You want to be the man, do you? Well, who do you think you are? You don't think I'm capable of looking after you? You don't think I'm man enough? You think you're more of a man than me?" he ranted.

"I don't think any of those things," she answered nervously.

"She thinks I'm going to let her go out and do whatever she wants to do. She wants me to give up being a man and what…become a woman? Is that what she wants? Well it's not going to happen. As long as I can breathe, it's not going to happen." His eyes darted around the room.

"What's gotten into you, Douglas? Just calm down a little, why don't you." She rested her hand on his shoulder.

"Don't use that condescending tone with me." He grabbed a vase and smashed it to the floor. Before she could react, he rammed his hands into her chest. Taken completely by surprise, she fell backward, landing on her behind. A shard from the broken vase pierced her palm. By the time she had dislodged it, he had disappeared again.

Drops of blood trickled down her arm as she got the broom and swept up the mess.

A few doors down the hall, Violet felt a sharp pain in her hand as she washed her face at the bathroom sink. The incident took her back to her childhood, when she had experienced odd sensations at odd times. This time, however, the feeling was more intense. She wondered what it meant, then forget all about it.

She had been patiently waiting for the cold weather to subside, but the chill persisted. While Robert came and went freely, she remained cooped-up in the apartment feeling like a bird unable to spread her wings. When she looked out into the murky sky, she tried to bring images of her tropical home to mind, but they never came.

Early one afternoon, Robert returned home looking more weary than he usually did. Violet took one look at him and knew instantly that something was wrong.

"What happened to you?" she asked.

"I lost my job. They fired me. Can you believe it? Those good for nothing idiots fired me."

"Why? How?"

"They told me since I was the last hired, I had to be the first fired. But that's a bunch of shit because there were two Irish guys hired after me, and they still have jobs to go to in the morning."

"What are we going to do?"

"I don't know. You know how long it took me to find that job?"

He had never appeared so vulnerable to her before.

As she watched him, she began to feel two things. The first was pity. The second was arousal. She got up from where she was sitting, walked over to him, and touched his face. Before she knew it, the two were entangled in a tight embrace. In another flash, they had both undressed, and their bodies were rubbing against each other on the couch. As their arms and legs melded and meshed everything was forgotten.

Angela Spencer was the name of the woman Violet had discovered with Robert the night of her arrival. Violet hadn't found her the least bit attractive. To her, the woman's face looked more like a mashed potato than anything else. The Caribbean emigrant worked as a manager at an insurance company and lived in a nice part of town, in a cute white bungalow.

Robert had great respect for her. He especially admired the fact that she owned her home. The sight of it cheered him up and made him believe that anything was possible. In his eyes, all of Angela's assets made up for her appearance.

On the same day that Robert lost his job and made love to Violet for the first time in many months, he sought further solace at Angela's bungalow. When he arrived on her doorstep, she greeted him with open arms. She was always happy to see him. She squeezed him close and ushered him into her home and led him to a warm plate of food. When he was done eating, she pulled him into her bedroom and pushed him onto her king-size bed, never once noticing Violet's scent.

When she was finished performing her many tricks, she looked over at him and grinned.

"I have something to tell you," she squealed with excitement.

"Me too," Robert echoed.

"Okay, you go first, then…It's bursting out of me, but I can wait."

He gave her a strange look. "I lost my job."

"Oh, you poor baby. When did this happen?"

"This morning."

"Well, don't you worry yourself about it. You know I'll take care of you. Whatever you need." She caressed his face.

"Thanks. I knew I could count on you, Angela." He

pecked her on the cheek and turned away with the intention of sleeping.

"Wait, wait, you didn't hear my news yet." She yanked his arm.

"What is it?" He yawned.

"We're going to have a baby."

Robert sprang up immediately. Now he was fully alert.

"What? How? I thought you were doing something."

"It doesn't matter how it happened, it just did. Isn't it wonderful?"

Robert shook his head in disbelief. "I can't afford another child, Angela. Didn't you just hear me tell you that I lost my job?"

"You don't have to worry about that, Robby. I'll take care of everything. I make enough at my job, and I have plenty of savings to fall back on."

"Oh, okay. That's good. Glad to hear it." He turned back around and closed his eyes.

Exactly eight weeks after Angela's announcement, Violet found out that she, too, was expecting. But when she gave the news to Robert, his reaction couldn't have been more different.

"How could you have let this happen?" he shrieked at the top of his voice.

Violet shrank back.

"What happened to those goddamn pills you were supposed to be taking?"

"I ran out of them." Her body quaked. Robert had never raised his voice with her before.

"What the hell do you mean, you ran out?"

"I...I just ran out."

He flew toward her and pinned her against the wall. Her heart pumped frantically as her mind raced. *What's going on? What's gotten into him? Will he really hurt me? What have I done to deserve this? All I told him was that I was pregnant with his child.*

His mouth was so close to her eyes that his breath created a fog.

"Please, Robert. Please," she pleaded.

The venom in his gaze flared, then subsided. He turned away abruptly.

Believing that the ugly episode was over, she sighed. But in a quick flash, he swung back around and slapped her squarely on her jaw. It stung. Staring down at his hand as if it were a foreign object, he appeared remorseful, but no apologies were made.

With the impression of his hand still on her face, she watched him as he fled to the kitchen. The image of her mother's troubled face came to her mind.

• • •

Both Eva and Ava sat in a trance with their hands on their faces as if they, too, had just been slapped.

"Boy, this doctor is sure taking his sweet time," Bernice said as she stretched her arms over her head. "Why don't you two go and find out what's keeping him."

Bernice looked at her daughters on either side of her. "Snap out of it you two." She slammed her hand down on the rubber mattress.

The twins jumped.

"What...okay, Ma," they said together. As they stood up, they heard someone enter the room in a hurry.

"Sorry, Mrs. Archer, but the doctor is going to be another three or four hours. It seems he had to deal with an emergency somewhere," a young nurse announced, out of breath.

"Somewhere like on the golf course," Bernice muttered.

"I hope that it's not too much trouble for you," the nurse said.

"Trouble? What else do I have to do at my age but wait," Bernice replied smugly.

"I'm sorry. We'll bring you something else to eat a little later." The nurse rushed back out.

"Watch you don't hurt yourself flying around like that," Bernice yelled after her. "So we have to wait. You two want me to—"

"Yes," Eva and Ava answered and sat back down.

"Okay then," Bernice continued.

CHAPTER 17

The Welfare Office and Other Catastrophes

ROSE FOUND IT very hard to sleep after Douglas's sudden departure. Every night she tossed and turned wondering where he had disappeared to and worrying about her dwindling food supply. She was grateful that the baby was still breast-feeding. It wasn't long before all she had left in her cupboard was a box of soda crackers. By this time she had begun to look skeletal.

When I knocked on her door, I couldn't believe how sickly and malnourished she looked. Her eyes were protruding out of her head. One glance at her and I regretted that I hadn't gone to her earlier.

"Sorry to bother you, but we had a party and I...I had so many leftovers, I thought I would bring some for you." I lied through my teeth.

She stared back at me apprehensively. I didn't blame her because she barely knew me. Before that day we hadn't even exchanged more than ten words.

"I just thought it would be the neighborly thing to do," I continued. I could tell that I was making her uncomfortable.

"I don't understand why you brought this for me," she said.

"I just didn't want the food to go to waste," I insisted, unintentionally mimicking her accent.

When she still wouldn't take the plate from my hand, I placed it down inside her door and walked away. When I looked back, I saw her picking it up.

The next day, when she returned the empty plate, I could see that the food had done her some good. Her face had more color and life.

"Did you enjoy it?" I asked.

"Yes, thank you, very much."

She nodded and turned to walk away.

"Oh, please wait, Rose, I have something more for you." I rushed back into the apartment.

"You…you know my name?" she asked puzzled.

"Sure I do."

"How?"

When I returned with a bag of groceries, she looked as if she had just seen a ghost.

"Oh, I just do. This is for you and your son." I pushed the bag toward her.

"This is too much." She shook her head.

"No, no it's all right. It's no problem," I said, trying to reassure her. I had to force the bag between her boney fingers.

"Okay, I'll take it for my son."

"Great. Little Thomas must be sleeping now, isn't he?"

"How do you know my son's name?"

"I know many things about you and her."

"Her?" She looked even more flustered.

"Her," I repeated as I pointed to the end of hallway where Violet lived.

Rose still had no idea what I was talking about. From the look on her face, I could tell she thought I was some sort of crackpot.

"Oh yeah, I forgot. I have something else for you." I dashed back into the apartment. "You'll be able to get some help here." I handed her a folded piece of paper.

She looked at the paper.

"It's the number and address for the welfare office. You can get some help—money—there."

"Thank you very much. You're very kind."

"Oh, you're very welcome, sweetie," I said as I watched her thin frame move back toward her door.

The welfare office was a drab looking room located in a run-down building downtown. The space could have easily doubled for any hospital emergency room with its sea of sullen, anxious faces.

Violet found the office by simply looking it up in the phone book. She had remembered someone back home telling her how the government gave poor people money to live on in times of need.

When she arrived in the office, she scrutinized the crowd. They didn't look at all like she had imagined. They were all shapes, sizes, and colors, all wearing the same desperate, sad expression.

Violet couldn't bring herself to look anyone directly in the eye. Nobody did this. It seemed to be an unwritten rule.

While some pretended to read the outdated magazines, others stared at the number counter or feigned sleep. The ones fortunate enough to have children fussed unnecessarily over them.

After getting a number, Violet sat down and fixed her gaze on the entrance. She watched as every new applicant arrived, all wearing the same troubled expression. When the woman from down the hallway arrived, carrying her tan-colored child, Violet sat up. She hadn't seen her since that first day. The weight loss was startling. The woman's already thin frame had withered, and the dark circles under her eyes were even more pronounced.

When their eyes met, the sensation they had felt on their first meeting was replicated. Again, neither knew what to make of it. Rose acknowledged Violet with a tiny nod of her head.

Violet reciprocated, then pointed toward the number dispenser. She watched as Rose walked over to it, then found somewhere to sit. As they waited, the two women snuck glances at one another. No words were exchanged.

Both women left the office that day humbled but grateful for the assistance that was offered to them and happy to have seen their new neighbor.

A short while after Violet's visit to the welfare office, Robert returned home from points unknown. The moment Violet saw his disagreeable face, she knew that it would be best for her to hold her tongue and not say anything that might provoke him.

As she folded her laundry in silence, she glanced up and watched him walk into kitchen. In that spilt second, she noticed that the fleshy back of his neck seemed to be the only thing about him that had remained completely unchanged. It reminded her of the man she once knew and loved. The pang of affection that followed was inescapable.

"Have you eaten yet?" she asked in a gentle voice.

Robert stormed out of the kitchen with a half-empty bottle of whiskey in his hand.

"Why do you have to know if I ate or not?" he barked angrily. "I'm a grown man. I can take care of myself. Why are you always asking me such damn idiotic questions?"

Violet was dumbfounded. While she reflected on just how much Robert's behavior reminded her of her father's, she felt the impact of two blows, one to her face and the other to her abdomen. Unlike the first slap, the punches didn't come as a surprise. They had been very much anticipated, since he had already shown what he was capable of. Doubled over in pain, she watched the upward and downward motion of the whiskey bottle as he huffed furiously and took continuous swigs.

She received many smacks and cuffs to each and every part of her body as time went on. While administering them, Robert thought nothing of the harm that he might be inflicting on his unborn baby.

As the violent eruptions increased, Violet became complacent, just as her mother had. She took every kick, thump, and whack in stride while she lay in wait for the next one. All she could do was protect her child as best as she could, the same way her mother had protected her.

Had anyone told the young defiant Violet, who almost willed her father to death, that she would end up a victim, she would have laughed in their face and said, "Who me?

Never—that would never happen to me." But somehow it had.

Douglas and Robert were two men who on the surface had absolutely nothing in common. Robert had been raised in a world of poverty and favoritism, while Douglas's world had been one of wealth and neglect. Both were products of their mother's whims. Even though Robert's ego had been over inflated, and Douglas's diminished, the pair had turned out similar in so many ways.

When the two men crossed each other's paths, they didn't feel any sort of commonality or connection. There was only discord, both believing that the other was an insignificant speck. They did their best to avoid each other's gaze and always kept a fair distance between them. There were never any forms of greeting or attempts at conversation. Neither knew that they shared a common means of communicating with their wives. Just as Robert's single slap had progressed to pushes, punches, and kicks, Douglas's single push also eventually developed into more severe actions.

On the day that Douglas had purchased the pills from the Stickman and shoved Rose, he had left the apartment and walked straight back to the same corner. The Stickman knew right away by Douglas's frantic movements that a mistake had been made. He exchanged the pills for identical looking ones and even gave Douglas three bonus ones on the house. This made Douglas very happy. He popped one immediately, then was on his way.

As he waited for the effect of the new drug to kick in, he walked many blocks to a strip of stores where he often liked to window-shop. His favorite of the shops was one that sold lady's lingerie. He stopped there from time to time to admire the delicate lace panties and bras on display. The sight of the women's underwear always had a soothing effect on him. He had been fascinated by them since he was a small child. At seven he had snuck into his mother's room, and tried on one of her frilliest underpants. When she discovered him prancing around the room, she took off her pointed shoe and cracked him over his head. There was still a triangular shaped scar where she had hit him.

As Douglas marveled at the silky undergarments, he started to feel lighter and much more relaxed. He knew right away that the new pill had taken effect. While he began to imagine himself floating, a beefy man exited the lingerie store carrying a tiny pink bag. He glanced at Douglas with a look that said, "I can relate, man."

Douglas looked at the man's bag with envious eyes. He wished that he too had the courage (and money) to do what the man had just done. The two stood awkwardly studying one another.

"What about those Knicks, eh?" the large man asked clumsily.

He towered over Douglas like an ancient oak tree.

Douglas, not familiar with North American sports, had no idea what the man was talking about. He smiled and nodded politely. An uncomfortable silence followed.

"Do you like to fish?" the man asked.

"Sure, fishing is nice," Douglas replied, not knowing what else to say.

"I like your accent…Some of my favorite places to go are up North, where it's nice and quiet."

"Quiet is nice," Douglas replied.

"Maybe we could go fishing one day," the man added.

"Sure, why not?" Douglas agreed, trying to figure out what was being said between the lines. He knew the conversation had something to do with silky panties and lacy negligees.

"Would you like to go back to my place?" Douglas heard the man ask.

It took a few seconds for the proposition to sink in.

"Your place, sure," Douglas heard himself reply.

Before he could reconsider, he found himself seated in a messy, lopsided jalopy, on his way to who knows where. A short, anxious ride later, the car stopped outside a high-rise building. When the man got out of the car, Douglas followed closely behind him. On the fifth floor, the man unlocked his apartment and motioned for Douglas to enter.

"My name is Johnny, by the way. Johnny Little," he said, breathing heavily down Douglas's neck.

Douglas smiled uncomfortably at the irony.

"I'm Douglas, Douglas Weiss," he said as he stepped into the man's place. It was unkempt but spacious.

"Good to know you, Douglas. I really like your accent, man. I hope you don't think that's rude of me to say." He signaled for Douglas to take a seat on his leather couch.

"No, it's not rude at all," Douglas replied shyly.

Once Douglas was seated, Johnny disappeared. When he returned, he was carrying two opened bottles of beer and had changed into a ruffled pink bra and panty set.

"What do you think? I just got these." He handed a bottle to Douglas.

Douglas nodded his approval.

Even though Johnny's protruding gut created an unsightly

picture, Douglas was still heartened.

"I have some that might fit you. Would you like to try?" Johnny took a swig of beer.

"Sure, I guess." Douglas was beginning to wonder if what he was experiencing was real or drug-induced.

"You sure like that word *sure*, don't you, man." Johnny sauntered back into his bedroom.

Douglas's eyes grew large when he saw the light-blue baby-doll set in Johnny's hands. He was in heaven.

"Can I use your bathroom?" Douglas asked.

"Of course, of course. It's right over there." Johnny smiled and pointed to a door with a poster of Mae West on it.

In the bathroom, Douglas held the baby-doll up to his face, and sighed. He stripped off all his clothes as quickly as he could and pulled it on. The fact that it was a few sizes too big didn't bother him at all, the softness was what mattered. He stood up on the toilet, looked at himself in the mirror, and grinned.

"It looks great, man. Beautiful!" Johnny switched on the TV. "Just great!"

As they sat there watching the tube, Douglas was pleased as punch. He wondered where Johnny had been his whole life.

As the days began to get longer and the gripping chill began to dissipate, Douglas remained shacked up with Johnny. Within the blink of an eye, almost two whole months had passed. The odd couple had spent their days lounging around, surviving on Johnny's disability check and handouts from the Salvation Army. They would have stayed cocooned indefinitely had Douglas not remembered that he had left

Rose without money or food. He made up a story and told Johnny that he had to leave, but would return. Needless to say, Johnny was sad to see him go.

When Douglas arrived back home, he found Rose just as he had left her. The welfare assistance and regular meals had kept her afloat and alive. The reunion was not a happy one. The conflict started right away.

"Government handouts are for retarded degenerates," Douglas blurted out as he popped a pill. He had been able to buy a fresh supply with money Johnny had given him.

Rose said nothing as Douglas continued his rant. She was not interested in adding any fuel to the fire. Her refusal to join in, however, didn't stop the argument. Douglas just continued on his own.

"Who told you it was alright to take money like some sort of common beggar?" he fumed. "Don't you know the Weiss's have never had to rely on charity? But then again I am not a Weiss anymore, am I? Those buggers just couldn't wait to get rid of me. Now they got their wish. I'm thousands of miles away from them. To hell with them. I should just take that money to spite them." She was glad to hear that he had resolved the disagreement on his own. When she adjusted her bra strap that had fallen down onto her shoulder, he stopped and stared. A bizarre look flashed across his face. He loosened his belt and took a step toward her. Fearing the worst, she scampered away.

He caught her and pinned her in a corner. With an ardent look, he reached down her dress and took hold of one of her breasts. She didn't know what to make of his sudden arousal. It stirred something in her. She gave in. Within seconds the two were fully enthralled. In the time that followed, sex seemed to be the only thing on Douglas's mind, and for the first time Rose participated happily and willingly.

When Rose announced some months later that she was pregnant, Douglas was so overjoyed to be having a child of his own that he did his best to control his violent outbursts. Rose was happy for the peace, but conflicted about the prospects of having another child.

The tranquility, however, was short-lived. Tension returned after Douglas telephoned his parents.

"We don't care if you have ten more children with that woman. They are your responsibility now, Douglas," his mother said curtly.

"Do you want me to live on handouts and suffer in poverty here?"

She responded with a click of the phone.

The beeping sound was just as bothersome as his mother's callousness. Incensed by the incident, he took a glass of cold water, went to where Rose was sleeping in the bedroom, and emptied it over her.

"This is all your fault!" he announced.

Waking from a dead sleep, Rose couldn't make heads nor tails of why she was wet.

"What…what…happened?" she slurred.

"You and that bastard's child of yours, that's what happened. If you had had my child first, none of this would have happened," he screamed at the top of his lungs.

Rose shook her head and thought, *Here we go again.*

CHAPTER 18

A Tea Party for Twin Souls

"YOU FORGOT, didn't you, Ma?" Ava yelled over the noisy fans in the kitchen.

"Forgot what?" Bernice asked. She wiped away some beads of sweat from her cleavage. The short walk her daughters had imposed on her had tuckered her out. Mr. Wong's leering and comment about them looking like three bowls of Jell-O hadn't helped either.

"You forgot what's happening tomorrow."

"What's happening tomorrow?"

"I can't believe you forgot," Eva yelled.

"Forgot what? Why don't you two just tell me what it is." She was already growing impatient.

"The tea party," Eva and Ava said together.

"Oh yes, of course. How could I have forgotten that, my goodness," Bernice said all flustered. "It must be this godforsaken heat that's doing it to me. Giving me these fake heart attacks and making me all forgetful. Now I feel like a real old biddy."

"You're not an old biddy, Ma, you're just aging gracefully, like you're supposed to."

"You're just saying that to make me feel good. Don't worry. I know what I am. I know I'm not getting any younger—or smarter for that matter." She moved her head closer to one of the fans.

"You know the saying. You're only as old as you feel," Eva yelled over the sound of clanging pans.

"Well I feel like a mummified mummy, so what does that make me?" She sighed.

"What are you sighing about, Ma?" Ava asked.

"How can you hear me sighing though all that racket?"

"I just can." The clank of a metal object hitting the floor sounded out.

"You better not be making a big mess with whatever you're doing in there…What is it anyway?"

"You'll see, you'll see. We want to surprise you."

"I'm too old for surprises, just tell me," Bernice replied grumpily.

"We're making all of your favorites," Ava confessed.

"Why did you tell her, Ava?"

"Because she wanted to know."

"My favorites, eh? What's the point of making my favorites if you're not going to let me eat them?" Bernice asked.

"Don't worry Ma, you'll be able to have some. We're going to use less sugar."

"Again, Ava? Why don't you just keep that mouth of yours shut."

"What's the point of using less sugar? You might as well

not make it all if it's going to taste like old shoes," Bernice continued.

"No it won't. We're using apple sauce instead of sugar."

"Ava!"

"Apple sauce? What's that going to taste like?" Bernice asked.

"It'll taste fine, Ma. You don't need to worry," Eva reassured.

"I hope so." Bernice sighed again. "I hope so," she added, drifting off to sleep.

The next day at exactly two o'clock, there was a faint knock on Bernice's door. Bernice and the twins had been sitting quietly in the living room, nervously nibbling and waiting for their guest to arrive. They were a sight. All three wore matching neon-green, frilly dresses. The quiet rapping put a smile on all their faces.

Bernice jumped up from her seat with the vigor of a woman half her size and age and jogged to the door. The twins were right on her heels.

Rose stood at the door holding her son, looking somewhat apprehensive. It was clear that the shocking green outfits caught her by surprise.

"So glad that you could make it," Bernice said with a big smile. "Please come, come in."

Eva and Ava stood behind their mother sniffing the air, hoping to identify their first guest.

"Don't mind them, they don't have any manners. Please, this way," Bernice added as she swatted at her daughters. "Stop that you two. It's Rose, alright?"

Rose followed Bernice into the living room where she

motioned for her to sit down in the love seat. Two kitchen chairs had been placed on either side of Bernice's armchair for the twins.

"Can we get you some tea?" Bernice asked as she moved the coffee table closer to Rose. "Please feel free to help yourself to anything you like."

"My goodness. Thank you very much. It all looks so lovely," Rose said as she surveyed the wide array of goodies in front of her.

"You can thank my daughters. They did all of the work. Just a little bit of milk and sugar right?" Bernice asked as she entered the kitchen.

"Yes, that would be nice, thank you." Rose wondered how Bernice knew the way she took her tea.

Eva and Ava stood grinning for what seemed an excessive amount of time before they finally sat down.

"Why don't you try something?" Ava said to Rose. "The date squares are my favorite."

"Sure, I like those too," Rose replied. She was feeling somewhat uneasy in the twins' company.

"Don't be shy now," Eva added.

"Okay." Rose picked up a date square, fed a small piece to her son, and took a bite.

"What do you think? Do you like it?" Ava asked eagerly.

Rose nodded her head. "Oh, nice...very nice," she added, after she remembered that the twins couldn't see her.

As Rose took small bites of the square, she felt as if the twins were monitoring her every move. She found this unnerving.

"Does the baby like it?" Ava asked.

"Yeah, I guess so."

There was a knock on the door. Eva and Ava immediately jumped to their feet and shuffled to answer it. Rose was grateful for the momentary reprieve.

"Is that the door again?" Bernice yelled from the kitchen.

"Yeah, I'm getting it," the twins replied in unison.

"I'll get it," Eva insisted.

"No, I'll do it." Ava forced her sister out of the way. "You always do everything."

Watching the twins jostle with each other in their outlandish outfits, Rose felt as if she landed in some alternative universe. With just a few maneuvers, Eva was able to muscle her sister out of the way. When she opened the door, Violet stood there with her daughter in one hand and a cake in the other.

"Welcome," Eva chanted enthusiastically. "So glad you could make it."

"Thank you for the invitation," Violet relied. "What pretty dresses you have."

"Ma made them," Ava replied.

"Very nice. She's quite the seamstress, I see."

When Violet entered the living room, she was pleasantly surprised to see Rose seated there, as if she had been waiting for her. She was excited by the prospect of finally being able to have a conversation.

"Hi," Violet said through a smile.

"Hi," Rose replied, equally pleased.

As the women remained locked in each other's gaze, Bernice returned from the kitchen carrying two cups of tea. She grinned when she saw Violet.

"I'm so glad that you were able to make it. Please sit," Bernice said as she signaled for Violet to take a seat next to Rose.

"Thank you," Violet said as she placed her cake next to the other treats and took a seat.

"Oh, my word. How nice of you to bring a cake," Bernice chimed.

"Luckily I had just enough flour and butter to make it," Violet replied cheerfully. It was clear that she was far more comfortable in the situation than Rose.

"With all the pies and cakes and cookies my daughters made, there wasn't even enough room for my tea service," Bernice explained, placing one cup down in front of Rose and one in front of Violet. "I put extra sugar in yours, Violet, the way you like it."

Violet smiled.

"Well dig in, ladies, enjoy," Bernice added as she grabbed a date square.

"Oh, oh sorry, where are my manners?" She wiped some crumbs from her mouth. "Violet, I give you Rose, and Rose, I give you Violet." She motioned playfully in front of the young women.

"You both have flower's names. Isn't that interesting." Bernice giggled.

The two women smiled at each other.

"Okay then, let's go you two. I have something to show you," Bernice announced as she began to nudge her daughters' shoulders. "We'll be right back. Help yourself to whatever you like."

It was clear that neither Eva or Ava wanted to move.

"What are you going to show your two blind daughters?"

Eva asked sarcastically as she followed along.

"Show is just a figure of speech. I need your help, then. Does that sound better? Let's just go." Bernice ushered Eva towards the kitchen.

"But I want to stay, Ma," Ava whispered. She was still seated.

"I said let's go," Bernice muttered under her breath.

Once Bernice and her daughters were gone, the two women looked at each other and shrugged their shoulders. Neither of them quite knew what to make of their hosts.

"Very nice of them to invite us to their home. When I saw the invitation, I wasn't going to come at first, but then I thought it might be a nice change," Violet said softly.

"Yeah, I wasn't going to come either, but then I thought about how helpful the old lady has been," Rose said. "They're kind of strange, no?" she added quietly.

"Not any stranger than anyone else who lives here," Violet replied. "You think anyone else is coming?"

Rose shrugged her shoulders again. "Your daughter is so precious. I love her bright eyes," Rose said, just beginning to feel at ease.

"Thank you. Your son is also very sweet. How old is he?"

"Seven months. And your daughter?"

"Six months."

"She's a good size, isn't she? How much did she weigh when she was born?"

"Seven pounds, one-and-half ounces. And your son?"

"Exactly the same."

As the two women chatted, they each had an eerie feeling that they had already shared many lengthy conversations before this meeting. While their babies fell asleep on their laps, the women listened to each other, and each was soothed by the sound of the other's gentle voice.

By the time Bernice and her daughters had returned, almost a half hour had elapsed. It had, however, seemed like only seconds to the pair. They continued to chat as if they were the only people in the room as Bernice and the twins took their seats.

"So those buns in the ovens came as quite a shock for you both, eh?" Bernice interjected, reaching for another date square. Violet looked up at Bernice, puzzled.

"How did you know?" she asked.

Rose touched her stomach lightly and said nothing.

"I know many things about you and your friend there." Bernice pointed her chin toward Rose.

Violet and Rose looked at each other. From the look on Rose's face, it was clear she was not taking Bernice seriously. Violet, on the other hand, was all ears. There were many things about Bernice's demeanor that she found interesting and endearing.

"I see you don't believe me, Rose," Bernice finally said.

Rose was silent.

"Please allow me to prove myself then." Bernice leaned forward in her chair. "Do you remember the very last dream you had?" There was a glimmer in Bernice's eye.

Rose tried hard to remember.

"Do you remember wandering about somewhere lost?" Bernice asked.

"That sounds like a dream that I had," Violet jumped in.

"Yes, yes and what about you Rose? Do you remember anything like that?" Bernice asked.

"Vaguely," Rose admitted.

"You see, the two of you shared the same dream," Bernice continued.

"Yeah, but that's a common dream."

"Okay, what about when you were small. You both had imaginary friends."

"Most children do," Rose insisted.

"What if I could describe what you did with them. Would you believe me then?"

"Okay, sure…maybe," Rose answered.

"You used to tell stories to your imaginary friend," Bernice asserted.

Rose smiled.

"Violet used to have tea parties with hers," Bernice continued.

Surprised, Violet covered her mouth.

"She's right, I did do that," Violet replied.

"Well, you see…" Bernice sliced a piece of Violet's cake and popped it into her mouth. "Mmmm. Very good," Bernice said with a full mouth.

"Just tell them, Ma. And please slow down on those sweets," Eva finally blurted out.

Bernice flashed Eva an annoyed look as she swallowed the last morsel of cake. "I know these things about you because I dreamt about them," Bernice replied as she quickly cut a second piece of cake.

"What do you mean?" Rose shifted her baby in her arms.

"Just like I said." Bernice reached for the knife again.

"Ma, what are you doing with the knife? I said, that's enough," Eva insisted.

"Alright, okay. That's my last piece, I promise. Back to your question Rose.

"You see, your whole lives have been played out for me in my dreams. Each night, I see a different part."

"How?"

"How is that possible?" Violet and Rose asked the questions one after the other.

"It just happens. I close my eyes and there you two are."

"What do you mean our whole lives?" Violet sat up straight.

"All your lives. From the time the star divided into two and became the two of you until right now."

"A star, divided into two?" Rose mused. "How lovely."

"The star—the soul that became the two of you."

"The soul?" Violet looked confused.

"The two of us?" Rose repeated.

"Yes, the two of you are really one."

Rose and Violet looked at each other again.

"You were both born in the month of September, were you not?" Bernice asked. Violet and Rose nodded their heads.

"Your exact time of birth is 2:01 a.m. on September 27, right?" Bernice continued.

"I don't know the time, but that's the right date," Violet added.

"I don't know the time either, but yes, that's the date," Rose concurred.

"How nice, we're twins then," Violet said with a chuckle.

Bernice got so excited she jumped to her feet.

"Bulls-eye! You hit the nail right on its head. You are twins," she yelled.

"Please calm down, Ma. You don't want to end up in the hospital again," Eva warned.

"Hush now, you two. I'm speaking to the women." Bernice sounded annoyed. "You see, you're twin souls because you share the same soul," Bernice now stood directly in front of her guests and gestured emphatically with her arms.

"Oh?" Rose said.

Sensing Rose's skepticism, Violet touched her arm with a look that said, *Let's just listen and hear her out.*

"Can you explain it some more?" Violet asked.

Bernice looked back and forth between Violet and Rose, then clapped her hands together.

"Okay. This is not for the faint-hearted. You have to believe what I'm telling you. I swear it's the God-given truth. Before you were both born, a very rare event occurred. The soul of a newly departed did something that it doesn't ordinarily do. It split into two parts. It did this because there was a shortage of souls going around. One part became Rose and the other became you, Violet. It was one of the most beautiful sights I had ever seen in my dreams." Bernice returned to her seat.

"But we weren't born in the same place," Violet said.

"True, but in the realm of souls, that distance is tiny… minuscule," Bernice glanced quickly at the untouched pumpkin pie. Rose and Violet's eyes remained glued on Bernice.

"It's a gift. You have to believe me. You two are very special, extremely special."

"So we are one person, one soul? Is that what you're trying to say?" Violet asked. "I heard my pastor talk about departed souls before, but never about twin souls."

"Well they do exist, believe you me."

"That's probably why I feel so strange when I'm next to her," Violet explained.

"I felt something too," Rose admitted, "ever since that first night."

As Bernice sat and watched the awe-inspired expressions of the two women, she felt pleased with herself. She reached over and whispered something in Ava's ear. Ava rose and whispered something into her sister's ear. The two then began to sing.

> *Mi chiamano Mimì,*
> *ma il mio nome è Lucia.*
> *La storia mia è breve.*
> *A tela o a seta*
> *ricamo in casa e fuori...*

"I heard them sing that song my first night here," Rose whispered to Violet.

"Me too," Violet replied with a bright smile. "Me too."

When Rose returned to her apartment after the tea party, she felt lighter than she had ever felt in her life. As she prepared her son for bed, she found herself humming the melody of the song that the twins had sung. She was happy that she could forget her worries momentarily. When she saw the full moon in the night sky, her mood was lifted even more.

Some doors away, Violet also glimpsed the moon. She stuck her head out into the darkness to catch some evening air. As she stared up into space, the breeze caressed her face. She replayed Bernice's words in her head and felt at home for the first time since her arrival.

CHAPTER 19
Strangers Become Friends

FOR A SHORT TIME after the tea party, things continued between Rose and Violet as they had before. The women remained neighbors who longed to be friends but rarely saw one another. After some time, however, chance encounters started to occur. It was as if some outside force was acting on their behalf. When these meetings took place, serious subjects were never broached. Both found it easier to keep things light and on the surface.

"How is the little man today?" Violet asked Rose one particularly humid day as they came across each other in the stairwell. Violet took hold of Thomas's hand.

"He's good, and Clara?"

"She's okay, but I think she has a tooth coming in," Violet replied.

"Oh, you poor girl, you." Rose made faces at Clara.

"She's not complaining too much though."

"That's good to know."

"Sure. Well, have a good day, Rose. Nice chatting with you."

"You too, Violet." She hesitated, then continued up the stairs.

Violet stood and watched her.

"Oh, Rose, why don't we meet in the park tomorrow—maybe around two or so? It wouldn't be so hot by then."

"Sure," Rose replied. "See you then." She waved good-bye.

"Yes, see you then." Violet waved back.

Violet and Rose began to meet regularly at two p.m. in the broken-down park with their children. They packed food, diapers, and all the other things they needed to spend the day. On one particularly gorgeous Wednesday afternoon, Violet who was normally late, arrived first. Eva and Ava were already there seated on their bench, taking in the surrounding smells and sounds.

"What a beautiful day!" Violet said to the twins.

"Spectacular," Eva and Ava said together, tilting their heads upward.

"You sound like you're in a good mood, Violet," Eva said. "Hiya, Clara."

"Clara, say Hi," Violet prompted her daughter cheerily as she stepped toward the swings.

"The Stickman smelled better today, didn't he?" Ava asked.

"Yeah, he looks like he cleaned himself up a bit. He was wearing a different shirt and pants and all, too," Violet answered.

"Really!" Ava was getting excited. "What did they look like?"

"Oh, some colorful shirt and white pants."

"White pants—really!" Ava's voice rose, as if she had just heard some important revelation.

"Big deal," Eva said.

"Yeah, it wasn't a big thing," Violet agreed.

"Why do you even care, Ava? He probably made himself up for his real girlfriend." Eva whacked her sister on her arm.

Ava smacked Eva back, then crossed her arms in protest.

Rose arrived shortly after, greeting the twins with her fresh floral scent and a quiet, almost muffled, "Hello."

Eva sensed that something was not quite right. "Are you okay, Rose?"

"Just a little tired," Rose replied as she rushed toward Violet.

Realizing that Rose wasn't in a talkative mood, Eva went back to sitting quietly, hoping to catch snippets of the women's conversation.

Rose greeted Violet with a long, warm embrace. This caught Violet off guard. The two had never hugged before.

"Are you alright?" Violet took a good look at Rose's face. She appeared more dishevelled than usual.

"Sure, I'm fine. I just didn't sleep that well last night," Rose sat her son in the swing next to Clara. The babies started to babble right away.

"Look, they're talking to each other," Violet said.

"Looks like they have a lot to say," Rose replied, distracted.

Violet watched Rose as she gave her son a push, then quickly pulled up her long-sleeved dress that had begun to droop over her shoulder.

"Aren't you hot in that?"

"No, it's fine. I'm fine." Rose looked away.

On closer examination, Violet noticed a fresh bruise just below Rose's collarbone.

"Are you sure you're okay?" Violet asked, gently touching Rose's arm. When Rose recoiled, Violet didn't know what to do. "Ah...sorry. I'm so sorry," Violet muttered.

Rose hung her head.

"You don't have to be ashamed, Rose. Look." Violet discretely lifted her blouse and revealed a cut on her abdomen that had just started to scab over.

"How long?" Rose asked in a whisper.

"A while now. And you?"

"The same."

"I could tell from before," Violet said as she tapped the swing, "but I didn't want to say anything to embarrass you."

"Me too," Rose admitted.

"It's hard to talk about."

"I know. I know."

"But we should. We should talk. It might help," Violet added.

"Maybe it will."

Eva and Ava nodded their heads sympathetically as they listened to every word.

Rose and Violet were too engrossed in conversation to notice when Douglas entered the park. Given that Eva and Ava were familiar with the smell of his expensive cologne, they were able to warn Rose of his approach.

"Rose, Rose!" Eva and Ava cried out together in somewhat of a panic.

When Rose turned around and saw Douglas purposely marching toward her, she stopped speaking mid-sentence and pulled her son out of the swing. There was no need for any explanation. She knew Violet would understand.

Before Douglas was able to utter a single word, Rose had already jogged past him. He was left to trot behind her. He showed his displeasure with angry grunts. The grumbling worried Violet and the twins who stood by helplessly.

By the time Douglas reached the apartment, Rose was already in the kitchen knocking about some pots and pans. When he entered, he was fuming, out of breath, and anxious to demonstrate his disapproval. He followed the noise of the clanging saucepans and found Rose. Once he was behind her, he bent down, took off one of his penny loafers, and—without any preamble—clobbered her in the head with it.

"That's what you get for talking about me in the street with lowlifes," he seethed. He was convinced of his accusation, even though he hadn't heard a single word.

Rose pretended not to feel. She didn't turn around or even flinch. As he hit her with his shoe, she opened a can of hashed beef, washed and peeled some potatoes, and put them on the stove. At some point in the flurry of blows, she decided that the park was no longer a good place for her and Violet to meet. When the idea of the perfect alternative came to her, she smiled. Douglas became even more incensed when he saw the grin and began to beat her with even more force. She just continued to smile and make dinner, acting as if the whacks were just currents of air.

Eva and Ava left the park in a hurry that day, directly after Rose. When they got back to the building, they listened closely in the hallway outside Rose's door, but they were only able to detect the tiniest of taps. Since this was all they heard, they knew that Rose was not in any danger.

They immediately reported everything that had transpired in the park that day to their mother. Bernice listened to the full account as she fanned herself with her hand and sucked on a mouthful of tiny ice cubes. "Well I guess that means there is no need for me to tell any more of their story then."

"What did you say, Ma?" Ava flopped down on the love seat.

"I said, I don't need to finish that story anymore."

"What do you mean, Ma?" Eva asked, joining her sister.

"Never mind. You'll see."

"What about the other story?" Eva asked cautiously.

"Now what other story would that be?" Bernice asked as she tapped the bottom of the glass for more ice.

"You know. The one about our father," Eva replied.

"Eva, Sh. Don't ask her that. Don't you remember what—"

"It's okay. She can ask. I can finish that story," Bernice answered calmly. She looked as if her thoughts were a thousand miles away as she played with the last remaining piece of ice.

"Now?" Ava asked.

"Yeah, sure, now." Bernice paused.

Eva and Ava waited patiently for their mother to continue.

"Well some time after he stopped helping me—you two were about fifteen months or so—Mrs. Misic came to our door and asked me if I would like to go to the movies with her. She knew I had been taking care of you two practically by myself and thought a little break would do me some good," Bernice continued hesitantly.

Eva and Ava both took careful note of all the tiny breaths their mother was taking between each word. They sensed whatever she was going to tell them would be difficult.

• • •

"*Way Down East* is playing at the Paradise with the heavenly Lillian Gish in it," Mrs. Misic said, chewing gum and taking a sexy stance at the door. She was so much more attractive back then with a twenty-five inch waist and real teeth.

"Oh, I really can't. My husband…" I began to say.

"Uh-huh, I know all about that creature. The babies are sleeping already, aren't they?"

"Yeah, I just put them down."

"So you don't have anything to worry about then. Just tell the big lug that you're leaving. I'm sure the girls won't even stir for the whole night."

"I don't know," I hemmed and hawed.

"Come on, you deserve a little fun."

"I'm really not sure if I should."

"It'll be my treat. I'll even throw in some of those Kandy Kakes. Those things are so yummy."

"I just never left them before."

"Oh, nothing to worry about. We'll be back in the flash of an eye. The picture is not that long, and the theater isn't that far."

"Okay, okay, I'll just go and check with him."

"Great, I'll run upstairs and grab my handbag," Mrs. Misic said.

I walked back into the apartment and went directly to your father's room. I was reluctant about asking him anything since his only interaction with the two of you since he stopped helping me was the odd toss-up and a few peek-a-boos here and there. Outside of that, he showed very little interest in you or anything else for that matter. He went to work at the meat plant, and when he came home, he would spend hours locked up in his cell, making model airplanes and cars and listening to opera. I know he also dabbled in making some moonshine-like concoctions because I found some under the bed once. That's what relaxed him after a hard day of butchering meat. I think it helped with his insomnia too.

As soon as I knocked on his door, I heard something crashing to the floor. I think I may have startled him.

"Yes, Bernie?" He sounded very excited.

I hadn't been paying him much attention either at the time, so I guess he was grateful for my interruption.

"Jovanna from upstairs asked me to go to the movies," I said matter-of-factly, as if people were always asking me to go places.

"Jovanna, the Serbian?" He pretended that he didn't know who I was talking about.

"Yeah, she wants to take me to the Paradise to see *Way Down East*."

"She wants to take you to the pictures? That sounds like it could be fun," he said sounding more animated than he had been in a very long time.

"Then would it be okay if I went? The babies have already been bathed and fed, and they should sleep until morning."

"Sure," he said, without any hesitation whatsoever. The door sprang open. "You should go."

"Are you sure?" I asked.

"I'm positive. I want you to go and enjoy yourself."

"Okay, I just have to get my jacket. And just in case the babies do wake up, you can give them a little water from their bottles in the fridge. You could put a little sugar in it if you like. It helps to calm them down."

"No problem, I can do that." He seemed confident.

I put on my jacket, kissed you girls good night, then said good-bye to him. I left the apartment looking forward to seeing the film.

Once I was gone, he continued to work on his model plane. Normally, he kept the door to his bedroom closed, but this time he left it wide open so that he could hear if you two stirred. He told me all this afterward.

It was a good thing he did, because Eva woke up with a start and began to cry. This, of course, woke you up, Ava, since you two shared the same crib. Your father listened for a while to see if the crying would stop, but when the volume increased, he began to get anxious. He wasn't accustomed to dealing with cantankerous babies.

Remembering the instructions I had given him, he ran quickly to the kitchen in search of your bottles. He went right to the crib in my room. He found you two standing, shaking the side of your crib, and wailing indignantly as you always did. Not knowing what to do, he picked up you first, Ava, sat down with you on my cot and offered the water. You drank a little bit but then stopped abruptly and started to cry again. Frustrated, he put you back into the crib and picked up Eva. He had similar results, so he returned Eva to the crib. When he did this, both of you began screaming.

"Come on you two, give me a break for a second," he

pleaded. "Why don't you just go back to sleep and stop with all this fussing?"

As screams, tears, and snot spurted from you both, he paced nervously back and forth. The more he marched, the more he found himself moving farther away from all the commotion. When he reached his room, he remembered his stash of moonshine.

When I arrived home a few hours later, the whole place was pitch black. I went directly to my room and found the two of you fast asleep, more or less in the same position as when I left. Thinking that everything had gone smoothly, I prepared myself for bed. But when I lay down on my cot, I noticed something strange. I felt damp spots and something that felt like sand sprinkled all over my bed. When I turned the lights on to see what it was, I realized it was sugar. Then I noticed the empty baby bottles that Ben had placed under the crib. I grabbed one bottle and saw the large amount of sugar that had been left at the bottom. That alarmed me because I never added more than one or two tiny spoonfuls to your water. I looked at the sugar again, and a little bell rang in my head. Something told me to smell the bottle. When I took a whiff, I knew right away what he had done, and I panicked. I tried to wake you to make sure that you were okay. But when you didn't open your eyes, I began to scream.

"Wake up, wake up! Please, wake up! Why won't you wake up?" I was petrified.

I lifted each of you out of the crib and, carrying one on each side of me like I normally did, I ran downstairs and hailed a cab.

"Take me to the children's hospital," I told the driver.

"Are those babies okay?" the driver asked as he got out and helped me into the back seat.

"I don't know," I replied in a shaky voice.

"Well, let's get you to that hospital then." He stepped on the gas.

I bounced you two in my arms, trying to revive you, but nothing I did worked. The only thing that reassured me during the ride was that you were both still breathing.

When we reached the hospital, the driver took one of you, I don't remember which one, and ran with me to Emergency. We huffed and puffed as I explained to a nurse what had happened. The medical team went to work right away. Within a few minutes each of you had a long tube down your nose and your stomachs were being pumped. After the pumping, they put intravenous needles in your tiny hands. I couldn't bear to watch.

When I asked if you would be okay, the doctor said, "We'll just have to wait and see, but I think they will be fine."

And so I waited and I waited, and some hours later, you two finally woke up. You don't know how thankful I was. But as soon as you were awake, I noticed something very strange. Your eyes were glazed over.

"Avaline, Evaline, Avaline, Evaline," I said as I waved my hands in front of your faces. You moved your tiny heads around trying to find where the sound was coming from.

I yelled for the doctor, and a nurse came running.

"What is it?" She seemed annoyed, as if I was interrupting her.

"It's my daughters. I don't think they can see me. Look," I said as I waved my hands in front of your faces again. "Look at their eyes. They look dead. They weren't like that before.

Look how scared they look." I was hysterical.

The nurse ran out and when she returned with the doctor, he did a quick examination with a tiny flashlight and started shaking his head. I began to bawl the second I saw this. I knew exactly what it meant. He tried to calm me down, but it didn't help. The tears wouldn't stop.

"It looks like they were poisoned by the alcohol. Maybe if they had been brought in earlier, we could have prevented the damage," the doctor began.

The words, *if they had been brought in earlier* echoed in my mind and I regretted ever leaving that night to see that godforsaken boring film. I felt completely responsible.

• • •

Tears streamed down the faces of Eva and Ava. Bernice was distraught. She sighed, got up, and raised her arms in the air.

"You see what I mean? Your father and every other man that has ever walked God's green earth are all cowards and imbeciles. They should all be struck down. Every single last one of them!" she screamed at the top of her lungs, then stomped off to her room.

The twins sat completely still.

"I don't think he really meant to hurt us. Do you?" Ava whimpered.

"No. I don't think he knew any better. He was just trying to do his best to handle the situation."

"And there's no real point in holding grudges against ghosts anyway."

"Yeah, you're right—should we go and check on Ma to see if she's okay?"

"I think we should leave her alone for a bit. I can still hear her crying."

"Yeah, you're probably right."

"I'm glad we know the truth, anyway. Her stories about all those childhood illnesses were never very convincing." Eva exhaled.

"I know. They were always changing."

The twins moaned, reached out for each other's hand, and held on tightly. As they sat there silently, their faces muddied with tears, the same lost memory came to both. It was a recollection of their father pushing them in a large pram. While they cooed and babbled during their stroll, they watched the strained expression on his face as a myriad of vivid colors danced all around him.

As tears continued to stream from their sightless eyes, a part of them wished that they had never insisted on hearing the rest of the story.

CHAPTER 20

A New Openness

WHEN BERNICE WOKE UP the next morning, her stomach was growling. Her mind wasn't on the persistent rumbles but, instead, on the secret that she had revealed the night before. She had wanted to rush back and apologize, and offer some kind of comfort to the twins, but found it impossible to gather the necessary strength. She was thankful that they had each other.

As she made her way to the toilet, she tried to force her brain to concentrate on something more positive, but was unable to do so. After her morning constitutions, she felt lighter and a little bit more relaxed, but not completely relieved. When she entered the kitchen, breakfast had already been prepared.

"Smells and looks good," Bernice said as she sat down in front of one of the three plates that were piled high with eggs, toast, sausage, and bacon.

"Thanks," Eva and Ava said together. They were already seated.

"Did you sleep okay last night, Ma?" Eva asked.

"Just great, thanks." She gulped down some juice. "I dreamt about Rose and Violet again."

"That's nice, Ma," Ava said.

The sound of chewing and the clinking of cutlery filled the silence as Bernice and her daughters began to eat.

"Ma, we…ah, we wanted to thank you for yesterday," Ava said.

"Thank me for what?" Bernice asked, her mouth full of eggs.

"You know, for telling us the story that you told us. It was very brave of you," Eva continued.

"Brave?" Bernice said as she looked back and forth between her two daughters.

"Yeah, Ma, we know it must have been hard for you to tell us, and we can see now why you never wanted to talk about it before," Ava added.

"You see, there was a rhyme to my reason."

"Yes, Ma, we see, but we wanted to tell you that it's not your fault, so you don't have to blame yourself," Ava offered gently.

"Who do I blame, then?" Bernice asked.

"No one. You shouldn't blame anyone. It was just something that happened, and it was not good, but we wouldn't be the people we are today if it hadn't happened," Ava replied, sounding wiser and more mature all of a sudden.

"But there are so many things you haven't been able to do because of what happened. And me, I know I've put so many—too many—restrictions on you."

"We know you were only trying to protect us, Ma."

"You did the best that you could with us. The best that you knew how to do. We know that," Ava added.

"I tried." The sobs began.

"Ma, please don't cry again," Eva, said, sounding as if she, too, was on the verge of tears.

"I can't help it. I should have let you two go back to the school for the blind when you asked me. I should have given you more freedom to try different things."

"But we're still alive, Ma. We could still do things," Eva insisted.

"But you're fifty-three years old already," Bernice said.

"Yeah, but we still have some life left in us. We could still go back to school," Ava offered.

"At your age?" She tried not to sound too condescending.

"Our age doesn't matter. We could still do it." Eva jumped in.

"You know, you two are absolutely right." Bernice forced a smile. "Age has nothing to do with how old you feel, right?"

"Right," the twins said in unison.

Bernice and her daughters finished their meal with their eyes glimmering. They were all pleased with the new openness that was beginning to develop.

As Bernice had predicted, Rose came and knocked on their door later that same afternoon. Wearing a bright summer dress, she appeared to be in a cheerful mood.

"Hi. So sorry to bother you," Rose said apologetically. "I just wanted to…"

"Yes, yes, of course. You and Violet are most welcome to

meet at my house anytime you like," Bernice replied before Rose was able to finish her sentence.

"How did you know what I was going to ask you?" Rose asked stunned.

"My dreams," Bernice declared. "I see lots of things in them."

Rose shifted uncomfortably. "Great then, would tomorrow be okay?"

"Tomorrow would be wonderful," Bernice replied.

"Okay, thanks. See you then," Rose said as she turned and walked away.

"They're coming tomorrow," Bernice yelled as she shut the door.

The following day was perfectly gorgeous. A day that shouldn't have been wasted inside, but the women gathered in Bernice's apartment weren't paying much attention to the weather. They were too busy enjoying each other's company. Rose and Violet sat together on the love seat and chatted while Bernice prepared lunch. Ava and Eva were on the floor, playing with the babies.

"They feel like little balls," Ava chuckled.

"Like watermelons," Eva agreed.

The babies were happy to be bounced around.

When lunch, which consisted of baloney and peanut butter sandwiches, was ready, everyone ate ravenously. Bernice watched Rose and Violet as she shoved pieces of bread between her lips. The two appeared to be growing closer with every passing minute.

"May I?" Bernice asked as she reached out her hand to touch Violet's stomach.

"Sure, go right ahead," Violet replied, looking down at her growing abdomen. "Eva and Ava, do you want to try too?"

"Try what?" Ava was fussing with Clara.

"To feel the baby inside Violet," Bernice replied.

Eva and Ava were both quickly on their feet with the babies in their arms. Rose and Violet watched them anxiously.

"Don't worry, they won't drop them," Bernice said trying to reassure the nervous mothers.

The twins groped at first, then Violet gently took each of their hands and placed them on her stomach. "You feel that? He's swishing around now. He's probably trying to swim." Violet laughed.

"Wow!" the twins cried together.

"It does feel kind of like a fish in there," Ava said.

"Yeah," Eva agreed.

Rose felt left out. "Let me have your hands, and you can feel mine too," she offered. The twins gave Rose their hands. They both smiled as they touched Rose's tummy.

"I can't believe how hard your stomachs are." Ava returned to her place on the floor.

"Yeah, our bellies are so soft and jiggly." Eva sat down next to her sister.

Rose and Violet couldn't help but laugh.

"What does sex feel like?" Ava blurted, then quickly covered her mouth.

"Ava!" her sister yelled.

"Please excuse my daughter. She forgot her manners," Bernice said as she stared crossly at Ava.

"I'm sorry, I was just wondering. We're all grownups here. And it's just that Ma told us stories about your experiences."

"You mean stories about our sexual experiences?" Violet asked.

"Yeah," Ava replied.

"How would she know about that?" Violet asked again.

"My dreams," Bernice answered.

"Yes, those dreams," Rose teased.

"They don't lie. Is everyone ready for dessert? I made some grape Jell-O." Bernice was trying to change the subject. When all four women nodded, Bernice took that as her cue to disappear into the kitchen.

"So will you tell us?" Ava asked softly.

"You mean about sex?" Violet smiled and nudged Rose. "What do you want to know?" she asked.

"How does it feel when it's inside you?" Ava asked.

"The whole sensation," Eva chimed in.

"You mean you two never?" Rose asked, looking quite embarrassed.

"No, never," the twins answered together.

"Not even close," Eva smirked.

"Well it feels wet, warm, and full—like it belongs in there somehow," Rose began. "I guess because that's what it was made for."

"When it's in just right, it's like the relief you get when you scratch a mosquito bite or the feeling you get when you've been holding your pee for a very long time and you finally get to go. You just say ahhh. But if it's pushed in when you're not ready, it could hurt," Violet continued. "It works better if you're moist already."

"How do you get moist?" Ava asked.

"Oh, it just happens naturally. When you get turned on and if the man touches you just right," Violet replied.

"It always feels better when you do it with someone you love rather than someone you don't really care for," Rose added.

"Our mother told us that bowel movements are much more satisfying and relaxing," Ava said.

Rose and Violet looked at each other and burst out laughing.

"Your mother certainly has a way with words," Violet snickered.

Everyone giggled.

"Well, the Stickman tried to have sex with me one time," Ava blurted out.

"What! Where?" Eva and Bernice yelled together.

Bernice ran back into the room holding her chest. "When was this?"

"Why didn't you tell me?" Bernice and Eva asked together.

"You see? I told you!" Bernice was upset.

"Don't worry, I didn't let him do anything. He just touched me in the garbage room one day, and I didn't say anything because it was no big deal. He didn't mean anything by it."

"What do you mean, he didn't mean anything? Where did he touch you?" Bernice was beside herself.

"Oh, he asked me if I wanted to, but I didn't want to do it, especially in that room, so he didn't get far. I grabbed his hand and got out of there."

"Good for you, Ava," Violet said.

"I don't know what smelled worse—him or the garbage," Ava continued.

Everyone except Bernice burst out laughing.

"Well, next time be more careful," Bernice scolded. "And

stay the hell away from him."

"I was careful. I handled it, Ma."

"And next time you should tell someone, like your sister," Eva insisted.

"Didn't I just tell you? I'm a grown woman. I can take care of myself."

"That good for nothing, smelly pig! The nerve!" Bernice muttered to herself as she returned to the kitchen.

Everyone laughed again.

"Rose, did you mean your husband when you said someone you don't care for?" Ava asked boldly.

The flushed look that came over Rose's face was lost on the twins. They could, however, detect the uneasiness in her hesitation.

"Sorry if my sister asked the wrong thing," Eva interjected. "What did you say that for?" She pinched her sister's leg.

"Ouch, what did you do that for?"

"It's okay, she can ask me that. Well, yeah, I guess I did mean him," Rose replied.

"Can I ask why you never really loved him?" Ava continued.

"It's not a matter of loving him or not. We were never really suited for each other, I guess," Rose offered. She suspected that the twins knew about her domestic situation even though they couldn't see the welts and bruises that decorated her body.

"I thought you two wanted to know about sex," Violet said, trying to change the subject. "Yes, of course," Eva replied.

"Tell us more," Ava insisted.

The twins were all ears as Rose and Violet continued with their titillating descriptions.

After Rose and Violet left that day, Ava shut herself in the bathroom and stepped into the shower. While she washed herself, she allowed her fingers to creep up between her legs into regions where no man had ever ventured. At that moment she wished she had let the Stickman have his way with her. She wasn't alone in her elation. In the bedroom, Eva reached up her dress in search of the same pleasure. While the pair explored the sensations of their bodies, they never once considered the age-old warning of the danger of such activities. They were already blind.

In their apartments, Rose and Violet smiled and reflected on the conversations of the day and looked forward to the next visit. Their moods quickly shifted and soured, however with the return of their respective husbands.

A few days later, there was an ugly downpour. The mood outside mirrored the one indoors. From the moment the two women arrived, the twins could hear the worry in each of their labored steps and in the silence before and after their greetings.

"Are you two okay?" Eva asked Rose and Violet.

"It's those awful husbands of yours again, isn't it?" Ava suggested.

The tense pause confirmed the twin's suspicions.

"Sometimes I just want to kill him," Rose said softly in a matter-of-fact fashion.

It was clear that she felt liberated by her words.

"I know. Me too," Violet echoed.

The two women began to cackle nervously. Not knowing what else to do, the twins joined in. From her bedroom, Bernice didn't even wonder about the laughter. She was just pleased to hear it. She wobbled out of her bed into the living room.

"Here, let me take those babies out of your hair," she insisted.

"Can you manage both at the same time?" Rose asked.

"Remember, I had twins," Bernice reassured them.

In a few minutes Bernice had returned to her room with the babies. Rose, Violet, and the twins were left to themselves. The tone in the room changed.

"I thought about tampering with Douglas' pills once," Rose confessed.

"How? When?" the twins asked together.

"I'm not quite sure how I would do it, or when. I guess I would have to wait for a good opportunity. All I know is that he's constantly popping those things."

"I sometimes think if I could catch my husband when he's at his most vulnerable, then I could really get him," Violet admitted.

"When would that be?" Rose asked.

"When he's on the toilet or sleeping. Sometime when he least suspects it," Violet answered with a sneer.

"I could just imagine the look on his face if you were to barge in with a knife when he's in the middle of doing his business," Rose snickered.

"I know," Violet howled.

By the tone and inflection of their voices, Eva and Ava were starting to believe that the two women were not as innocent as they seemed.

Visits to Bernice's soon became a regular part of Rose's and Violet's routine. On the love seat, or sometimes reclined on the twins' double bed, the four women would discuss anything and everything under the sun. Special attention was always given to sex and vengeance. As the women's tummies grew, the twins became more concerned about the mounting domestic tensions that the two women were facing.

CHAPTER 21
The End of Summer

VIOLET LAMENTED the end of the warm weather as she strolled back home from the pharmacy. The only signs of the changing season were the reddish and yellowy leaves that spotted the crab apple bush in the park. Each time she passed it, she marveled at the slight shifts in color and the thinning leaves. Back home, the vegetation always remained the same—green, in varying shades.

Even though the place on her leg where Robert had kicked her the night before still smarted, she was in an upbeat mood. It was her birthday, and she wasn't going to let anything spoil that. The thought of celebrating it so far from home was a bit daunting, but the fact that she had people to celebrate it with warmed her heart.

She had wanted to dress up a bit in honor of her birthday, but she knew her large belly wouldn't fit into her one nice dress. She opted instead to wear one of the pair of matching maternity dresses that Bernice had made for her and Rose.

When she arrived at Bernice's, she saw that Rose had decided to do the same. The two chuckled and pointed at each other when they saw this.

"I have a surprise for you two," Bernice said, holding the wiggling babies around their chubby middles.

"Oh, I love surprises," Violet said. She walked with a slight limp over to Rose.

"What happened to you? Are you alright there?" Bernice asked, concerned.

"I'm fine," Violet said, trying to remain cheery. "I'm okay."

"What did he do this time?" Ava asked, coming from the bathroom.

"Oh, nothing out of the ordinary, just the usual." Violet wished they would change the subject.

"What's the surprise, Bernice?" asked Rose, trying to save her friend from any further interrogation.

"Oh. Well first of all, Happy Birthday to you two."

"Yeah, Happy Birthday," the twins echoed.

"Thank you," Rose and Violet replied in unison.

"Today, I think you two should go on your own—maybe to the café down the road or something—you know, just to spend some time by yourselves. We'll keep an eye on the babies, of course," Bernice offered.

"Yeah, we'll take good care of them," Ava added.

"Are you sure it would be alright?" Rose asked. Something in her voice suggested she wasn't completely comfortable with leaving her son.

"I wouldn't have suggested it if it wasn't alright," Bernice replied.

"We might look a little silly, dressed in the same dress," Rose offered.

"Ah, who cares what you look like? Nobody's even going to notice anyway. And besides, it's your birthday. You should go out and act like two young people for a change. You need to enjoy yourselves a little." Bernice handed the babies over to the twins, reached into her bosom and retrieved a one-dollar bill, and pressed it into Violet's hand.

"Get some coffee on me," Bernice said with a smile.

Violet turned to Rose. "I guess we don't have any choice in the matter." Violet said happily.

The two women grabbed their handbags, kissed their babies, and left the apartment.

"Bye and thanks," Violet said as she looked back.

"Yes, thank you," Rose echoed.

The two women kept a watchful eye out for their husbands as they strolled to the café. Rose was the most vigilant because she had gone to the police station some days before to file a report on Douglas. She had given his name, their address, and a full account of his abuse. She had even shown some of her fresher bruises, but all they said was that since she wasn't in any imminent danger nothing could be done. She had left there feeling as if she had wasted her time.

"That Bernice is a good one," Violet began.

"Yes she is…my, it feels so strange being without Thomas," Rose said.

"I know what you mean. I feel like I can fly." Violet spread out her arms as if they were wings. This made Rose smile.

The café was a dingy space with seven small tables crammed into it. The front counter occupied most of the room. The place was deserted, save for a young girl at the cash. The women carried their coffees to the very back. They smiled at each other as they took their seats.

"Happy Birthday," they crooned as they clinked their mugs together.

"You look lovely today, by the way," Rose said. She took a sip of coffee. "You always seem to look lovely, no matter what," she continued.

"You too," Violet said, returning Rose's compliment.

Even though their troubles had left their marks on the women's faces, they still managed to maintain a somewhat youthful appearance.

"You know what we need?" Violet suddenly asked.

"What?"

"Something that would change our lives." Violet reached for her purse, rummaged for a few seconds, then pulled out a brand new tube of lipstick.

"Lipstick?" Rose mocked.

"Yeah, put some on. It'll make you feel better." Violet handed Rose the lipstick.

"But, I don't even have a mirror," Rose stalled.

"I'll be your mirror. Go ahead," Violet insisted. The purplish-brown shade was a bit too dark for Rose's pale complexion, but it brightened up her face nevertheless. Violet gave Rose the thumbs up.

"Very nice," Violet said. "My turn now." The color was better suited to Violet's brown skin. "How do I look?" she asked, pushing out her lips.

"Perfect," Rose beamed. "Just perfect."

"You know, I brought that lipstick the day before I left home. I wanted to look my best for that husband of mine, but it turns out he really didn't care how I looked after all," Violet explained as she returned the lipstick to her bag.

Rose nodded sympathetically. She knew all about what had happened the night Violet arrived. "What should we do then?" Rose leaned closer to Violet. There was no need for her to extrapolate. Violet knew exactly what she meant.

"What do you suggest?" Violet asked.

"What we talked about at Bernice's," Rose replied.

"We were just joking. Did you really mean those things?" Violet looked away.

"Didn't you? I thought you did," Rose replied.

"It was just silly chatter—fantasy, that's all." Violet looked uneasy. She knew that she wasn't speaking truthfully. "Anyway, when is your due date again?"

"You know when my due date is. Why don't you want to talk about this?"

"Well, first of all, can't you see that we're in a public place?" Violet whispered.

"We're the only ones here."

"What about her?" Violet pointed to the young woman behind the counter. She wasn't close enough to hear them, but she was staring at them strangely.

"Okay, I get it. You don't want to talk about it. What would you prefer to talk about instead?"

Violet pursed her lips again and smiled. "Lipstick!" They laughed out loud. Then Rose took a quick sip of her coffee, grabbed her purse, and jumped up. Violet watched.

A few minutes later, Rose returned with two large pieces of chocolate cake. "Happy Birthday," she yelled as she placed the plates on the table and pretended to blow out imaginary candles.

Violet grinned and followed suit. Both women clapped loudly. The girl behind the counter rolled her eyes and shook her head. As the pair drowned their sorrows with the cake, neither noticed that they were eating in perfect sync.

By the time Rose and Violet returned, Bernice had prepared a smorgasbord of food in honor of their birthday— roast beef, potatoes, spinach, and pie. After everyone had stuffed themselves, Eva and Ava changed into a pair of black dresses and gave a stunning performance of their whole repertoire. They sounded even better than the records. Rose's and Violet's spirits were so uplifted that they each applied another coat of lipstick after their meal. They both agreed that it had been a wonderful day.

Violet hummed to Clara as she walked over to the light switch and flicked it on. She was still elated from the celebration.

"Why so happy?" Robert boomed from the couch, looking very agitated. He had been sitting and stewing in the dark, waiting for Violet to return. Violet shifted her daughter in her arms as she anticipated Robert's next move. He lurched toward her and greeted her with a smirk that was quickly followed by a slap.

"Where have you been?" he demanded, slapping the other side of her face for symmetry.

She stood stone-faced.

"And what's that you have on your lips? Who are you wearing lipstick for?"

"Whoever I find, once I leave you," she said, without a trace of fear in her voice.

His eyes opened as wide as humanly possible. He was stunned.

Before he could react, Violet dashed to the bedroom and pulled the door closed behind her. She placed Clara into the crib and listened to what was happening in the next room. It was quiet. Just as she was beginning to believe that the tirade was over, the door swung open. Robert charged at her and grabbed her by the neck. Trapped, she struggled to catch her breath.

"So who was the lipstick for again?" he demanded.

"No one," she said, squirming in his grasp.

"And where are you going?"

"Nowhere," she moaned.

"You're damn right. You're not going anywhere. You know what will happen if you do."

With a sharp twist of her body, she was able to free herself and rush out of the room. Robert barged after her. Once he caught her, he continued the beating. With every slap, kick, and punch, he accused her of committing all sorts of nasty and vile deeds with men of every stripe. Throughout, she remained silent and stoic. Her unflinching face expressed that she could take all that was being thrown her way and then some. He erupted when he noticed that his efforts were going to waste.

"If you're going to be a slut, then I'm going to have to treat you like one," he bellowed as he ripped off Violet's dress. This took Violet completely by surprise. Her impassivity quietly shifted to terror.

"Please don't," she pleaded quietly as she tried to hold him back.

He paid no attention. Pushing her down on the couch, he pulled off her bra and cupped both of her breasts before biting down hard on one of her nipples. She screamed and tried to push his head away, but her flailing arms and legs were easily controlled and pinned back. As she struggled, he ripped off her underwear. With one hand he undid his belt and pulled his pants down. He covered her mouth as he forced himself inside.

His thrusts were so aggressively violent that they caused ruptures in her vaginal wall. She shrieked in pain. Had he been able to penetrate any deeper, he would have punctured the embryonic sack of their unborn child. She attempted to bite his hand, but wasn't able to get a good enough grip. With one slight movement, she was finally able to clamp down on the edge of his shoulder.

"What the fuck!" he screamed, retaliating by mashing his large hand into her face. Unable to breathe, she stopped struggling and gave in. Remaining completely still, she closed her eyes and emptied her head of all thoughts except those of her children and of revenge. On his final thrust he rested atop her.

"It would be best to be both loved and feared," he roared before slapping her one more time for good measure.

In the kitchen, he grabbed his bottle of Johnny Walker. Once his thirst was satiated, he left.

Violet opened her eyes and looked down at the blood-smeared sofa beneath her. The amount of blood and the throbbing, burning pain was alarming. The walk to the bathroom was agonizing. She winced as she watched the blood trickle out of her and into the toilet. The conversation at the café came back to her as she ran the shower to wash off Robert's musk. A part of her wanted to cry, but she refused to shed a single tear. She knew at that moment that there was no more time for idle thoughts. Action—action had to be taken.

The next day in the safety and comfort of the twins' bed, Violet and Rose lay together while Violet recounted the events of the previous night. Eva and Ava listened eagerly from the foot of the bed. Rose was not at all surprised by what she heard. She knew their husbands were capable of so much worse.

Rose rested her hand lightly on the upper part of Violet's arm. "Maybe you should go to the doctor to make sure the baby is okay," she suggested.

Violet cupped her hand under her abdomen. "Oh, he's been moving around like crazy, he's okay. Just a little upset, maybe."

"What about the police?" Ava interrupted. She had been wanting to make this suggestion for a long time but had never found an appropriate moment.

"Yeah, why don't you call the police. He raped you," Eva echoed.

"He's done worse than that to me before, and I never called the police," Violet answered calmly.

The twins had no comeback.

"What would they do, anyway?" Violet continued. "Back home you call them and they end up chastising the woman instead, asking her what she did wrong to drive a man to beat her. It's pure foolishness. That's why my mother never bothered with them."

"She's right. I went to them, and they said there was nothing they could do," Rose said.

Violet looked at Rose with surprise. This was the first she was hearing of Rose's encounter with the police.

"It wasn't even worth going," Rose added. "The laws are not made for us women."

"And this is not our country either," Violet added.

"No, it's not," Rose agreed.

"Why don't the two of you just rest," Eva suggested, detecting the fatigue in Violet's voice and movements.

"Yeah, we'll just go and help Ma with the babies," Ava added.

"Some sleep would do the two of you good." Eva trailed after her sister.

When the twins were gone, Violet turned to Rose and stared at her lovingly. "Look at us. We look like a pair of mountains lying here." She tittered.

"More like hippos," Rose replied with a laugh.

"So now what?" Violet asked, changing her tone.

"Now what? I don't know exactly. I guess we have to come up with some sort of a plan or something. You know, something that makes sense for both of us."

"I think we have to put a lot of thought into it before we begin."

"Right, we need to do some solid planning," Rose agreed. "But let's just lie here for now and rest. You must be exhausted." Rose pushed back some hair from Violet's face.

"Yes, I am," Violet stretched her feet out on the bed. "I am."

For the rest of the afternoon, Violet and Rose remained sprawled on the twins' bed, napping and quietly beginning to discuss some details of their plan. While they did this, the twins stood at the bedroom door, attentively listening to every word.

The moment Rose opened her eyes the next morning, she was overcome with a deep feeling of sorrow. She knew it was normal to sympathize with those who were in similar situations, but what she felt was much stronger than that. At that moment, Bernice's talk about twin souls came to mind. Logic told her that it was a farfetched idea, but her heart told her otherwise.

"Everything is going to be alright, Letty. Don't worry, everything is going to be alright," she whispered to herself as she got up to check on her son.

She had expected to be woken up by the baby, but he hadn't made a peep. When she got to the crib, she let out a piercing scream. The baby wasn't there.

"Thomas! Thomas!" she cried, knowing full well that her son was still too small to get out of the crib on his own.

"Thomas…little man!" she continued to yell as she rushed from the bedroom to the living room. She stopped abruptly when she saw Thomas, fast asleep on the couch with Douglas hovering over him, staring indecisively. The discovery both scared and confounded her. She had no way of knowing what was going on inside Douglas's head. But her instincts told her what to do.

"What…what were you doing…?" Rose stammered angrily as she grabbed her son and held him tightly. "What were you doing with him?" she demanded again. When Douglas didn't answer or even look up, she nudged his shoulder. "Answer me, damn it. What were you doing?"

Getting no response, she began to shove more forcefully. Douglas remained completely motionless for a few beats, but then, without warning, the zombie within him awakened. In one quick swoop, he grabbed Rose's arm, stood up, and pushed her so forcefully that she ended up on the other side of the room. The baby, luckily, landed on top of her and was not hurt. The stunned child cried for a bit, but she was able to lull him back to sleep. Carefully placing him on the carpet, she maneuvered her large belly off the floor, and walked back over to Douglas. He acknowledged her with only a blank stare.

"What were you going to do to him? Tell me!" Rose said, yelling straight into his face.

Both were surprised by her sudden fervor. It was a definite departure from her usual passivity. Douglas scowled at her and walked away. She was not satisfied. "I said, tell me!" She hurried up behind him and shoved his back. "Tell me, I—"

Douglas grabbed a glass ornament from a nearby table and threw it at her head. A ridge of the glass caught her on the ear. She watched as tiny droplets of blood trickled slowly onto the carpet.

Confident that he had ended the argument, he went to the kitchen. Rose seethed and watched the red droplets as they soaked through her white nightgown. Her breathing became more pronounced as she went in pursuit of her husband.

He pulled out a knife just as she stepped up behind him. She stared calmly at it, without the slightest bit of concern. It was as if she had been expecting this all along.

"Is that what you were going to do? You're going to kill me? Why don't you do it right now? Kill me, you coward. At least the police will know who did it," she screamed.

He turned his head slightly. "You went to the police!"

"Yes I did. What are you going to do about it?" She could feel the fury building up inside him. He remained motionless, with his back still away from her. She stepped even closer to him. He flung the knife to the floor. She tapped his shoulder. "I said, what are you going to do about it?"

He snapped. Turning abruptly, he took hold of her, twisted her around, and propelled her away from him. The force of his thrust made her fly into the sharp edge of the glass kitchen table. She heard a popping sound and shrieked, clutching her belly. She knew that something terrible had just happened. The pain and the warm blood-streaked liquid that oozed down her thighs confirmed it. Douglas looked on in terror.

In the hospital, Rose lay asleep. Her ear was bandaged and she was hooked up to an intravenous drip. Her abdomen was still large, but not as large as it been hours before. Douglas was seated next to her with his head in his lap, sobbing. A doctor stood in front of him.

"It seems that the impact fractured the fetus's skull and killed it instantly," the doctor explained calmly. "Were you there when it happened?"

"I was in the other room," Douglas lied as he dried his eyes.

"It's unfortunate, but these things happen," the doctor continued.

Douglas nodded his head as the tears began to gush again.

"Well, you're still young. You could always have more children." The doctor touched Douglas's shoulder. "When your wife wakes, someone will come to talk to you about what you would like to do with the remains." The doctor moved toward the door. "Take care."

Douglas wiped his face with his shirtsleeve. "Okay, doctor. Thank you very much," he blubbered.

"You're welcome," the doctor said as he disappeared into the corridor.

When Rose woke up, she found the room empty. She rang for the nurse and propped herself up. "Would it possible for me to see my baby?" she asked the nurse in a weak voice.

The nurse took one look at Rose's large, sad eyes and decided to forgo the normal procedures. She nodded. "I'll be right back."

When she returned some minutes later, she clasped the lifeless body of Rose's child, wrapped in a pink blanket, next to her chest.

"A girl," Rose moaned. She had hoped for a girl. The swaddled baby didn't seem dead at all. It looked like any sleeping child. As the nurse moved closer, Rose hoped silently that it all had been a big misunderstanding.

Her body seized when the nurse placed the bundle in her arms. At first she couldn't bear to look directly at the lifeless form, but then she found the courage to glance down. The baby's shriveled face was slightly yellowish. It looked more old than young. A thin tuft of light-colored hair poked through the top of the blanket. Her eyes were squeezed tightly shut, and her mouth puckered. Her skin felt cool, yet still alive.

Holding the baby in her arms, Rose had never felt more heartbroken.

"What color were her eyes?" Rose looked up at the nurse and clutched her daughter closer to her heart.

"I'm not sure," the nurse replied. "Let me see if they wrote it down." The nurse retrieved the chart and leafed through it.

"Hazel, it says that they were hazel."

"Hazel," Rose repeated, gazing down at her daughter. "That was the color of my mother's eyes."

Rose wept, realizing she would never see her child's eyes. "Hazel," she whispered. "That's what I'm going to call you."

Before the miniature body with its smashed skull was put to rest, a short service was held in the hospital chapel. While Rose stood beside the chaplain, still dressed in her hospital gown, she mumbled a silent prayer for her daughter. In it, she promised herself that she would never allow Douglas to harm her again.

When Rose returned home, she went directly to Bernice's to pick up her son. Violet was already there waiting. When the two women saw each other, they fell into a long embrace. They held each other and cried for what seemed like hours. Bernice had some tea prepared for them by the time they sat down. She knew they would want to be alone.

On the love seat, they cuddled up next to one another without saying a word, listening to each other's hushed inhalations and weighted exhalations.

CHAPTER 22
The Beginning of the End

ANGELA SPENCER DIDN'T know that she had been spared the full extent of Robert's violent temper. Occasionally he berated her verbally, but never once did he lay a single finger on her. This was not by chance. It had everything to do with Angela's no-nonsense attitude. She wasn't the type of woman who would allow herself to be beaten. Robert discovered this one day when he made the mistake of raising his hand to her. Within seconds of his fingers reaching up, Angela had grabbed a screwdriver and jabbed it toward his right eye.

"Don't you dare," she had scowled in a voice that was no longer sweet. "If you ever, ever try that again, I'll dig your eye out," she threatened, bringing the tool within inches of his pupil.

After that day, Robert understood that whenever he felt

the need to slap, kick, or punch anyone, he had to return home, even if Angela was the source of his frustration.

Since Angela gave Robert whatever he wanted whenever he wanted it, he treated her accordingly. He catered to her every whim and to all her ailments throughout her pregnancy. And when it came time for the baby to be born, he was in the delivery room, holding her hand. When he saw that Angela had produced a baby boy who resembled him in every way, he was extremely proud, and Angela's value rose in his eyes.

Once the baby was brought home, however, tensions mounted. Angela's inexperience as a mother and the child's insistent crying proved disastrous. Everything came to a head one evening when the baby woke from a nap as Robert relaxed in the comfort of Angela's cozy living room.

"Can you please deal with that?" Robert asked, annoyed.

"Why don't you go and see what's wrong this time," Angela barked.

"How am I going to take care of him? Can't you see I have no tits?"

"If you'd been paying any attention, you'd know I stopped breastfeeding a few weeks ago. The formula is in the fridge. You just have to heat it up."

"I don't know anything about heating formula."

"All you have to do is put it in a pot. It wouldn't hurt if you helped a little, you know."

"What have I been doing all this time?"

"Only when it suits you."

"Only when it suits me?" Robert was incensed. "You call getting up at the crack of dawn to change a dirty nappy 'when it suits me?'"

"That's all a part of having a baby."

"Maybe if you managed the child better he wouldn't be waking up every two minutes for something."

"Manage the child better?" She sat up. It was now her turn to be riled.

"I think I've been managing just fine, no thanks to you. You're always telling me it's my turn and complaining about how tired you are. I'm wondering what you're so damn tired from. It's not like you have a job or anything important like that."

"I'm tired, Angela, because I'm not getting any goddamn sleep with that goddam kid hollering all night long."

"What kind of man calls his child that 'goddamn kid'?"

"One that's had enough and is fed up and just wants to sleep." He pulled himself up off the couch. "Look, I'm gone, alright?"

"Good, you go. And don't come back, you good for nothing asshole," she yelled, hurling a cushion at his back.

Violet was not at all pleased to see Robert. Swinging his arms, he gave the impression that he lived nowhere and belonged to nobody. The man that she had known would have never walked the streets looking so unkempt, dressed in un-ironed pants and a stained T-shirt that had been pulled out of shape. Back home, he was always clean, and his slacks were always carefully pleated, even if he was just going for a stroll.

Violet sensed that he was slipping deeper and deeper into some sort of slump. Even though she tried not to be concerned, she couldn't help but notice. Since the rape, he had not forced himself on her, but other forms of ugliness continued.

"Get me my Johnny," he ordered as he sat himself down.

He always called his whiskey by name, as if it were his closest and dearest friend.

When Violet returned with the half-full bottle, he grabbed it out of her hand, caressed its long neck, as if to say, *Hello how are? So glad to see you again.*

After he polished off the bottle, he got up, searched for Violet's purse, and took some money from it as she watched. She knew better than to let her temper flare. She wasn't looking for a fight.

In the days that followed, Robert spent most of his day in front of the TV, falling more and more into his funk. As he slipped away, Violet wondered again what had become of the man that she once cared for. Taking full advantage of his disengagement, she went and came as she pleased. All he would say on her departure was, "Pick me up some more Johnny, while you're out," and on her return, "Did you get the Johnny?"

After one week of this Violet begin to get a little irritated. "Don't you have someone expecting you somewhere?" she prompted.

Robert was sprawled out on the couch. "No, I just have you, my dear. You know you are the love of my life," he replied and closed his eyes.

Violet shook her head in disbelief.

After the loss of the baby, Douglas had become more sedate. This was due to grief as well as to his increasing visits to the Stickman. Eventually, much like Robert, he began to spend his days in an extended siesta, only leaving the apartment to purchase his pills.

When he left for longer periods, he always ended up at

Johnny Little's place. It had become unavoidable, since it was the only place he found true peace.

A strong gale blew like an omen the day Douglas returned to Johnny's after a short time away. Johnny was so delighted to see him, he could hardly contain himself. Douglas was equally excited, but when Johnny moved in to embrace him, he quickly moved away.

"I'm so glad you came. Sit, sit, get comfortable. I have something to show you. Wait right here." Johnny vanished.

When he returned, he was dressed in a pink baby doll set with a frilly tutu. When he spun around, he looked like a circus bear. He handed Douglas a matching set in his size.

"Now we can be twins," Johnny beamed happily.

When Douglas didn't react with his usual wide-eyed, almost embarrassed grin, Johnny knew something was wrong.

"Are you okay?" Johnny crouched down beside Douglas.

Douglas cast his eyes downward.

"Do you have a headache or stomachache? Did you not sleep well last night?" Johnny asked.

Still no reply. Biting his lip, Johnny gave Douglas a serious look.

"Is everything alright at home?" Johnny stuttered, knowing that the question would not be a welcomed one, since they never discussed personal matters.

Douglas sat erect. "Home?" he repeated. "Why would you ask such a question? What does it have to do with you?"

Johnny knew nothing of Douglas's wife, Thomas, or the dead child.

"Sorry. I was just trying to find out what was wrong. That's all. You're looking so glum and even the baby-dolls didn't cheer you up."

Douglas snarled at Johnny. He wanted to sucker punch him, but he knew better. Johnny was more than twice his size. "Whatever's going on with me is my business. Do you understand? None of your fucking business."

From the tone of Douglas's voice, Johnny could tell that his friend was in a great deal of pain. Not knowing what else to do, he sat down next to him, raised his arm as if to stretch, and placed it around him. This was just the medicine Douglas needed. Within a few seconds, he groaned, then started to weep. Johnny tightened his embrace and began to gently rock back and forth. As the two men swayed to and fro, Douglas stared directly at Johnny and told him about his mother and her lingerie, Rose, and the dead child— omitting, of course, all the parts about the abuse. When he was done, Johnny told him about the uncle who touched him and the mother who never believed him. When all the confessions were made, they embraced—both feeling much lighter.

While Douglas and Robert passed the time away with their respective "Johnnies" and the weather got progressively cooler, Rose and Violet continued to meet at Bernice's. One evening, the pair decided to take a stroll before returning home, thinking that the air would do them some good. They dressed the babies up warmly and headed out.

"We wouldn't mind watching them, if you two want to go on your own," Bernice offered from her doorway as the two women walked away.

"Oh, thank you, Bernice. It's okay. You've done so much already," Violet replied.

"Oh well, enjoy your walk."

"Thank you," the two women replied in unison as they left with their children.

Outside, they walked through the deserted streets.

"When are you going to start?" Rose asked.

"Soon."

"You're waiting for the right moment?"

"Yeah, I guess." They continued along their way.

While Violet and Rose strolled, Eva paced around the apartment trying to figure where the uneasy feeling in the pit of her stomach was coming from. Since Rose and Violet had begun to visit regularly, the twins and Bernice had been more cheerful than before. The stale smell of loneliness that permeated the whole apartment also seemed less prominent. But each time the pair left, traces of the odor would curiously return, and the joyfulness would dissipate.

"It really stinks in here," Eva announced as she went from room to room opening all the windows.

Ava was resting in bed while Bernice took a bath.

"Where is that godforsaken draft coming from?" Bernice yelled.

"Eva opened all the windows," Ava tattled.

"Now why in the hell would she do that?" Bernice screeched.

"It stinks in here, Ma," Eva yelled from the kitchen.

"Maybe it's you that stinks. You ever think of that?"

"It's not me. It's the apartment. Can't you smell it?"

"Well, you need to close those windows or one of us old ladies is going to catch her death of cold." Bernice banged on the bathroom wall.

"Speak for yourself, I'm not old," Ava said.

"Yes, we are old, Ava. Face it." Eva swung her leg absent-mindedly across the bed, accidently squeezing her sister's arm.

"Oww!" Ava screamed.

"What's wrong?" Bernice shrieked.

"Eva's just not paying attention to what she's doing, that's all," Ava griped. "What's gotten into you anyway?"

Eva pouted.

"Yeah, what's wrong with you?" Bernice toddled out of the bathroom in her robe.

"What did you say to him, after he did it?" Eva asked faintly.

"What did she say?" Bernice asked Ava.

"I said, what did you say to him after he did it?"

There was silence.

"What did you do? Did you argue? Did you ask him to leave?" Eva continued.

"Your father…" Bernice started, then stopped.

Ava wanted to strangle her sister for bringing up the subject again, but then she realized she wanted to hear the answer just as much as Eva did. The sisters listened as their mother sat down in one of the kitchen chairs at the foot of their bed.

"Take your time, Ma," Ava encouraged. "You don't have to talk about it if you don't want to."

"It's okay…I will…You see, I found out that your father was a very sick man after the incident," Bernice said as she settled into her seat. "Before, I thought something was wrong with him, the way he was spending so much time locked in that room, but after what happened, I was sure something wasn't quite right, so I told him that he should go to a doctor and get his head checked out."

"How was he acting afterward?" Eva asked.

"Oh, he'd disappear for a few days or so, then when he came back, he was even more like a prisoner in that room. I could hear him crying in there sometimes."

"How did you get him to go to the doctor?" Ava asked.

"I just knocked on the door one day and told him that I thought he should go."

"So what did the doctor say?" Eva asked.

"The doctor said that he was in a serious state of depression, and he gave him some medication to deal with it. The problem was, the stuff made him more of a zombie than he was before."

"Did you forgive him for doing what he did?"

"I've tried. I haven't even forgiven myself for leaving you two with him that night." Bernice's voice quivered.

"Please don't, Ma," Ava said. "You don't have to say any more."

"I'm sorry. I'm so very sorry. I wish I could have given you a better father. You don't know how many times I wished I could take that night back and give you back your sight. If I could give you mine, I would do it in a second."

"We know, Ma," The twins said in unison. "We know."

The three women remained motionless, not knowing what else to say.

The next morning, Bernice was overcome by an acute feeling of sadness the moment she opened her eyes. It kicked her in the chest and grabbed her by the throat. She crept quietly to the cabinet in the living room and picked up a blue urn. Holding it close to her chest, she snuck into the twins' room. They were in the same position as she had left them the

night before. Their heads were slumped to the side with glob-
ules of drool dripping from opposite corners of their mouths.
They looked like overgrown babies.

As she watched them sleep, she wanted to apologize for
the all the wrongs she had done them, for keeping them so
isolated, for taking them out of school, and making them
so fearful. She had so many regrets, more than she could
withstand.

She touched Eva's foot first, then Ava's. Their heads
popped up together.

"Is it morning already?" Eva asked.

"Yes, Eva, it's morning, you sleepyhead," Bernice replied.

"We must have been tired," Ava said.

"I guess you were, Ava," Bernice replied.

"Eva, Ava," the twins repeated together.

"Wait a second there," Eva said.

"You said Eva and Ava. How very sweet of you, Ma," Ava
said.

"Sweet? What did I do?" Bernice asked.

"You didn't call us 'you two' like you usually do," Ava
said.

"It's nice hearing you say our names again," Eva added,
getting a little choked up.

"No need to get mushy about it," Bernice interjected.
"Enough of that, I'm holding something in my hand right
now. I wonder if you can guess what it is."

"What color is it?" Ava asked jumping right into her
game mode.

"Blue," Bernice replied.

"Is it bigger than a bread box?" Eva asked, also getting
into the spirit.

"No."

"What is it made of?" Ava asked.

"It's ceramic."

"Does it have a lid?"

"Yes."

"Then it's that urn of our father's ashes that you keep in the cabinet," Ava replied.

Bernice was dumbfounded. "How did you know that it was there?"

"We do have hands you know, Ma," Ava replied.

"How do you think we entertain ourselves when you're not here?" Eva continued her sister's thought.

"How did you know it was ashes—and your father's, at that?" Bernice placed the urn on top of the dresser and sat down.

"Should we tell her how we knew it was ashes?" Ava asked Eva.

"Go ahead. Tell her," Eva answered.

"We smelled it and then we…we—" Ava was unable to say what she wanted to say.

"We tasted it," Eva said bluntly.

"You what!" Bernice was even more startled than before. "You tasted the ashes?"

"We guessed what it was by touching it and smelling it, but we wanted to give it one final test, so we tasted it," Eva said.

"But when we knew what it was, we both decided that we would eat a little more," Ava added.

"That's downright crazy. Why would you want to eat your father's ashes?"

"To be close to him," Eva replied.

"To be close to him?" Bernice was puzzled.

"Yeah, to be close to him," Ava repeated.

"When did you two crazies do this?" Bernice asked.

"Oh, years ago," Ava answered.

"Long time ago. In our twenties," Eva added.

"That's when we started, but we took little samples every now and then, whenever we felt like it. It was Eva's idea. She said that when we did it, we were honoring him."

"It was our way of getting to know him better, I guess," Eva continued.

"I thought it felt a little lighter than before. It's a wonder that you two didn't get poisoned or something. And how did you know that it was your father's ashes and not someone else's?"

"Who else's would it be?"

"And how did you know that the container was blue?"

"It just felt blue," Ava answered.

"All these years we wondered why you would want his ashes around."

"Yeah, when you always acted like you hated him."

"But you didn't really hate him altogether. You did love him a bit, didn't you?" Eva asked.

"I don't know about that," Bernice replied smugly.

"Then why keep the ashes all these years?"

"I guess I never knew what else to do with them. What was I supposed to do? We never had any special places and he died so suddenly. There was never a chance for him to give me any instructions on what to do with him after he passed."

"Why didn't you just bury him in the cemetery like everyone else?" Ava asked.

"Cremation was cheaper."

"So why were you going to tell us now that the urn has been there—why now, after all these years?"

Bernice fell silent. The twins listened as she formulated her thoughts.

"I guess I wanted you to know that he has been here all the time."

"Why didn't you ever tell us before?" Ava asked.

"I guess I was afraid."

"Afraid of what?" Eva asked.

"Oh, of the truth, I guess," Bernice admitted.

"What truth? That you really did love him? That truth?" Eva demanded.

"Maybe. I did. I never really thought about it before. But yes, maybe deep down under all that resentment, I did care for him."

"So you did forgive him,?" Eva asked.

I guess I did...I guess so."

"That's nice to hear, Ma. Very nice."

"Yeah, very nice," Ava added. "And don't worry Ma, we won't eat any more of the ashes."

"That's good to know, Ava," Bernice replied, sounding somewhat relieved.

"It didn't taste all that good anyway. It was like eating dirt."

CHAPTER 23
The Art of Retaliation

AFTER A LONG STRETCH of cool fall days, winter set in with a vengeance. The frigid air of mid-October reminded Violet of the day of her arrival. The weather and her transformed husband were two things she knew that she could never get accustomed to. The only saving grace was that in the midst of this first cold snap, she gave birth to a healthy baby boy she named George, for no particular reason. Just as with the birth of her daughter, Robert was nowhere to be found.

After some stints on the couch, Robert packed up some underwear, shirts, and pants and left one day without any warning. Violet was glad to see him leave, but his departure meant that her plans had to be placed on hold.

A short while after Robert's leaving, and only few weeks after giving birth, Violet came home to find a familiar-looking blue airmail envelope on the floor. She swallowed hard and anticipated the worst as she ripped it open. The wording was very brief and to the point.

Dear Miss Violet,

I regret to inform you that last Friday your mother, and my dear friend, passed on to a better place. She had been ill for some time but didn't want to trouble you.

You have my humblest condolences.

I hope this bad news finds you in good health.

All the best,
Mrs. Payne.

Violet gasped. Her eyes remained completely dry. Mrs. Payne's words only confirmed what she had already known. A vision of her mother had come to her when she was pushing out her son. Her mother, wearing her Easter dress, was waving good-bye and mouthing the words, *I love you.* The day mentioned in Mrs. Payne's letter confirmed that her mother had died on the same day her son had been born. It was a sad but beautiful irony. God had given her one great gift in compensation for a terrible loss. Violet was grateful that her mother had died without knowing that all of her assumptions about Robert Black had been correct.

The next time Robert made an appearance at the apartment, he was not alone. He was carrying a snugly bundled-up baby with him. When Violet first saw the blanket slumped over his shoulder, she thought he had brought home his dirty laundry for her to wash. But on closer examination, she realized what it was. She watched as Robert placed the sleeping child on the couch with the greatest of care.

When the infant's face was uncovered, she was shocked by how much the child resembled her own son. Robert's features had been stamped on both. She and Clara moved closer to get a better look.

"Robert, whose child is this?" she asked knowing full well that the child was clearly his.

"Who else's? Why would I be carrying someone else's child with me? This is my son, Robert Junior," he said proudly.

"Stop poking your brother," Robert said gruffly to Clara, who was now using her fingers to probe the unfamiliar mass.

Violet winced. The confirmation hurt her in ways that she herself did not understand. What stung the most was how gentle and attentive he was to the child. He had never given either of her children such attention. Never before had she felt such a deep sense of betrayal.

As she continued to study the infant's face in disbelief, Robert went in search of her purse. She tore her eyes from the baby long enough to see what he was up to. She quickly ushered Clara into the bedroom, closed the door, and returned to face Robert.

"What are you doing?" she demanded.

He was too busy counting the money to reply.

"Leave it alone. What kind of man are you anyway, stealing from your children—"

Before she could finish what she was saying, he flung the purse in her face.

"Just shut up and mind your own business," he snapped.

"My own business? That *is* my business. It's my purse. Give me back what you took and get that fucking bastard out of here," Violet heard herself screech as she grabbed for the money.

Robert had never heard Violet speak this way before. The harsh words sounded strange coming from her mouth.

"What did you say?"

"You heard me," she said, standing her ground. "Take your fucking bastard and get the fuck out of here."

Robert didn't wait to hear any more. He fired off his own expletives. Then with the passion of a prize fighter trying to make a comeback, he pummeled her with a barrage of punches. She made a valiant attempt to defend herself, but her weak hands were no match for his force.

Once he succeeded in knocking her to the floor, he pocketed the money, collected his son, and left.

While Violet writhed in pain, she forced the corners of her mouth upward into a provocative smile. The smile, however, disappeared the moment she heard a faint whimpering. She followed the noise into the bedroom. There she found her terrified daughter. Violet's heart ached to see her daughter in such a state. She immediately scooped her up, held her tightly and rocked her in her arms.

"It's okay, sweetie. It's going to be okay. It's going to be okay...Mommy is going to make it okay. We'll be okay... Mommy is going to make it okay."

The very next morning Rose left Thomas in Bernice's care, braved the cold, and went to pay a visit to the Stickman. His putrid scent was just as potent now as it was in the heat of summer. She made sure to stay a reasonable distance from him.

"Excuse me, sorry to bother you..." she began.

"What can I get for you, beautiful? I have Bennies, Acid Head..." the Stickman replied.

"I need something very strong," Rose said, covering her nose.

He showed her some pills that looked exactly like the ones that Douglas took.

"Are those the ones that the nervous little man who walks like a woman buys?"

He knew instantly who she was talking about.

"Yeah, those are the ones Dougie gets. He's one solid guy, my best customer. If I had kids, he would have been putting the little buggers through college."

"What do they do exactly?" she asked.

"They relax, calm someone down." He pulled out another package of similar-looking pills.

"These here, on the other hand, do the opposite—they excite, stimulate, fuck someone up."

"I'll take them. Those are the ones that I need," she said without hesitation.

"Well, honey, you shouldn't take them both because mixing the two could be dangerous. Not recommended at all."

"No, I just want the second ones, thank you." She looked around to see if the coast was clear.

"Nice choice. How many do you want for now?"

Rose had to stop to think.

"I think I'll take five for now."

"Here you go sister." He handed her the pills in a tiny, plastic bag.

As Rose made her way back to the apartment, the smell of the Stickman lingered like a bad memory.

That night in the darkened kitchen, Violet dragged a chair across the floor, leaving a trail of black scuff marks behind. Stepping on the chair, she felt around in the cupboard where Robert kept his stash of whiskey. She didn't ordinarily tamper with his things, but the need had arrived.

Her knees began to feel a bit wobbly as she held the bottle in her hand.

"I'll kill your ass if you ever touch my Johnny," she remembered him saying to her when he caught her snooping in his not-so-secret hiding space. Even though he was nowhere to be found, she was still a bundle of nerves.

She took a deep breath and then reached into her jeans pocket, pulled out a small plastic baggie containing a finely ground brown substance. Breathing heavily, she poured the brown stuff into the whiskey, shook it, then carefully returned it to its original location. Stepping down, she gasped for air, knowing that there was no turning back.

Three days after Rose had bought the pills from the street pharmacist, Douglas returned home more tired than usual. He dropped his pants and set up the make-shift bed on the couch with linen that Rose had left out for that purpose.

Behind the locked door and small barricade of a bookshelf and chair, she lay listening to his every move. She had come to know what each rattle and bump meant. The heavy thud was his belt buckle hitting the floor. The creaking was him finding a comfortable position, and the final faint pop belonged to his pill bottle.

She knew to wait exactly twenty-two minutes after the pop before proceeding. This was the amount of time it took for him to fall asleep. She had timed this out on numerous occasions. The reverberation of his snore was her final cue. She tiptoed out of her room and assessed the situation with the precision of an experienced jewel thief.

First, the exact position of his pants had to be memorized. Then she had to stabilize the belt buckle to prevent it from clinking. With the pants in hand, she scurried to the bathroom.

She locked the door and fished out his pills. Her heart started to race as she held them in her unsteady hands. The action seemed much easier when she rehearsed it in her head. It was so much more nerve-racking than she had imagined.

She had to still her hands and calm herself before continuing. "Stop shaking, will you? There's nothing to worry about. He's fast asleep," she whispered to herself. But her body paid no attention. The trembling just increased.

"Stop it, I said," she repeated.

There was still no agreement between her brain and body, but she proceeded nevertheless. With her uncooperative hands, she emptied the bottle into her palm and counted the pills. There were exactly sixteen. She took five, chucked them into the toilet and flushed. She retrieved her stash from her bathrobe pocket and put them in the bottle, shaking them gently for good measure.

With the container safely back in Douglas's right-hand pocket, she crept back and carefully placed the pants back where she had found them. She didn't exhale fully until she was back in bed, behind the barricade. Her heart almost beat out of her chest as she lay staring at the ceiling. Sleep didn't come easy and wasn't at all sound.

Washing dishes at the kitchen sink, Violet pretended not to notice when Robert entered, carrying a new bottle of whiskey in the crook of his arm. Her eyes never left him as he went to the cupboard and finished off the last of the whiskey that she had tampered with.

"What are you staring at? You've never seen anyone have a drink before?" he blurted, tapping the bottom of the bottle to make sure nothing was left to waste.

She busied herself at the sink. In the corner of her eye, she watched as he placed the new Johnny Walker down on the countertop, caressed its curves, and kissed it delicately as if he was engaging in some sort of foreplay. She tried to contain her distaste. She was happy when the foolish charade was over and the seal to the new bottle was cracked open. The guzzling sound followed by the slam of the cupboard door, told her that he was done.

She adjusted the faucet and kept her eyes cast down as he dragged his feet out of the kitchen. A sigh of relief escaped her when he was finally gone.

That night, after she had bathed and put the children to bed, she repeated all the steps from the time before with Robert's new bottle. This time her legs didn't shake quite so much. The pang of guilt she felt as she returned the bottle was quickly pushed aside.

In the nippy days that followed, whenever Robert was home, he paid a visit to his good friend in the high cupboard. Violet's tampering had not changed the taste nor had it produced any immediate side effects. This eased her mind a little and allowed her to sleep somewhat peacefully.

When Robert's mother died suddenly, Violet was concerned that her plans would be ruined, but then she realized that Robert, being who he was, wouldn't stay too long in a place where his precious mother no longer existed. She knew the trip would be short and purposeful.

The day after he received the news about his mother, Robert showed up at the apartment sniveling like an overgrown baby. Violet was taken aback. She could not help but feel a small bit of pity for him. As he stood weeping shamefully in front of her, she was tempted to offer him a tissue to wipe away his globs of snot, but she didn't dare. She just stared at him, silently wishing that it had been him who had died in the place of his mother.

"He was worse than a little girl," Violet related as she told of Robert's pathetic condition.

"But it was his mother, after all," Ava said.

"I know, I'd just never seen him so helpless before," Violet answered.

"Didn't you say that all men are big babies, Ma?"

"Yeah, I guess they are," Bernice agreed, bouncing Thomas and Clara on her lap. "These two are almost getting too big for this." The kids laughed with delight.

"Should I stop? I think they might be getting too tired," Bernice teased. "I think I'll stop then."

"No, no," the toddlers repeated together, using one of the few words they now had at their command.

"Okay, I'll keep on going," Bernice told the tots.

"Be careful, Ma. Remember you shouldn't exert yourself too much," Eva said. There was a hint of worry in her voice.

"Oh, this is nothing," Bernice replied.

Eva was closely monitoring her mother's breathing.

"So how are those plans of yours coming along?" Bernice asked as she settled the babies on her lap.

The twins turned their attention to Violet and Rose. The night before, Bernice had told them she had dreamed about Violet tinkering with the whiskey and Rose switching the pills.

"What plans?" Rose answered defensively.

"We're not planning anything," Violet said. She didn't sound very convincing.

"It's okay, you don't have to hide it. We already know all about it," Ava chimed in.

"How?" Rose asked. "The dreams again?"

The twins nodded their heads.

"How else?" Bernice said.

"But you said that you saw Violet in the hardware store the other day, Ma," Ava interjected.

"And Rose with the Stickman."

"Stop with all the babbling," Bernice insisted.

"Well that's what you told us. I'm just repeating what you said."

"We also overheard your conversations," Eva added.

Rose and Violet squirmed in their seats.

"Oh, come on Bernice, we really don't have to talk about this. It's really just between Rose and me. We didn't want to involve the three of you in this anyway." Violet adjusted the sleeping infant in her arms.

"Yeah, it's our problem," Rose added.

"But you're our friends. So your problems are our problems. It's as simple as that." Bernice got up and deposited Thomas on Eva's lap and Clara on Ava's.

"But you've been so nice to us. We don't want anything to happen to you," Violet continued.

"You don't have to worry your pretty little heads about us. Nothing is going to happen to us—and nothing is going to happen to you two, either. Everything will work itself out in the end." Bernice stretched and returned to her armchair.

"How do you know that for sure?" Rose asked.

"I just know, is all. I just know." Bernice rested her head.

Rose and Violet looked apprehensive.

Early in the afternoon, a few days later, there was a faint unfamiliar knock on Violet's door. She had no idea who it could be. When she opened the door, she found Angela Spencer standing smartly dressed, arms on her hips, exuding an air of superiority. Violet recognized her right away and wondered what had brought the woman back to the scene of the crime. She inspected her adversary from head to toe. The woman was as ugly as she had remembered her.

"Hi, good afternoon. I'm Angela." Angela stepped forward and held out her hand.

"How can I help you? Robert's not here," Violet replied coldly, ignoring the outstretched limb.

"I didn't come to see Robert. I know he's gone to his mother's funeral. I have something that I wanted to discuss with you."

Violet was repelled and intrigued at the same time. *What could this woman want with me?* she wondered.

"Can I come in? I'd prefer not to have this conversation

out in the hallway," Angela said as she tried, politely, to force her way inside.

"Whatever you have to say, I'm sure you can say it out there." Violet purposely blocked Angela's way. She couldn't help but see the irony of the situation. The last time they had met Angela was rushing to leave; now she was pleading to enter.

"Please let me in. I won't take up too much of your time," Angela appealed.

"Why should I let you in?"

"Because of this." Angela raised her hand and showed Violet a large engagement ring. Violet stared at the ring blankly. "So you're getting married. Why should I care?"

"Robert gave me the ring," Angela confessed.

The sudden pang of jealousy took Violet by surprise.

"So are you going to let me in now?" Angela sneered.

Violet's eyes remained glued on the ring as she stepped aside to allow Angela to pass.

Angela sat down on the couch as if it belonged to her, crossed her legs, and placed her hand on top of them, flaunting the ring.

"So, Robert gave you that?" Violet asked, eyes fixed on the ring.

"Yes, just before he left."

"You do know he's married already," Violet heard herself say.

"Yes, I know," Angela replied.

An uncomfortable silence followed, during which Violet pried her eyes away from the ring long enough to take a good look at Robert's mistress. She wondered how Robert could have fallen for such a unsightly woman. Her manicured nails, coiffed hair, and expensive clothes did little to improve her looks.

Angela fidgeted as she stared back at Violet. Her insecurity was showing in her restlessness. It was clear she felt threatened by Violet's simple beauty.

The uncomfortable silence was shattered by the cries of Violet's newborn son. The crying puzzled Angela. She had forgotten that Violet had given birth a few months after she had. When Violet returned with the baby, Angela was transfixed. She couldn't believe how much the infant resembled her own.

"I guess that's Robert's?" Angela asked rudely.

Violet was stunned by the audacity of the question.

"What's his name?" Angela asked.

"Robert Junior," Violet shouted over the baby's wails.

Angela's jaw dropped. If it were possible for her eyes to pop out of her head, they would have done so.

"Hush now, Robert," Violet said, trying to add insult to injury. Had baby George been able to speak, he would certainly have corrected his mother.

"Robert...Robert Junior," Angela repeated.

"Yes, that's his name," Violet plopped herself down next to Angela and pulled out her breast. Her closeness unnerved Angela even more.

"Well...well, I...I don't want to keep you, so let me get to why I came..." Angela stumbled over her words as she stared down at the suckling child.

"Well now...you see what Robert's intentions are toward me, so I think it would be best if you just give him a divorce."

"Divorce? Robert has never ever mentioned anything

about a divorce," Violet replied, trying to play the role of the resentful but devoted wife.

"Well he has to me, many times."

"He may have asked you to marry him, but the reality is, he's not free to do so," Violet continued. "Is that all you have to say?" Violet scoffed as Angela scribbled something on a tiny piece of paper.

"Well, I just thought you should be aware of the situation." Angela sprung to her feet. "I left my number if you ever need to reach me." She waltzed to the front door and let herself out. Violet shook her head as she looked at the piece of paper.

"What would I ever want with that…Now that one's trouble, George. We better watch out for her." She caressed the baby's cheek. George was too busy to reply.

CHAPTER 24

The Plan Starts to Bear Fruit

WHILE ROBERT HADN'T yet experienced any side effects, the same could not be said for Douglas. His symptoms began to show almost immediately. The first noticeable change came one day when he and Johnny were returning from the grocery store. As they trampled their way over a mess of damp leaves, Douglas felt a shooting pain in his leg. After a few minutes, it stiffened up. By the time he reached Johnny's apartment, both legs were so stiff that his wobble was temporarily corrected.

The other symptoms, curiously enough, mimicked the conditions of the first trimester of pregnancy. They included nausea, bloating, fatigue, and sudden mood shifts. One moment he felt happy, the next, sad. Never once did he think the pills were to blame. He was fully aware of the changes, but he chose, instead, to ignore them and pretend that everything was alright.

The nausea and bloating, however, worsened. When it got to the point that he became uncomfortable, Johnny took care of him—happily. He made up the couch with soft pillows and warm blankets and placed a bucket within reach. In addition, he made bland foods and warm tea for Douglas's upset stomach.

While the waning remnants of autumn winds stirred, Johnny rushed around his apartment like a doting mother. "Here's dinner," Johnny said, presenting Douglas with a steaming cup of soup.

Douglas opened his eyes. His skin was paler than usual, his lips parched. "I'm not hungry," Douglas said weakly.

"But you have to eat. Remember, you need your strength," Johnny insisted.

"I'll eat a little later," Douglas promised. "I don't feel like eating now."

"You never do, but that doesn't mean you shouldn't eat." Johnny touched Douglas's cheek gently. "My God, you're burning up!"

"I feel fine," Douglas said, trying to sound as normal as possible.

"Why do you keep saying that? You're not fine. You haven't been able to keep any real food down in days, and you don't even have the strength to make it to the toilet sometimes."

"I'm just comfortable here."

"You know damn well you're not just *comfortable*. I said it before, and I'll say it again. You need to go see a doctor and find out what's going on with you."

"I don't believe in doctors, and there's nothing the matter with me. I'm just a little tired."

"Tired from what? You've barely moved from this spot in days."

"I told you. It feels comfortable here."

"Come on, Douglas, we both know there's something wrong. I hope you're not still taking those pills because I'm sure they'll just make whatever you have worse."

Douglas looked up at the ceiling.

"You *are* still taking them, aren't you?"

"They make me feel better," Douglas confessed. He reached into his pants pocket to feel for his pills.

"They just might kill you." Johnny raised the cup to Douglas's mouth.

"Go ahead, drink just a little of this. It'll do you some good."

Douglas took a sip.

"So, will you go to a doctor?"

"Sure."

"When?"

"Soon."

"How soon?"

"I'll go tomorrow, if you'll stop bothering me."

"Good! Do you want me to go with you?"

"No, I'll be fine on my own."

"You sure you'll be able to make it there all by yourself?"

"Positive," Douglas said as he pried the soup from Johnny's hand and drank it on his own.

The next morning, Douglas woke up early, lifted himself off the couch with much difficulty, put on a jacket, and left Johnny's apartment. He got off the bus a few short blocks from the Stickman's corner.

"I'm all out," Douglas said as he approached the Stickman. He was out of breath.

"What happened to you, man? You look like someone beat you up or something," Stickman said. "And what's up with your walk?"

"I'm fine. I just need more pills." Douglas paused to catch his breath.

"Sure, sure, anything for my number-one guy." The Stickman reached into his inside coat pocket and fished out some pills.

Douglas paid him. The Stickman smiled and slipped the money into his pocket. "You take care of yourself, you hear me?"

"Yeah, yeah," Douglas replied as he stumbled away.

Rose was puzzled to see Douglas return so early in morning. He dropped his pants and walked into the bathroom with all the energy of a ninety-year-old.

Assuming that Douglas would be in the bathroom for some time, Rose decided to take advantage of the situation. She moved briskly to Douglas's pants and picked them up. *Should I do it now? Is there enough time?* Rose had to make a split-second decision. "What the hell," she muttered under her breath. She dug her hands into Douglas's pocket and pulled out a full bottle of pills. *He must have just brought some more.*

She dropped the pants, dashed into the bedroom to retrieve her own stash. Once the switch was made, she returned the bottle to its rightful place. As she did, she felt a presence behind her.

"What are you doing with my pants?" Douglas yelled. He was furious.

"Nothing. I'm not doing anything," Rose mumbled. The pants fell to the floor and the pill bottle rolled out. Douglas dropped to the floor to retrieve it.

"Get your own fucking pills," he yelled. "These are mine." He rose with the bottle, stumbled, and collapsed on the couch.

Down the hall, Violet, who was mopping the kitchen floor, sensed that something was wrong. She listened carefully to see if she could hear anything. Unable to shake off the feeling, she put down the mop, walked to her front door, and stuck her head out into the hall. She didn't hear anything, so returned to her chores.

"You know, I should have just killed him, right there on the spot," Rose said, trying to control her rage. Violet sat next to her on the twins' love seat. Baby babbles and Bernice's chuckles floated in from the next room.

"What about the pills?" Violet whispered. "Do you think they're working?"

"No use whispering. We can still hear you," Ava said as she stuck her head out the kitchen door and pulled it back like a jack-in-the-box.

"Okay, we'll speak normally…So are they working?" Violet continued.

"I think so. He's not looking so good."

"Did he try anything with you?"

"Yeah, he tried to kick me, but he couldn't even lift up his leg. It was pathetic."

"Oh?"

"It was no big deal. Is yours back yet?"

"Not until next week."

"Did you get some more of that stuff?"

"Yeah, I'm ready for him when he gets here."

"Good."

"Good," Ava echoed from the kitchen.

In Johnny's care, Douglas returned briefly to his normal self, but then he took a turn for the worse.

"You know you're really starting to look like a piece of shit," Johnny said bluntly as he watched Douglas emerge from the shower with a towel wrapped around his emaciated torso. Aggressive bouts of vomiting and the runs had brought him to that point.

"You're more and more like a goddamn skeleton every day. Can't you see yourself in the mirror?"

Douglas ignored him and slipped on some lacy panties under the towel, then his pants.

"Did you even go to the doctor that time you said you were going? Do you still have the runs?"

Douglas nodded as he reached for the plastic bottle in his pocket and popped a pill.

"I told you to stop those fucking things. They're messing you up," Johnny continued. "You told me you would stop."

Douglas stared at Johnny as if he were in a trance.

"Say something goddamn it. What the fuck is wrong with you?"

"Okay!"

"Okay what?" Johnny was beyond irritated.

"You told me to say something so I said okay."

"You're not even making sense. I think you may need to get that head of yours checked out too."

"Okay," Douglas repeated.

"Okay what?"

"Let's get my head checked out. I know there's something wrong with it. Let's go." Douglas sounded almost like a robot.

"I was just kidding about your head, but I think you really need a doctor to take a good look at you. This time I'm going to go with you to make sure you go, alright?"

"Okay," Douglas said again.

"Does that mean you're going to let me take you?"

"Yeah."

"Finally! You don't know how good that sounds to me." Johnny hugged Douglas, who stood almost lifeless in his arms.

"We'll get you all better now. You'll see, we'll get you better," Johnny said rubbing Douglas's back.

Douglas's rigid body suddenly erupted, spewing vomit. Johnny stepped out of the puddle, looked down at his soiled clothes, and wiped dribbles of it from the corners of Douglas's mouth.

"You'll be okay. You'll be okay. Don't worry." Johnny was extremely concerned.

In the emergency room, Douglas rested his head on Johnny's shoulder. His eyes were shut tight as he waited to be called. They were still that way when Rose walked by with Bernice. Bernice noticed them first.

"Isn't that your...?" She pointed to Douglas and Johnny.

Rose's eyes darted back and forth between the two men. She didn't know what to make of the scene.

"Who's the big guy?" Bernice asked.

"Your guess is as good as mine," Rose said, motioning toward the elevator. "Come on. We have to go up to the fifth floor."

"Should we say something to them?" Bernice asked.

"No, we shouldn't," Rose said as she pulled Bernice toward the elevator. "We're going to be late for your appointment."

Johnny watched as the two women entered the elevator and disappeared. He had no way of knowing why they had been staring at him.

"Douglas Weiss?" A nurse with cat-eye glasses stuck her head out from behind her station.

"Yes, yes…he's here. One moment please." Johnny nudged Douglas awake. Then he walked him into the examining room and left him there.

"What seems to be the problem?" the doctor asked as he began to grope under Douglas's chin.

"Ah, I'm tired all the time," Douglas mumbled, still half-asleep.

"You seem to be very dehydrated," the doctor said. He listened to Douglas's heart.

"I've been vomiting too, and…yeah, shitting like crazy."

By the time the doctor finished his examination, Douglas was dozing off. The doctor shook his shoulder.

"Sir…Mr. Weiss?"

"Yes." Douglas jerked.

"You are extremely dehydrated, so we need to get your electrolytes back up to where they should be." He opened the cupboard above his sink.

"You can have these. They should make you feel better." He handed Douglas a small package of Pedialyte. "If you need more, you can get it at any drug store without a prescription."

"Thanks," Douglas said through a yawn.

Johnny sprang to his feet when he saw Douglas staggering out of the examining area. "What did they say was wrong with you?" Johnny asked.

"Said something about being dehydrated!" Douglas replied. "He gave me this." Douglas passed the box of Pedialyte to Johnny.

"Dehydrated!? Of course you're frigging dehydrated. I could have told you that. You've been shitting and vomiting like nobody's business. What kind of place is this anyway? I knew I should have stayed in there with you."

"I'll just drink this and I'll be fine," Douglas said. His eyes began to close again.

"Pedia...shit. These things are not even for adults. They're for kids," Johnny snarled. "Maybe I should just go back in there and have a conversation with that quack."

"Oh, don't worry about it. Let's just go. I just want to lie down. Now you know why I didn't want to come." His words were slurred.

"Are you sure? I can go in there and rough him up for not taking good care of you."

"No, let's just go."

"Okay, whatever you say. Are you sure you don't want to drink one if those things before we leave—for what it's worth."

"Sure, why not. Give me one."

Johnny quickly ripped open the box. Douglas guzzled the contents down like he hadn't had anything to drink in days. Johnny watched with great concern.

"Mrs. Archer? We can take your grandmother now," the technician said to Rose as she opened the door to a room that contained some daunting X-ray machines.

Bernice smiled at the woman's mistake. Neither she nor Rose saw fit to correct it. "Took them long enough," Bernice complained under her breath.

"I'll be waiting out here for you when you're done, Bernice," Rose said.

Sitting there alone, Rose's mind raced back to the scene she had just witnessed downstairs. There was no need for her to wonder what had brought Douglas to the hospital. His fragile state said it all. The identity of the large man and his relationship to Douglas was a whole other story.

CHAPTER 25
The Final Straw

ROBERT WENT DIRECTLY to Angela's bungalow on his return from his mother's funeral. Angela's temper had been brewing since her visit to Violet. It had reached its boiling point the minute Robert stepped in the door.

"Why didn't you tell me how much that child looked like ours?" Angela snapped as she stood with her arms crossed. She saw no need for a warm greeting.

"What child?" Robert threw his luggage down and braced himself for an earful.

"Why didn't you tell me?" she repeated.

"Tell you what?" he asked as he flopped down into Angela's recliner. "Why do you have to start up right away with me? I just came back from burying my mother, goddammit. Can't you see when someone is tired? Can I at least get some water or food or something first?"

"Why didn't you tell me how much your wife's son looks like ours?" she asked again, ignoring Robert's request.

"When did you see my wife's son?" Now she had his attention.

"I paid that simpleton of yours a visit while you were gone."

"Why the hell would you do that, Angela? What business do you have with her?"

"Never mind that. Why didn't you tell me that child's name was Robert Junior too?"

"That's not his name. Who told you that?"

"Your wife, that's who!"

"Why would she tell you that? His name is George."

"So then why did she say it was Robert Junior?"

"I have no idea."

"How sly of her! She's not as stupid as I thought," Angela mumbled to herself.

"Good. Now that's settled. Can I please get something to eat?"

"When are you going to leave her, anyway? You keep telling me that you will, but you never do. And what about finding another job? When are you going to get around to doing that?"

"Give me a break, Angela! Why do you need to bring all of this up now? I just got back from putting my mother in the ground. Didn't you hear me? Have some mercy on me why don't you!"

Angela unfolded her arms and sighed.

"Okay, okay…" She clenched her jaw and headed for the kitchen.

"That's more like it," he said with a smile as he pushed

himself back into a reclined position.

"Some whiskey would be nice too," he yelled, then quickly covered his mouth when he realized that he had said the wrong thing.

"You know full well that I don't allow that in here. This a Christian house," Angela yelled from the kitchen.

"Yeah, yeah, I know," Robert grumbled as he rubbed his head and closed his eyes.

Violet had just stepped out of the bathroom and was on her way to the kitchen when Robert entered the apartment. She quickly took note of his empty hands, and his unshaved face. He followed close behind her.

In the kitchen, she put some water on the stove and started cutting up some vegetables while Robert went in search of the usual. "I gather the funeral went well…I hear there'll be a wedding soon," Violet said casually.

Robert paid no attention. He was too busy with his drink.

"I saw the ring," Violet continued. She threw the vegetables into the pot.

This got his attention. "What ring?" he asked.

"The one you gave that Angela woman."

He gulped, spitting out half his drink.

"What! I didn't give her a ring."

"She showed it to me. It had a large diamond."

"I can't afford a pot to piss in, how am I suppose to afford a ring with a diamond?"

"She said you brought it for her."

"We'll she's big liar then. I didn't buy her anything."

"Why would she lie?" Violet asked as she emptied a bowl of leftover chicken into the pot and adjusted the flame.

"Because that's how she is." He downed some more whiskey.

"So is that what you want?" Violet added some spices and began to stir the pot.

"That? What do mean, is *that* what I want?"

"To marry her?" she asked, staring down into the pot. "That's what she said you wanted—to marry her." Violet hadn't realized just how much Angela's visit had upset her until that very moment.

"Now, how in the hell can I marry her when I'm already married to you?" Robert shouted. He was getting even more agitated.

"Some marriage!" she muttered under her breath. She hoped that he hadn't heard her.

"What did you say?"

It was too late. She felt the mood suddenly shift.

"Nothing. I didn't say anything." She looked away.

"You did say something. I heard you." He moved closer to her with the bottle of whiskey still in his hand.

"No, I didn't," she reiterated, holding her breath. She knew exactly where things were heading.

"Don't lie to me," he shouted. "I can tell when someone is lying." He forced her chin upward.

She could feel his indignation. "I'm not lying," she said, as calmly as possible. The confidence had left her voice.

"Can you look me straight in the eye and tell me you didn't just say something?" he demanded.

"I didn't. I didn't..."

"Liar!" he yelled as he smacked her face with the back of his hand.

The impact of his knuckles caused her nose to bleed.

"Now you remember what you said?"

Wiping the blood away, she scowled up at him with her nostrils flaring and returned the slap. This took him completely by surprise. He touched his cheek, grunted then whacked her with more force than before. Satisfied that everything was settled, he turned away and took another swig of his drink.

The second slap caused even more bleeding. But this time she didn't wipe any of it away. Instead, she amassed all her strength, grabbed one of the kitchen chairs, and swung it at his back. The bottle fell out of his hand, spilling whiskey all over the floor and his shiny leather shoes. Before he was able to react, she followed the first hit with a second, and then a third. Each strike was accompanied by an excruciating scream.

"Take that you bastard," she yelled, feeling a degree of freedom she had never experienced before.

When Robert regained his bearings, he moved a few steps to the stove, lifted the simmering pot, and hurled it at her. The boiling liquid landed on the left side of her neck, shoulder, arm, and upper torso and caused her skin to bubble immediately. She screamed. The agonizing sound that emerged from the depths of her lungs didn't even come close to representing the amount of pain she felt. As she stood hunched over and shrieking, still not fully realizing what had happened, the scorching liquid dripped from her body onto the floor along with pieces of chicken and vegetables.

"What have I done? What have I done?" The sight of her burnt flesh told him that he had gone too far. His knees began to buckle as he watched the blisters erupt. Not knowing what else to do, he rushed to the sink, ran cold water over some kitchen rags, and placed them on her back and neck. She moaned painfully and peered up at him with a look of terror.

"Sorry, sorry, sorry," he said repeatedly, making sure to enunciate carefully so that she would understand the full extent of his remorse. This was by far his most sincere apology. The one lone tear that sprang from the corner of his eye was testament to this.

Rose heard Violet scream and ran with her heart jumping out of her chest. When she reached the apartment, Bernice and her daughters were already there banging on the door. Rose joined them, knocking even louder, with more urgency. Their pounding only stopped when they heard the sound of approaching footsteps. They all braced themselves as the door swung open.

Their hearts sank when they saw the sullen expression on Robert's face. They expected the worst. All they could hear were soft animal like grunts. An unsettling feeling swept through Rose's body. She looked up at Robert and pleaded silently for permission to enter the apartment.

"I called an ambulance already," he finally said. "She's in there." He pointed toward the kitchen.

Rose hurried in. She found Clara sitting large-eyed and petrified in the living room. She stopped and scooped up the traumatized toddler and passed her to Eva. "Take her back to your place. Bernice, please get the baby. He must be in the room."

Without asking permission, Bernice entered the bedroom and found the baby. His eyes were just as wide and frightened as his sister's. She placed him in Ava's arms. Ava couldn't see the baby's expression, but she felt the terror in his tiny, rigid body. "I'm going to stay here. You go ahead," Bernice told her daughters.

Rose was relieved and overjoyed to find Violet fully conscious and on her feet. She reached out and touched Violet's tear-stained face, wanting desperately to comfort and reassure her.

"You'll be alright. Everything will be alright," Rose repeated as she stroked her face. Violet whimpered and turned her body to show Rose what Robert had done. There was no need for Rose to ask any questions. The blistering skin and the remnants of soup covering the kitchen floor told the tale.

By the time Bernice reached the kitchen, the sound of the fire truck and ambulance could already be heard in the distance. Bernice set out right away to clean up the mess. She knew that Rose was all Violet needed at the moment.

"Where's the injured person?" the paramedic boomed as he pushed his way through the door.

"Here. She's here," Rose replied, moving out of the way.

"Your husband said that you had an accident. Is that correct?" the man asked as he pulled some disposable gloves out of his kit.

Rose and Violet looked at each other, though neither of them said a word.

"Yes, yes. That's what happened," Bernice replied from the other side of the room.

"I can be clumsy sometimes," Violet added weakly. She knew that reporting Robert would prove useless. A warning and a slap on the wrist was not enough for him.

The paramedic looked suspiciously at Violet's injuries. The women could tell that he knew they were lying.

"Oh, it doesn't look too bad. The rags helped a little, but you're going to have to be treated. Could take some time to heal, but after that you should be as good as new, I think," the paramedic said.

Violet, Rose, and Bernice were encouraged.

In the hospital, Violet's skin was coated with ointment and carefully covered with gauze. She was kept in the burn unit for seven days. During that time she received daily visits from Rose. Each time, Rose brought greetings and baked treats from Bernice and the twins.

When she arrived one miserable snowy day, she brushed off the snow, put down that day's offerings, then peeled off her winter wear and cuddled up next to Violet in her bed.

"You wouldn't believe where I saw your husband today." Rose hugged Violet and adjusted the covers on the bed.

"Where?" Violet asked as she took Rose's hand in hers.

"The laundromat."

"Did he leave the kids with Bernice?"

"No, no, he had them both with him."

"Wonders never cease!"

"And Bernice said that he cleaned the whole apartment. Said she couldn't believe how spic and span everything was."

"My goodness, what's come over him?"

"Guilt, I guess."

"After all this time."

"Well look what he did to you!"

"Compared to some of the things he said and the awful way he's been carrying on, this was nothing." Violet held up her bandaged arm.

"We'll never mind that, the twins made one of your favorites today." Rose slipped out of bed and retrieved the package.

"It's chocolate fudge. They said they only made a tiny amount so that Bernice wouldn't be tempted to eat it." Rose handed Violet a piece of fudge and jumped back into bed.

"Mmm, this is good. So how is that anti-man of yours?"

"I don't know for sure if he's a homosexual," Rose replied in a hushed voice.

"From how you described him and that fat man, it sure sounds like that to me."

"Well, I have no idea what's going on between the two of them. But Douglas isn't getting any better. Every time I see him, he's looking more and more decrepit, like a ghost."

"That's good then, isn't it?"

"I guess."

"Don't tell me that you're having second thoughts now. Are you?"

"No, well, maybe just a little bit."

"You come all this way and have second thoughts? I forbid you."

"Okay, okay, I'll try not to think about it then."

"Good, pass me some more of that fudge. It's delicious."

Just as Rose stepped off the bed, Robert arrived carrying an armful of yellow carnations.

"Hi, I hope you don't mind that I came," he said. His eyes moved nervously back and forth between Violet and Rose.

The two women didn't quite know what to make of his appearance.

"I left the children with the old woman down the hall," he continued.

The air in the room suddenly became heavy.

"Ah, I think I'll leave the two of you alone." Rose slid past Robert and collected her things.

"Are you sure? You don't have to go you know," Violet said.

"Yeah, yeah, I'll come back tomorrow to see you."

"Okay, tell Bernice and the twins I said thanks."

"Sure. Bye." Rose left.

"I'm sorry I didn't come sooner, but I was fixing up things for you at home," Robert said.

"Yes, I heard."

"I brought these for you." He held the flowers.

"Thank you. You can put them over there." Violet motioned toward an empty vase on the windowsill.

He placed the carnations in the vase and took a seat. His rigid posture betrayed his uneasiness.

"So how have you been keeping?" he asked with genuine concern. "You're looking better."

"I'm fine. They said I can leave in two days."

"That's good. I'm glad to hear that."

The two sounded more like strangers than husband and wife.

"I just wanted to tell you that I didn't mean to hurt you like I did."

Violet gave no reply.

"It's just, things haven't turned out like I expected them to. Everything has gone to hell. First I couldn't find a job. Then I found an awful one, then I lost that one, then there were mouths to feed, and it's just a lot of pressure for a guy, you know. Back home I had something. I was somebody. I didn't have to worry about the things I'm always worrying about here…and then I also had my mother. I didn't have to worry about anything when she was around. Now she's gone and everything's changed. I don't know if I'm dead or alive, coming or going. I don't know what I should be doing...but none of that is an excuse for how I've been acting."

Violet was unmoved. His visit, the flowers, and his words were too little and far too late.

"Well, I think I've talked enough. It looks like you want to sleep, so I've leave you to get some rest." Robert made his way toward the door.

Violet watched him leave in silence.

When he was out the door, she swung her feet to the side of the bed and walked over to the window. She pushed the vase out of the way and wiped off some condensation so that she could get a better look outside. The temperature of the glass told her that it had gotten considerably colder. As she stared out over the skyline, her thoughts traveled back home where skylines and frosted panes didn't exist. She imagined the turquoise ocean, green hills, and pastel-colored buildings, and her mother's face and reflected on how much things had changed and what still had to be done. The appearance of a few speckles of snow told her that winter was now settling in like a long-lost relative.

For Violet's homecoming Bernice prepared a special meal of pork chops, apple sauce, and mashed potatoes.

"Anyone want seconds? I think I have few more chops left." A strange, pained look came over Bernice's face as she stood up.

"Everything alright there, Bernice?" Rose asked.

"Ah, it's just gas, is all. So does anyone want any more?" she repeated.

Everyone spoke at once—they'd all had enough.

"Suit yourself. All the more for me then." Bernice shuffled into the kitchen with her plate.

"Don't overdo it, Ma," Eva said sternly. "You remember what the doctor said about overindulging."

"I already gave up all my sweets. What does the man want me to do, starve to death?"

"You would be the last person to starve to death, Ma!" Ava giggled.

Rose, Violet, and Eva all laughed.

"Laugh at me all you want. I'll outlive all of you," Bernice shouted, sounding slightly out of breath.

While laughter continued in the living room, Bernice clutched the edge of the table and grabbed her left shoulder.

"You okay in there, Ma?" Ava yelled from the living room.

"I'm just fine. Just peachy keen." She moaned quietly as she held her grip.

CHAPTER 26
Death and Other Stories

ROBERT BARGED INTO Angela's bungalow. "So you told my wife that I asked you to marry me? Where is this ring that I was supposed to have given you?" he demanded.

Angela was in the process of trying to soothe the baby.

"It's my ring. I bought it myself, like everything else around here," she said pointedly. She handed the colicky child over to Robert. "Where in the hell have you been all this time? This damn kid is driving me crazy."

"Why did you have to go over there and lie to her?" Robert patted the baby's bum.

"Why do you care whether I lied to her or not?"

"Did I ever tell you that I wanted to marry you?"

"Not exactly, but I knew that—"

"That's right. Look, just don't go back over there again. Do you hear me? Just leave her alone." He returned the baby to Angela.

"What's gotten into you? Why are you acting so weird and protective of her all of a sudden? You've never had a nice word to say about the woman before. What happened—"

Before she could finish, he turned around and left as suddenly as he had arrived. This strange behavior baffled and angered her.

"Where in the hell are you going? You just got here," she yelled after him.

He was already out of earshot.

"You piece of shit," she screamed at the closed door. The baby continued to cry.

The day after the first real snowstorm, Rose stepped up to the second-floor landing with her groceries and got a glimpse of Douglas and his large friend stamping the excess snow off their shoes just outside her door. She found the sight quite odd, since Douglas had never brought anyone home before. The way the two interacted, like an old married couple, was also unsettling. When she slipped through the door, Douglas was perched by himself on the couch. The heavy footsteps of the large stranger could be heard coming from the bedroom.

"All my T-shirts and underwear are in the top drawer on the left-hand side. And there should be a couple of jackets hanging in the closet," Douglas bellowed from his seat.

"What about the shoes?" the man asked from the bedroom.

"Yeah, take those too," Douglas, replied.

Rose gave Douglas a questioning look as she placed her bags on the floor.

"Johnny's helping me move some of my things out,"

Douglas coughed. His eyes looked bloodshot and his skin yellow.

"You're...you're moving out?" Rose asked as she picked up her son. She couldn't hide her surprise.

Douglas nodded, then turned his attention back to Johnny.

"Don't forget my ties and trousers." Douglas's voice was weaker.

"Yeah, yeah, I got them all," Johnny said, emerging from the bedroom carrying two large garbage bags. He stopped in his tracks when he saw Rose and Thomas.

"Oh! Sorry. I didn't think anyone else was here," Johnny said with his eyes glued to the child.

"That's just Rose and her...and Thomas," Douglas said as he made a quick dismissive gesture toward Rose.

Johnny acknowledged Rose with a slight movement of his head. He hadn't recognized her from the hospital.

"Can you grab me some of the figurines too? Take some of the more sturdy ones, so they don't break," Douglas said softly to Johnny.

"Got yuh." Johnny started making his way around the living room.

"I can get you a box for them," Rose offered.

Johnny looked at Douglas for his approval. Douglas gave it with an upward tilt of his head.

"That would be great," Johnny replied.

Rose went to the bedroom and returned with an empty shoebox.

When she handed Johnny the box, he kept his eyes downcast. She watched as he carefully selected the keepsakes.

Many questions entered her mind, but she didn't dare ask any.

"I think I have enough now," Johnny said as he walked over to Douglas. "Would you be okay carrying that?"

"Yes, sure, it's light. Let's go then." Douglas struggled to pull himself up off the couch. Without being asked, Johnny grabbed him under the arm and helped him up. He gathered the bags and they moved slowly out of the apartment.

When they were gone, Rose locked the door quickly and sighed.

From a tiny opening in the door, Bernice observed as Johnny and Douglas walked toward the landing at a snail's pace. Douglas stopped and rested his head on Johnny's arm, Johnny stroked his face tenderly, then they continued.

When they were out of sight, Bernice toddled toward her daughters. "You wouldn't believe what I just saw."

"What?" Eva and Ava asked together.

"The oddest couple I ever laid my eyes on."

"Who was it?" Ava asked.

"Douglas and his boyfriend."

"Oh!" Eva replied, surprised. "How do you know that they are boyfriends?"

"It's as clear as day. Clear as day, I tell you."

When Rose and Violet stopped by Bernice's place later, they found her in an upbeat mood.

"Come right on in ladies, I have a little treat for you," she beamed.

"What would that be? What kind of treat?" Rose and Violet asked together. They placed their children on the floor to play.

"I have a story for you two," Bernice grinned.

"We haven't heard one of your stories in a while." Violet leaned over and cozied up next to Rose.

"What is it about?" Rose asked smiling.

"About my husband," Bernice replied.

"Your husband?" Rose was intrigued. They had heard all the same stories Bernice had told her daughters.

"Where are the twins tonight?" Violet asked.

"Oh, they both decided to take a nap."

"Are they're not feeling well?" Rose asked.

"They're just a little blue. They get this way every year when winter shows its ugly face," Bernice replied.

"Oh?" Violet said.

"Well, first I want to tell you two something before I start my story."

"What is that, Bernice?" Violet asked.

"That the three of us have something in common."

"What would that be?" Rose asked this time.

"The three of us, we all want—or wanted—to get rid of our husbands," Bernice said.

"What do you mean?" Violet asked.

"I mean I wanted to kill my husband, too."

"You never said anything like that before," Rose said.

"It wasn't something I wanted to say in front of the girls," Bernice admitted.

"They're not girls, Bernice. They're grown women. Remember you said you were going to stop treating them like children," Violet insisted.

"I know, I know what I said. You're absolutely right. So do you want to hear the story or not? I actually have two to tell," Bernice replied.

"Two stories in one night! Now that's a treat," Violet grinned.

"Yeah, what did we do to deserve such indulgence," Rose added.

"Are you going to be quiet already, so I can start the story?" Bernice was getting ruffled.

"Sure, sure. Sorry," Rose put her hand to her mouth.

"Thank you," Bernice said as she reached to take a sip of water.

• • •

There was, as anyone could imagine, a lot more tension in the house after that night I left the twins with their father. I couldn't even bear to look at the man, let alone speak to him. So I took to writing him notes instead. Whenever I wanted him to get something at the store or take the garbage out, or say anything that needed to be said, I would write it down and leave the note on the kitchen table for him to read. By this time, the medication that the doctor prescribed for his depression had sedated him so much that he barely even noticed that I had stopped speaking to him.

"The doctor said I have high blood pressure and I should really keep an eye on it," he announced to me one afternoon after coming home from an appointment.

After I heard this, I knew exactly what I had to do. Each time I prepared and dished out his meals, I made sure to sprinkle an extra amount of salt onto his food. The poor guy was so out of it that he didn't even taste the difference. That, or he was too afraid to say anything. He just swallowed down his food the same way as always.

I began to see the effect of the salt right away. He started putting on weight, his face got puffy like a cotton ball. He also started to become more and more winded. On the day that I wrote the note that said "Buy milk and fix the leaky faucet in the kitchen," I could see that it wouldn't be long. He was grasping at his chest when he returned from the store with the milk and he was wheezing like a banshee when he stuck his head underneath the sink. He was so intent on pleasing me that he disregarded all his symptoms and warning signs.

"I'll deal with the faucet in a moment," he said as he lay on the floor trying to catch his breath.

I said and did nothing. When I returned to the kitchen the next morning, he was still in the same position, but he wasn't breathing. He was dead.

• • •

"That's how it happened," Bernice stated with no hint of emotion in her voice. She took another sip of water.

"So you killed your husband with salt?" Rose was stunned.

"Yes, that was the poison I chose," Bernice responded proudly.

"Salt is not a poison, Bernice, it's a condiment or a spice," Rose countered.

"Poison or not, it worked," Bernice replied.

"But wait, wait. Didn't you tell us before that he died on the way back from the store?" Violet said, jumping in.

"Yeah and the milk was supposed to have been spilled all over the ground," Rose added.

"What does it matter where it happened? All you have to know is that it happened," Bernice insisted.

"But which was it, Bernice?" Violet asked. "Was it on the way back from the store or on the kitchen floor?"

"It doesn't really matter, does it?"

"It was neither." Ava lumbered into the living room with her sister.

"You don't know what you're talking about," Bernice replied as she looked up at her daughter.

"Yes we do," Eva replied. "Mrs. Misic told us."

"What business is it of that witch?" Bernice was agitated.

"She was telling us the other day that her brother back in Europe just died," Eva said.

"He drank himself to death," Ava added.

"And she said it was a shame that he had to die the same way our father did," Eva continued.

"She doesn't know what she's talking about," Bernice stated adamantly.

"I think she does," Eva said.

"Me too," Ava agreed.

"Okay, okay, so I didn't do it, but I did think about it, even though the poor guy probably didn't deserves to die. I just told that story because I wanted to show my solidarity with Rose and Violet. It doesn't matter anyway. He's dead. How it happened is irrelevant. Go get the chairs from the kitchen, I have another story that I wanted to tell."

"What if we don't want to listen to any more of your stories?" Eva asked, only half seriously.

"Oh, just go get the chairs and stop testing me. I promised these ladies two stories tonight so I'm going to deliver on my promise. I know you want to hear it too," Bernice said firmly.

The twins dropped their heads in silence and retreated

into the kitchen. Bernice began her story the second Eva and Ava returned with the chairs, not even waiting for them to be properly seated.

• • •

This story of the man with the beautiful buttocks takes place exactly thirty years after Ben's death. By that time we had gone through the period of adjustment and acceptance, and the twins had graduated from being two needy little girls to being a pair of quasi-independent women. We had already settled into our predicable lives, doing the same things day in and day out. But one night that tired schedule got a kick in the pants.

It was one of those miserable muggy summer days and I was feeling quite gooey from stewing in my own sweat the whole day. But as luck had it, there were just enough dirty clothes for a load of laundry, so I had a good excuse to go down to cool off in the basement.

"Why are you doing laundry on a Thursday, Ma? You never do it on a Thursday," Ava asked as she heard me emptying out the hamper.

"I just feel like doing it," I told her and off I went without any more explanation.

When I got down there, I was glad to find the place deserted. I shoved the soap and the clothes into the washer and spread myself out over the empty chairs. Just as I was getting comfortable, a roguish-looking young man with a small bag appeared like an apparition out of nowhere. I knew he didn't live in the building because I had never seen him before. It was a bit unsettling the way the little bugger strutted around like he owned the place. He started looking me up and down. Of course I pretended that I didn't notice a thing.

When he walked to the end of the washers and started putting his load of mostly off-white T-shirts in the machine, my eyes somehow accidentally landed on his muscular buttocks. They were surprisingly round and rather attractive. As I continued to stare at the stranger's bottom, an odd sensation started to stir in me. I began to feel warm in parts that hadn't felt warm in a very long time. I suddenly got the urge to reach out and touch that young man's derrière. I didn't dare, of course. I could tell from his suggestive stance that he knew exactly where my eyes were planted. I'm sure he was accustomed to women of all shapes and sizes admiring his worldly goods.

When he turned around and flashed me a smile, I could see right away that he recognized the longing in my eyes. Without saying a word, he moved closer to me. As I watched his approach, my heart started to beat erratically. I had no idea what I was in for. When the young man walked directly past me and continued on to the exit, my heart sank. But it began to race again when I realized that he had only gone to lock the door.

When the bolt was securely fastened, he dimmed the lights and then made his way back toward me. I closed my eyes as I listened to his footsteps. Within a few seconds, I felt his breath on the back of my neck and his arms stretching out around my waist. It was uncanny how our breathing was in such perfect sync. He kissed me softly on my shoulder and then started to caress my flabby tummy. I welcomed his touch. I had never felt such a jumbled mixture of danger and pleasure in all my life. Next, he twirled me around to face him and then like a wasp with his stinger, he plunged his tongue in my mouth. At this point my whole body froze and I thought that I was going to go into convulsions, but I didn't. I just offered him my tongue in return. So for the duration of the wash, rinse, and spin cycles we kissed, caressed, and performed lewd acts in the dark.

When we were done, he kissed me one last time, pulled his pants up, collected his wet clothes, unlocked the door, and disappeared. My body was still trembling as I rearranged my clothes, turned the light back on, and threw my things in the dryer. Sitting there, waiting for my clothes to dry, I knew that I would never see that man again.

"What's that strange smell?" Eva asked me as she sniffed the air when I got back to the apartment.

"I don't smell anything. You're just imagining things," I insisted as I deposited the bag of laundry and hurried past her.

"She's not imagining anything. I smell it too," Ava said.

I couldn't tell them that it was the musk from the man with the most beautiful bottom. "Oh, it's nothing, nothing at all," I yelled back to them from the bedroom. I cuddled up in my bed and went to sleep without washing—for the first time in my life.

That night I slept the sleep of angels and woke up the next morning in a state of ecstasy with the taste of the young man still on my lips. About two months later I began to suspect that I was pregnant. I never thought there was any way on God's green earth that I would end up pregnant at the age of fifty, but I did.

In the time that followed, my feelings toward the pregnancy wavered back and forth as the child inside me grew.

My already fat stomach and the twin's blindness helped me to conceal my condition until the very end.

On the evening of September 27th, 1949, I woke in the middle of the night with heavy contractions. I got up and went directly to the bathroom. My water broke the moment I stepped into the bathtub. As I pushed the baby out, I tried my best not to scream. I wanted to maintain my secret until the time it was necessary to reveal it.

When the baby was out, its blue color sent me into a tailspin. I placed my mouth over his and tried desperately to breathe some life back into him, but the tiny thing didn't budge, breathe, cry, or open his eyes. I was frantic. Without even bothering to cut the cord, I placed the limp child down on a towel and started light compressions on his chest. After only three attempts, he finally took his first breath. But after exactly ten inhales and exhales, the breathing stopped again. His last breath was taken at exactly 2:01 am. Before I allowed myself to shed a single tear, I mustered up all the strength that I could to cut the cord and separate the dead baby from me.

"Your name will be Gabriel, after the angel Gabriel," I whispered. I said a short prayer, kissed him and swaddled him in the towel, then placed him in a plastic bag. I carried it out the front door. Down the hall, I stood in front of the incinerator door for an eternity...waiting for some divine intervention. None came. So I said another prayer, this one longer. I closed my eyes and released my baby down the chute and listened as he flew away from me. When I got back to the apartment, I went into my room, sat down on my bed, and cried the same way I had cried when the doctors gave me the news about the twins being blind.

• • •

"That's a bunch of malarkey, Ma," Eva declared the minute her mother had finished.

"Yeah, we would have known if you were pregnant," Ava added.

"And since when do you pray? You never pray, Ma," Eva continued.

"And what about what you said about men and bowel movements?" Ava asked. "If you really believed that, you never would have done what you said you did with that strange man."

"I believe her," Violet interjected. "Can't you hear the pain in her voice?"

"Ma is a great actor. Don't be fooled," Eva insisted.

"I agree with Violet. I think there just might be some truth to that story. How else could she tell it with such conviction. The story reminded me of my Hazel," Rose added with a sniffle.

"I'm glad to see I have at least two people on my side," Bernice finally said. "I told that story for a reason, you know. I needed you to know how deeply we are connected."

"Who?" Eva asked.

"Who else but Rose, Violet, and me, of course," Bernice continued.

Rose squinted her eyes. Violet scratched her head. It was clear that neither of them had any idea what Bernice was talking about. The twins shook their heads in disbelief.

"You two don't have to listen if you don't want to," Eva said. "Why don't you go and rest, Ma?"

"I'm not going anywhere," Bernice asserted. "They need to hear this. I'm sorry I didn't tell them before."

"I want to hear, Eva," Violet replied.

"Me too," Rose agreed. "Go ahead, Bernice, continue."

"Well you see, my Gabriel died on September 27th, 1949, at exactly 2:01 am and on the exact same day, you were born. Don't you see now?" Bernice explained.

Both Rose and Violet shook their heads.

"That time, that day, that's when the star, the singular soul of my little Gabriel, split into two, one part becoming you, Rose, and the other you, Violet."

Violet and Rose stared at Bernice blankly, not knowing what to think.

"It all makes sense, if you think about it. I didn't figure it all out right away. But then, after a while, it all became clear to me. Then I saw your birthmarks and I was convinced. I knew for sure."

"What birthmarks?" Violet asked, looking at Rose.

"The one that each of you has on your right shoulder. I'm surprised that you haven't noticed them before," Bernice continued.

The women examined each other's shoulders.

"Why didn't you bring it up before if it was so important, Ma?" Eva asked suspiciously.

"Oh, there's a time and place for everything. Right ladies?"

"She's right. We both do have the same roundish birthmarks in the same spot," Violet announced.

"And my Gabriel had the same one in the exact same place."

"So what does it really mean then, Bernice?" Violet asked.

"That not only is the bond between you and Rose very deep, but the one between me and you two is almost as strong."

Rose took another look at Violet's shoulder.

Eva and Ava found Bernice's story of the man with the beautiful buttocks hard to swallow. This, however, did not stop them from enjoying it in their own way. By the time Bernice had finished with the tale, both had become moist between their legs. Something told them that Bernice had told the story to show them that sex was still possible for a woman in her fifties. Although they never said anything, both were grateful for this. That night as they lay at extreme ends of their bed, they masturbated to the memory of the man with the beautiful buttocks.

CHAPTER 27

One Down, One to Go

THE PHONE WAS RINGING off the hook when Violet arrived back home.

"Yes, hello," she answered.

"Hi, yes, is this Robert's cousin?" a strange female voice asked.

"Cousin?" Violet replied somewhat surprised.

"Yes, he told me that he was staying with his cousin and her children. It's so nice of you to have him."

"Yes, I guess it is," Violet said, playing along.

"Yes, my name is Jill. Robert probably mentioned me before. I was calling to remind him about the babies' medical appointment tomorrow." The sound of crying babies could be heard in the background.

"Babies' appointment?" Violet repeated, trying to hide the surprise in her voice.

"Yes, it's at three," Jill replied. "Do you know if he's over at that elderly lady's place who he helps out sometime?"

"You mean Angela?" Violet asked, smiling inwardly.

"Yes, I think that's her name," Jill answered.

"I'm not sure where he is right now. But I'll let him know that you called."

"Okay. Thank you very much. Bye."

Before hanging up, Violet overheard Jill hushing her children. "Don't worry, Daddy is going to be here soon," she told them.

Without a second thought, Violet went and retrieved the small piece of paper that she had been keeping in her dresser drawer. She dialed the number.

"Yes hello, Violet, how can I help you?" Angela replied on the other end of the line.

Violet was impressed by Angela's ability to identify her voice so quickly.

"I think you need to ask Robert who Jill is," Violet advised, then hung up the phone abruptly. She didn't see any need for pleasantries.

While the snow blew every which way and created white-out conditions, Douglas lay incapacitated on Johnny's couch. Johnny was crouched over him praying for two things: Douglas's full recovery and the guts to express his true feelings.

Johnny gently stroked Douglas's arm and then took a seat next to him. Sliding his fingers down Douglas's leg, he delicately inched it toward his groin. With his had cupped over his genitals, Johnny reached up and pressed his lips to Douglas's, kissing him tenderly.

Douglas stirred when he felt Johnny's warmth against him. He wanted to scream out in protest, but the sensation was too enjoyable. Inwardly, he wanted Johnny's hands and lips to linger and cure him of all of his aliments. Outwardly, he resisted.

"What are you doing? Get off of me!" he yelled. The hesitation in his voice and the softness of his eyes, betrayed him. "What do you take me for? Who gave you the right?" he continued half-heartedly.

Johnny stole another kiss then quickly pulled away. Douglas clenched his fist and feebly cuffed Johnny in his left eye. This took Johnny by surprise. He watched in shock as Douglas gathered his strength, got up, dressed, and marched toward the door.

"You can't go outside dressed like that," Johnny yelled. "It's snowing. You're going to catch your death. Wait, let me help you."

"I don't need your kind of help. Just leave me alone," Douglas insisted as he pushed the door shut behind him. Johnny's apprehensions kept him from following.

Outside, Douglas waded through the thick snow for a short while before he was able to hail a cab. Getting in the vehicle proved to be difficult, but he managed. He lay himself down along the length of the back seat.

"You alright there? You need me to take you to the hospital?" the driver asked as he glanced behind him.

"No, 274 Sackville please," Douglas replied, tucking his hands under his ear.

"Are you sure? You don't look so good."

"Yes, I'm sure."

"Okay, you're the boss." The driver turned around and started the car.

With his eyes closed, Douglas shook gently, thinking

about the taste of Johnny's lips. He had found the kiss more gratifying than any that he had ever received. As the frozen city went by in a blur, his mind was lost in the thoughts of what could have happened had he stayed.

It took his last ounce of remaining energy to get out of the cab. The blast of frigid air caused his muscles to constrict. He was unable to move even a step. The driver scrambled out from behind the wheel to help.

"I'll take you to the hospital now, if you want. No charge," he offered.

"No, I don't need to go to the hospital. I just need some help upstairs," Douglas maintained.

"Alright. Alright, whatever you say, boss." The driver put his arm around Douglas and helped him toward the building.

Upstairs, he deposited Douglas on the couch and left. After a few minutes, Douglas was overtaken by a bout of nausea, forcing him to crawl on all fours to the bathroom. He hugged the toilet as he vomited out the entire contents of his bile-filled stomach.

Rose was assaulted by the foul smell the moment she entered the apartment. She followed the odor into the bathroom, where she found Douglas passed out on the floor. He looked and smelled as if he hadn't eaten or bathed in weeks.

"You poor pitiful soul," she whispered to herself.

After cleaning him up, she dressed him in a pair of pajamas and carried him to the couch while he slept. Once she was done, she stood and watched the movement of his chest. She knew that it wouldn't be long.

That night as she lay in her bed, her thoughts wandered. She imagined how calm things would be when she was completely free. For the very first time in a long time, she thought about her small town and what it would be like to read poetry again. As her mind raced, an odd sense of peace and the promise of happiness coursed through her body. It was a very welcoming feeling.

Douglas woke disoriented, breathing very heavily. He wondered how he had gotten from the bathroom to the couch and who had dressed him. Staring at his heaving chest, he had a brief moment of lucidity. In this moment he questioned whether he was going to die. He wanted to get up and go to the bathroom, but he seemed to be incapable of the tiniest of movements. He ended up empting his bowels right there on the couch. He knew that was a bad omen.

As he lay delirious, wallowing in his filth, his thoughts rambled. In his disorientation he came to two important realizations. The first was that he did not love Rose. He had been certain of this the moment Johnny kissed him. His second realization, something that he had been suppressing his whole life, was that he had always wanted to be a girl. This yearning had haunted him since he was a boy in his mother's undergarments. He concluded that it wasn't the brassieres that he wanted but the soft supple breast instead. With these thoughts in his head, he fell back into a deep sleep.

At exactly three o'clock in the morning, he woke again, wheezing. This time, the more he tried to catch his breath, the harder it became.

Rose was awakened by the strange hacking noise. She got up to sneak a peek. Douglas's face was beet red, and the stench that surrounded him, putrid. She covered her nose. Douglas's wheezing became more frantic the closer she got to him.

"Help…help…me…please! Call an ambulance…please!"
he huffed. Looking down at him, she didn't feel any sort of
panic or alarm. She watched and listened calmly as his color
slowly turned from crimson to blue and the spaces between
his breaths began to taper.

"I think your time is up," she murmured.

The puzzled, desperate look on his face told her that he
hadn't understood.

"Please call…" he whimpered.

When she made a slight movement, a spark of hope lit
up his face. It quickly faded as he watched her walk past the
phone and back into the bedroom.

She sat listening in bed. The wheezing increased, then
slowed down again. In the silence, she heard Douglas call out
something. It sounded like a name. When he repeated it a
second time, she heard "Johnny!" This didn't surprise her at
all. She just continued to rest and listen. After the name was
called one last time, there was a sharp hissing sound, then
three labored gasps followed by absolute silence. She lay back,
closed her eyes, and went to sleep.

The next morning she woke feeling a sense of weightlessness.
It was as if she had spent the night drifting through space.
She got out of bed, wrapped a blanket around her sleeping
son, and rushed him past the couch and out to Bernice's.

When Bernice opened the door, Rose handed Thomas
over to her. Without saying a single word, Rose headed home.
Bernice's expression told her that all was understood.

Back at the apartment, Rose walked over to the window and stood there briefly looking out onto the street. The
snow was blowing everywhere, and people were running for

cover. She reached out and touched the windowpane. It was warmer than she expected. Taking in a few deep breaths, she turned around and looked at the couch. Douglas was now a lifeless, motionless lump, his body curled up in the fetal position. There was something about the way he lay, with his mouth slightly open with an odd-looking kind of smile, that reminded her of a dead rat. His odor had ripened overnight. With one hand pinching her nose, she lifted his wrist to check for a pulse. There wasn't one.

"What's your emergency?" a sleepy operator asked on the other line.

"I think my husband suffered a heart attack or something in his sleep last night."

"Does he have any vital signs?"

"I'm not sure. I don't think so."

"What is the address?"

After giving the details, Rose hung up, then picked the phone up again and dialed '0'.

"Operator speaking, can I help you?"

"Yes, I would like to make a long-distance call."

When Rose gave Douglas's mother the news, the woman sounded as if she had more important things on her mind.

"That's a terrible shame. Of course I will make all the arrangements to bring his body back here," she said with only the slightest hint of worry in her voice.

The only thing left for the paramedics to do when they arrived was lift Douglas's stiff carcass off the couch and onto the gurney. The smell didn't seem to bother them.

Two uniformed police officers entered as the cadaver was being wheeled out.

"So the deceased was your husband? Is that correct?" one officer asked as he pulled out his note pad.

"Yes," Rose answered.

"And his name?"

"Douglas Weiss."

"Do you know what happened?"

"No," Rose replied.

"Was your husband taking any medication that you knew of?"

Rose paused. "Yes, he keeps his pills in his pants pocket." She motioned toward the slacks that were draped over the arm of the couch.

One officer picked up the pants and and found the pills in a matter of seconds. "Jackpot," he said, shaking the bottle. "This is probably what did the poor guy in. We're going to need to take this with us."

"Sure, sure, take whatever you like," Rose answered. Her tired, rumpled appearance made her appear sympathetic. She purposely widened her large eyes and flashed the officers a forlorn look.

"Don't you worry your pretty little head, Mrs. Weiss. We'll get to bottom of this." He patted Rose's shoulder.

"We should also take the pants and all of the other articles of clothing he last wore," the other officer added.

"Sure, of course. They're all there." She watched as the police collected Douglas's belongings.

"Okay, that should do it. If we have any questions, we'll be in touch. And if you need anything, anything at all, just give us a call at the station," one officer said. He pulled a card from his pouch and handed it to her. "The number is right there."

Rose peered down at the card.

"Take good care." The officers left.

Rose began to feel light-headed. Within seconds, her knees gave out and she flopped to the floor. She felt both exalted and drained as she sat there. A soft tap at the door brought her back. It took some effort to get up again.

Violet stood at the door with her arms opened wide. The two women fell into each other's arms. Disbelief was plastered over both of their faces.

"It's over, Violet. It's over," Rose intoned.

"I know. I know." Violet stroked Rose's faced and pushed some unruly strands of hair away.

"What now?" Rose asked.

"We'll just wait for the other one," Violet whispered.

Rose nodded. Bernice watched them quietly from her doorway.

Since Angela had received the call from Violet, she had been fuming and waiting impatiently for Robert's return. When he finally appeared late one evening wearing a new wool coat, she was livid.

"Where in the hell have you been?" she demanded, as she sauntered over to him.

"What do you mean, where have I been? You know exactly where I am when I'm not here." He removed his rubber galoshes, then pecked Angela on her cheek. She sprang back.

"Have you been drinking!?"

"No, of course not," he lied. He wiped his mouth with the back of his hand.

"Then why do you smell like a rum shop? You have some

nerve showing up here smelling like that when you know how I feel."

"Okay, I had a little sip. What harm could that do?" He staggered over to the armchair.

"Didn't I tell you what happened to my father?"

"Oh, I don't want to hear about it now, okay? I'm feeling awful," he replied.

"What's wrong with you? What is it?"

A squeamish look came over his face as he touched his stomach.

"What is it?" she repeated.

He sprang up and ran to the toilet.

"What the hell?" She followed behind him. Groans came from the bathroom.

"What the hell is wrong with you?" she demanded, banging on the door.

"Can you just leave me in peace for a minute?" he yelled.

"No, I'm not going to leave you alone. I don't care if you shit your insides out, I just need you to answer one question."

"Can't you just wait?"

"No, I can't."

"Okay, Angela, okay. What's the damn question?"

"Who the hell is Jill?"

There was silence on the other side of the door.

"Who is she?" she repeated.

"Look, can we talk about this when I get off the toilet? Just give me a minute, alright? Okay, baby? Will you please do that for me, darling?"

Angela folded her arms and waited for him to finish.

"So who is she?" Angela didn't wait for the door to be fully open.

"I don't have the foggiest idea." He averted his eyes and walked sluggishly back to the armchair.

"So you're telling me you don't know anyone by that name?"

"No, I don't. Okay?" he replied looking squarely in Angela's eyes. "Why don't you sit with me for a while. It'll make me feel better."

Angela didn't move a muscle.

"So where were you then?"

"I told you. I was with Violet."

"That whole time?"

"Yeah, she needed me to watch the kids and then I did some job hunting."

"Oh?" Angela's body relaxed. "Any prospects?"

"No, not really. It's crazy out there," He pulled Angela closer to him. "Come."

Angela fell into Robert's lap.

"That's my girl," he said touching his head to hers.

"So what was all that in there? Are you okay?" she asked.

"Probably something I ate."

"Did she cook for you when you were there?"

"Who yuh mean? Violet?"

"Yeah. Did you eat any of her food?"

"Of course I ate her food. What other food was I going to eat."

"Are you sure she didn't poison you?"

Robert looked at Angela as if she were crazy.

"Is it just a coincidence that you feel sick after coming from her place?"

"That's ludicrous!"

"Ludicrous! Think about it."

"I know her. Violet wouldn't even think of doing some-thing like that. She doesn't have a mean bone in her body."

"Don't be so sure about that. She's a woman, isn't she?"

"Yes, she is. She is a woman."

CHAPTER 28
A Twist of Fate

A WEEK AFTER Douglas's death, Rose was awakened by a loud thumping knock at the door. *They've come for me,* she thought. She had already packed some clothes for Thomas and made arrangements with Bernice for when the time came.

When she opened the door, she got the surprise of her life. It was not the police but Douglas's large friend. His extra-long face and smaller paunch looked as if they had been whittled away by worry. He held a box in his hand.

"Sorry to bother you, but I thought I would bring these—" He broke down.

Rose took the box and let him in.

"I just wanted to…. I'm so sorry." He could not get hold of himself.

"Are you alright?"

"Yes, yes, I just found out and…I don't know what I'm

going to do. I know he was sick but I didn't expect this." He wiped his face. "What am I going to do...what—" He bent over as if he were in physical pain.

Rose put her hand on his shoulder.

"You...you loved him didn't you?" she asked, knowing the answer to her question.

"Yes, very much...I loved him very much."

She was touched.

"Did he suffer?"

Rose looked him squarely in the eyes. "Yes, he did."

"He did?"

"Yes, I made sure he did."

"What?" Johnny didn't understand. "You made sure he suffered?"

"Yes."

"Why would you do such a thing? Aren't...weren't you his wife?"

"Yes, I was his wife, and he made me suffer, so I did the same to him."

"Why?"

Rose took a deep breath. "He killed our daughter."

"What!"

"Sit. Please sit." Rose gestured toward the couch."

Johnny sat down reluctantly.

Rose proceeded to tell Johnny everything that had transpired between her and Douglas from the very beginning. She felt she owed this much to the only person who had truly loved Douglas. When she was done, she felt a sense of relief. Johnny was devastated by what he'd heard, but for some reason he left Rose's place that day feeling somewhat satisfied, since Rose's words had brought him closer than ever to his beloved.

After Johnny's visit, Rose agonized over whether he would go to the police with the information she had given him. She had many worry-filled days until she received a call from an officer. He told her that they had determined that Douglas's death was caused by his excessive drug use. The pills had done so much damage that he died with the internal organs of a one-hundred-year-old. The call did not, however, take away the pangs of guilt she had started feeling after Johnny's visit. A part of her regretted that Douglas had not been able to fully experience all that Johnny had to offer.

To calm her nerves she embarked on a flurry of activities. She began cleaning and rearranging the apartment and getting rid of all of Douglas's things, with the exception of a handful of his figurines and the color television. It took her a good part of the week to do so, since she insisted on doing it on her own.

After she finished throwing the last of Douglas's belongings down the chute, she was exhausted. As she walked back to her apartment, she caught a glimpse of Robert staggering home. The disturbed look on his face was bothersome. He had hardly laid a hand on Violet since the soup incident, but his drinking had increased.

She watched him as he opened the door and slammed it shut. She remained standing outside the door as a precaution.

"Have you been poisoning me?" Robert blurted out angrily, as he stepped into the living room.

Violet was nowhere to be seen.

"I said, have you been putting anything in my food?" he repeated, searching the apartment.

"Can you please keep it down? The children are sleeping,"

Violet said, coming from the kitchen, and wiping her hands on her shirt.

"I've been shitting like a madman. Did you put something in my food to make me do that?" he demanded.

Violet shot him a dismissive look.

"Stop looking at me like that and answer!" he ordered. Violet's new-found confidence confounded him. "Have you?"

"No, I haven't been poisoning your food. Don't you think you would be dead by now if I had?" she replied brashly.

"Then why do I have the runs?"

"I don't know," Violet answered, holding her breath.

Well, if I find out that you've been poisoning me, I'll kill you. Do you hear me? I'm serious as shit." He brushed by her and left.

She exhaled once he was out of sight.

The phone rang a few minutes after his departure.

"Hello, this is Jill," a voice stated giddily. "Is this Robert's cousin? Sorry to bother you again."

Violet smirked. "Yes this is Robert's cousin. Sorry, you just missed him."

"Oh no! Did he say where he was going?"

"I think he was going to do some work for that elderly lady again."

"How nice of him. He's such a great guy, isn't he?"

"Hang on, I have the number right here."

Violet smiled as she read Angela's number into the receiver.

Angela was lying on the couch watching TV. When the phone rang she sprang up to get it, thinking it might be Robert.

"Hello?"

"Hello. This is Jill. Sorry to bother you, but I'm looking for Robert. Is he there?"

Angela couldn't believe her ears. "Excuse me, what did you say?"

"This is Jill. I was wondering if Robert was there I was given—"

Angela slammed the receiver down, then picked it back up and banged it down again repeatedly.

"That son-of-a-bitch!" she yelled. Her body began to tremble as she charged into the kitchen.

Rummaging furiously through the cutlery drawer, she grabbed the sharpest knife, returned to the living room, turned off the TV and the lights, and took a seat in the armchair. She sat there unflinching, breathing heavily, with the sound of Jill's cheery voice resonating in her head.

Her son screamed from his crib, but she didn't hear him. Her full attention and focus was on the front door as she anticipated Robert's arrival. The baby, not having any other choice, cried himself back to sleep.

She sat up straight and repositioned the knife when she heard the key turn in the door.

"Why is it so dark in here?" Robert muttered, moving across the room to turn on a lamp. He didn't notice Angela's watchful eyes.

"Angie, darling. Angie, where are you, sweetie?" he crooned as re-crossed the room.

"I'm right here," she replied hoarsely.

He was startled to see her seated with the knife on her lap. The sinister look on her face was no less alarming.

"Are you alright, Babe?" he asked nervously. "I'm sorry I'm late. I got tied up."

She remained silent and stone-faced. He had never seen her in such a state before.

"Are you okay, Angie?"

"I'm fine, Robert. How are you?" she replied dryly in a weird, bass voice. "Where are you coming from just now?"

The phone rang before he was able to formulate a reply. "Hello," he said into the receiver. A look of terror transformed his face. "Sorry you have the wrong number," he stammered before hanging up the phone.

"Was that Jill?" Angela asked coldly.

"Jill? No! It was the wrong number," he stuttered. When the phone rang again he froze. "Pick it up!" Angela ordered.

He didn't budge.

"Pick up the fucking phone," she yelled lurching out of her seat toward it.

She spoke calmly into the receiver. "Hello. Yes. He's right here. I'll pass you to him." She held the phone out toward Robert. He refused to take it.

"Take the fucking phone, Robert. It's for you. It's Jill. The same Jill you said you didn't know."

Robert kept a close eye on the knife. Angela had brandished that same knife in front of him on two separate occasions before, but this time it seemed more menacing.

"Take the fucking phone! Your woman wants to talk to you," Angela yelled even louder.

Robert knew enough not to make any sudden movements. He kept his arms glued to his sides.

"Coward!" she screamed. "You're a fucking coward." Putting the receiver to her ear she said, "Sorry, he can't come to the phone right now. Too bad you won't be able to say your final good-byes." She let the receiver fall and returned to her armchair, slowly placing the knife back on her lap.

Robert stood paralyzed.

"So that was Jill," she scowled.

He said nothing.

"So I guess you *do* know someone named Jill after all. No more mystery there. So who is she? Are you fucking her?"

Robert shifted nervously from one leg to the next.

"Answer me. Who is she?"

"Yes, I do know Jill," he began. "You see…she…was my woman."

"What do you mean *was?*"

"She was, but we're no longer together," he said, tripping over his words.

"Don't lie to me. Robert." She held up the knife.

"Okay, okay, I'm still with her. Is that what you want to hear? Are you satisfied?"

"So where did you meet her?" Angela sat forward in her seat.

"What does it matter where we met?"

"Just answer the question."

"We met at a bus stop. It was raining, and she took pity on me, okay?"

"So why didn't you tell me about her before?"

"There was no reason to."

"What do you mean there was no reason?"

"Because I didn't want to hurt you. And then she got pregnant."

"Pregnant!" Angela gripped the knife even more tightly.

"Is that thing necessary?"

"What, the knife? Yes, it is very necessary. So what did

you have with her, a girl or a boy?"

"She…she had a boy…and two girls. Triplets."

"Triplets?" Angela echoed. Tears began to well up in her eyes. "Triplets!" she repeated. "You must have fucked her good and hard for that to happen."

"I'm sorry," he said, trying to sound apologetic.

"So what did you name them?" she asked, wiping her tears.

"Roberta…Jill and…Robert Junior." He inched closer to her, sensing that her defenses were weakening.

"Robert Junior?" she moaned, trying to compose herself.

Just as Robert was about to reach her, the sudden shrill of the unhooked phone caught her off guard. She flinched. In a flash he was able to wrestle the knife from her.

"Listen you crazy bitch, don't you ever try that shit again with me," he yelled. He threw down the knife and stormed out the door.

"I just wanted to hug him," Rose said. "He really loved Douglas."

She was snuggled up on her couch with Violet while the snow blanketed the streets outside. It had become a nightly ritual since Douglas's death.

"I wonder if Douglas loved him back," Violet said.

"I don't know, but I guess none of it matters now."

"No," Violet replied soberly.

"So you're not stopping?"

"No, why should I? Give me one good reason."

"The children."

"He's never taken care of them."

"Well, I'll understand if you change your mind."

"I have no plans to do that," Violet insisted. She leaned her head on Rose's shoulder and closed her eyes.

Bernice was feeling particularly frazzled that evening. She didn't know what had come over her. As she tossed and turned in bed, her thoughts shifted from the two women to her daughters and back to her aches and pains. She wasn't sure which was the most worrisome. Two husbands dying, one after the other, would seem a bit suspicious, she thought. She had wanted to mention this to Rose and Violet, but she could see that they had already decided to do things their way. The fact that Rose hadn't been implicated in her husband's death was encouraging, but she wasn't sure that Violet would be so lucky. She wished that her daughters could be as young and strong-willed as the two women. It troubled her that they weren't. Passing on parts of her own story had eased her burden somehow, but it hadn't changed their realities.

As Bernice monitored her irregular heartbeats, she wondered how much life she still had in her. The inevitable didn't scare her, but the periodic tightness in her chest and shoulder did. With thoughts of death and dying in her head, she decided to write down some words of wisdom for her daughters in the form of a letter, thinking that it would do them some good after she was gone. Her desire was to relate all the life lessons that she had learned. Since she knew that Rose or Violet would have to read it for them, she would leave some wisdom for them, too. She decided to start the letter that very night. Reaching for some paper and a pen from her nightstand, she sat up, fluffed her pillows, and began to write.

Even though Violet had not expressed it to Rose—or anyone else—she was starting to feel tiny pangs of doubt about continuing with her plans. Her children were the only reason for the hesitation. She had grown up without a father, and she knew what that was like. She also knew what it was like to live with a tyrant, and she didn't want that for them either.

As she weighed her conscience, Rose's words, and her own desire to be completely free of Robert, she decided that the time had arrived. *No more doing things in small measures. No more waiting to see what would happen.* After she put the children to bed, she went to the kitchen and carefully poured a full pouch of the brown rat poison into Robert's last remaining bottle of Johnny Walker. She made sure not to waste a single grain. *Rat poison to kill a rat. How very fitting,* she thought.

Just as she had replaced the cap and was shaking the bottle, she felt a stream of warm air on the back of her neck. The tiny hair follicles stood at attention. She didn't have to turn around to know who it was. How he had entered the apartment undetected was beyond her.

"So I was right!" Robert exclaimed. He grabbed the bottle and forced Violet around to face him.

"You are poisoning me."

"Yes, I am." Violet did not falter.

"You all want me dead, I see."

"Maybe because we think you deserve to die."

"That's for God to decide, not you." He raised his arm to hit her.

Violet raised her arm defensively, but then lowered it to her side. She knew now what her only recourse was. She looked him straight in the eye and started to concentrate. In her trance she thought about her mother, her father, Angela, and the women on the other side of the island. She thought about every punch, kick, cut that Robert had ever given her, the black eyes, blistered skin, and fractured bones. She thought about the times he had taken her by force, all the blood that she lost and all the scars and bruises he had left all over her body. She thought about all the tears she had shed and how helpless and worthless she felt. She remembered the smell of sex that lingered the first night of her arrival and the care he had shown the other women's child, while her own children went without because he had stolen from her. The memory of the boiling soup and each and every one of his blows coursed through her body.

Her concentrated glare confounded Robert. He was unable to move his arm. It was suspended in midair.

"What the fuck is wrong with you? Why are you staring at me that way? You look like the devil." He cursed without fully realizing that she had been controlling him.

She said nothing as she held her gaze.

Within seconds, he was unable to speak or move and was having difficulty breathing. The longer she stared at him, the more constricted his air passages became.

He gasped for air as she wished him dead. She was determined to succeed this time.

He grabbed his throat, trying to catch his breath. His eyes started to water. Within a few seconds, he fell to the floor and was dead. The bottle of whiskey lay shattered next to him, like a true friend.

There was no need for her to check his pulse or heart. She knew she had accomplished what she had wanted.

She called, and the police arrived ten minutes later.

"Tell us again—how exactly did this happen?" one officer asked as he scratched his head and gave his partner a puzzled look.

"I stared at him, I told you," Violet replied, stoned-faced.

"That's all you did?"

"Well, the rat poison wasn't really working, so I had to try something else."

"You were poisoning him?"

"Yes, but he was hardly here, so it wasn't really working."

"What were you putting it in?"

"His booze." Both officers noticed the broken bottle on the floor.

"And why did you want him dead, ma'am?"

"Why would I want him alive?" Violet began.

She went on to explain all the violence and mistreatment Robert had inflicted on her, starting from the very first slap. Since she had provided them with a very convincing motive and confession, she expected to be taken into custody right then and there, but was told there was no need for that just yet.

A few days later, the same officers returned. They told her that no trace of rat poison had been found in Robert's blood. He had apparently died of a brain aneurysm. The rupture had been so explosive that it had destroyed his whole brain. With their condolences, the officers offered her a referral to a mental health facility—which she politely declined.

After they were gone, Violet went straight to Bernice's.

"Two for two," Bernice cheered as she attempted to raise her arms in triumph. This calls for a celebration."

"Why don't we leave it for Saturday, instead. Isn't that the twins' birthday?" Rose suggested.

"Yeah, that's a great idea," Eva agreed.

"Let's have a big bash. We can do all the cooking," Ava added.

"Sounds good." Violet seemed a bit distracted.

"Why don't you two go to Rose's?" Bernice offered, sensing Violet's malaise.

The two women looked at each other.

"Some time alone would be nice." Rose put her arm around Violet.

"Sure. That would be great," Violet agreed.

"Go on then," Bernice said shooing off the women.

The moment the two stepped into Rose's apartment, they grabbed each other and held on tight.

"We did it!" Rose crowed.

"Yes we did. Yes we did." Violet wiped a tear from her cheek.

"We're free now."

"Yes, we are. We're free." The words felt strange coming out of their mouths.

"How about some schnapps?" Rose proposed, pointing to a bottle and some overturned glasses that had been carefully laid out on the coffee table. "I bought the bottle especially for this occasion."

Violet forced a smile, while Rose poured the liquor. The two sat and drank in silence, allowing the gravity of the moment to sink in. After a few minutes, Violet murmured something. It took Rose a couple of seconds to realize that she was singing.

Mi chiamano Mimì,
ma il mio nome è Lucia.

The singing got progressively louder as she went along. Rose's eyes sparkled with great admiration and affection as she watched Violet. She had never heard her sing before. Rose was so inspired that she grabbed Violet's hand and pulled her toward the window. She stuck her head out and began to sing herself. She welcomed the blast of cold air that greeted her. Violet laughed and joined her.

Mi chiamano Mimì,
ma il mio nome è Lucia.
La storia mia è breve.
A tela o a seta
ricamo in casa e fuori...

They sang at the top of their lungs, grinning from ear to ear. Bernice and the twins heard them from their apartment and smiled.

"Good for them," Bernice intoned. "Good for them."

The next day, the women decided to brave the cold and take the kids to the park. Eva and Ava went along.

Outside, even though everything was covered with a thick layer of dirty slush, it still seemed bright and cheerful. As the group approached the Stickman's corner, Ava braced herself. When she didn't smell anything she began to worry.

"Wait...wait...how come I can't smell him? Where is he?" Ava asked.

"You can't smell him because he's not here," Eva replied bluntly.

"How do you know?"

"Because Rose told me. He hasn't been here for a little while. He disappeared after Douglas died. Right, Rose?"

"Yes, that's right."

"How come you didn't tell me, Rose?"

"I thought you'd lost interest in him."

"No, I didn't. I still like him. I mean, I still think about him…What happened to him? Where did he go?"

"I have no idea where he went. I just know that he vanished into thin air when the police started asking questions about Douglas."

"What am I going to do now?" Ava pouted.

"Maybe find a new boyfriend. A real one that doesn't smell," Eva teased.

"Oh, you were just jealous anyway," Ava snapped.

"Jealous of what!" Eva screeched.

"Stop arguing, you two. Who wants to push the kids on the swings?" Rose interjected.

"I do," Eva and Ava answered together.

"Are they going to fit in the swings wearing those puffy snow suits?" Ava asked, forgetting all about the Stickman.

"Yeah they will," Rose insisted.

"Great," Ava said.

"Fabulous," Eva echoed.

"Good," Rose added.

They walked the rest of the way in silence.

CHAPTER 29
A Quiet Ending

STREAMERS OF VARIOUS COLORS and lengths hung haphazardly all around Bernice's apartment when Rose and Violet entered with their children Saturday evening.

The toddlers ran through the room pulling at the decorations.

"You and Eva decorated, right Ava?" Violet chuckled.

"Yes, how could you tell? Pretty spiffy, eh?" Ava beamed. "Ma wasn't up to the job, so we did it."

"Are you sure there is nothing wrong with her?" Violet whispered glancing toward Bernice's bedroom. "Maybe we should take her back to the doctor."

"I'm just fine. I don't need to see any doctor. I'll be out in a minute," Bernice shouted.

"Here, this is for both of you. It's from both of us," Rose hugged Eva, then Ava, and then placed a flat square present in her hand.

Ava examined it with her fingers.

"I know what it is already," she laughed. "It's an album."

"I'm not saying anything," Rose replied as she took a seat. "You'll know for sure when you open it."

"Oh, can we open it now? Please, please, pretty please?" Ava begged.

"Can we?" Eva moved closer to her sister.

"Sure, why not? It's your birthday, isn't it? You can do whatever you want," Violet added.

Ava immediately tore away the wrapping paper. "See I told you. It is an album. I was right." She passed the LP to her sister.

"But you don't know which one," Violet teased.

"What in tarnation! What did you two do to this place?" Bernice cried as she held on tightly to the doorframe outside her room.

Violet went to her and helped her to the armchair.

"It looks like there was a tornado in here," Bernice continued.

"Don't worry. It looks wonderful, ladies, very festive," Rose said.

"Thanks, Rose," Ava said.

"Yeah, yeah, whatever," Bernice snapped. "What's that now? A disco album? Is that what you brought them? What's the world coming to?"

"Disco!" Ava and Eva screamed.

"I love disco! Go put it on right now, Eva," Ava ordered.

Eva sped off to her bedroom. Within a few minutes, loud disco music blared from the room.

"Oh my gosh, I love it!" Ava screeched, bobbing her head to the music.

"I love it too," Eva agreed, moving her head in sync with her sister's.

"Then let's dance!" Rose jumped up and took Ava by her hand. Violet did the same with Eva. Bernice watched on in wonderment.

"Look at you all. What's gotten into you?" Bernice asked.

"Disco!" Eva and Ava shouted together as they continued to dance. Bernice felt a deep sense of satisfaction. She had never seen her daughters or Rose and Violet as happy as they appeared at that very moment. This pleased her greatly.

When the festivities were over and it was time to leave, Bernice showered Rose, Violet, and their kids with kisses. They were all puzzled, because she had never done that before.

"What's gotten into you, Bernice?" Rose asked.

"Just saying goodnight is all. I had a really great time tonight. Did you?"

Everyone smiled and nodded in agreement.

"Good night, Bernice, sweet dreams," Violet added.

"Yes, sweet dreams, Bernice," Rose echoed.

That night, Bernice lay back in bed. As her eyes shifted from the blank white walls to the darkness beyond her curtains, she found herself deep in thought, replaying all that had happened since Rose and Violet entered their lives. The fact that the twins now had someone else besides her was very encouraging. As she lay there feeling the constrictions of her chest, she was thankful for her active mind and imagination, and glad that they had not deteriorated with her health. A deep wave of satisfaction washed over her as her eyes closed and she began to drift off to sleep.

She dreamt of the future for the very first time that night. In it Rose and Violet were twenty years older. Violet had arrived home to a small house, dressed in a nurse's uniform, looking tired and stressed. Stepping inside, she found the place desolate and uncomfortably quiet. She threw down her keys and purse, sat down in the living room, and sighed. In another part of town, Rose had returned home dressed in office attire. She looked pale and gaunt. She entered the bungalow and walked through the dark house directly to the kitchen. There she deposited her purse, grabbed a glass of water, flopped down in a chair, and moaned.

"Violet," she said out loud. She got up and walked over to the phone on the wall, picked it up, and dialed.

"Hi Rosie," Violet answered on the other line.

"How was your day, Letty?"

"Awful, just terrible, those people at the hospital are getting on my nerves. How was yours?"

"About the same."

The two women chuckled.

In a subsequent vision, Bernice saw Eva and Ava ten years into the future. They were completely gray and looked more like her than ever. Dressed in black, they scurried around tidying up the apartment in a jovial mood. When there was a knock on the door, they both rushed to it like a couple of eager puppies. At the door stood a pair of male identical twins, each carrying a box of chocolates.

"We got your favorites," one of them said, shaking the box.

"Goodie," Eva and Ava screeched with delight. "Come in, come in."

The men greeted Eva and Ava warmly. Then they each took a seat in one of the two loveseats that were now in the room. The boxes of chocolates were placed on the coffee table.

"Make yourself comfortable," Ava said.

"We'll be right back with the tea," Eva added, hurrying into the kitchen with her sister.

The men nodded, smiled, and fidgeted as they waited. The sisters returned with a tray of treats, then took their seats next to their sweethearts.

"Are you two in the mood to hear a story tonight?" Ava asked, placing her arm around her beau.

"Sure, why not?" the twin men replied in unison.

"What's the story about?" Ava's beau asked as he bent forward and poured the tea.

"It's about two women, named Rose and Violet, who share the same soul," Eva answered.

"Sounds intriguing," Eva's beau said.

"It is," Eva replied. "I see the moon," she started with a smile.

"And the moon sees me," Ava joined in.

"God bless the moon and God bless me," the sisters concluded.

"Not so very long ago, there was a big shake-up in the heavens," Eva began. "The problem was that there weren't enough souls to go around. So it was decided that souls had to be divided and shared."

"So in the heavens that night," Ava continued, without missing a beat, "there were many tiny explosions, and the stars popped like popcorn and divided. One particularly brilliant star separated into two souls and each made their journey down to Earth."

The twin beaus smiled brightly as they listened to the sisters' story.

Once Bernice's vision had faded, she began to question the whole notion of togetherness. She had speculated all along about its attainability, since everyone comes into the world alone, spends the majority of their lives submerged and locked into their own subconscious, and eventually leaves the Earth in the same fashion they arrived. The type of togetherness that her daughters shared, she believed, didn't fully count, since it was brought on by circumstances. She knew it was still possible to experience loneliness because she had witnessed it in her children's melancholy. Although she was encouraged by her dream vision of her daughters' future, she was disappointed that she wasn't going to be there to witness their bliss first hand.

With the images of her dreams still floating about in her head, Bernice reached out for the large envelope and the pen on the nightstand. After scribbling something on the front of the envelope, she carefully placed it on her chest and lay back down.

As she closed her eyes, she said a silent prayer for her daughters and another one for Rose and Violet.

"Please take good care of them," she concluded.

The electricity that surged through her body and the flickering light she saw in the distance, told her that her time had arrived.

The next day when lunchtime had come and gone without a peep from Bernice, the twins entered her room, bracing themselves for the worst. They had listened each night as their mother got more and more restless in her sleep. They had also noticed a peculiar odor that seemed to be getting more and more pungent as the days went on. The scent had been even more powerful that morning. Neither Eva or Ava understood its significance. The night before—after the tender good-byes to Rose and Violet—Bernice had dragged herself into the twins' room and kissed them goodnight on their foreheads, the way she used to when they were children. Eva and Ava had taken this outpouring of emotion as a sign.

When they opened Bernice's door, the scent of lavender filled their nostrils. "That's strong," Ava remarked.

"I know," her sister agreed. "I don't hear anything. Do you?"

"No."

The scent became more powerful as they got closer. When their hands touched their mother's chest, their suspicions were confirmed. They knew that she was no longer with them. She was cold and not breathing. Falling over her stiff body in fits of sobbing, they discovered the envelope.

"What's this?" Ava said, picking it up. "Do you think it's a will?"

"Ma wouldn't leave something that important just lying on her like that. It has to be something else." Eva took the envelope from her sister. "Go and get Rose and Violet," she ordered.

Ava wiped her eyes quickly and ran out of the room. Eva opened up the envelope and pulled a pile of papers from it. She held the sheets close to her and reached for her mother's cold hand as she waited for Ava's return.

"How did it happen?" Rose asked.

"In her sleep," Eva replied.

"That's the best way to go," Violet said as she bent and touched Bernice's face.

"What are all those papers?" Rose asked.

"Ma left them on top of her in an envelope. Can you read it to us?" Eva asked as she held the papers out towards Rose.

"Should we call—" Rose began.

"No. I think Ma would have preferred it this way."

"Of course," Rose replied as she took the stack of papers from Eva and handed the envelope to Violet.

"It says 'Read after I'm gone' on top and 'Please stay together' in capital letters at the bottom," Violet said.

"Do you want to sit down in the living room? Or do you want me to just read it here?" Rose asked.

"Here," Eva, Ava, and Violet all said together.

"Ma would have wanted us to," Eva added.

"Okay, I'll read it here." Rose leafed through the pages. "Are you ready?"

"Yes," all three women said again in unison.

"Okay, here goes. Dear Eva, Ava, Rose, and Violet, since I'm dead now, I thought I would leave you with some wise words. But before I get to that, did I ever tell you why I never liked summers? I'm sure you've probably all wondered why. Well, it all started the summer my father left and my mother died…"

The End.

Acknowledgments

This book was many years in the making. I like to believe that I became a writer somewhere in the process. There were many people who helped me along on that journey.

I would first like to acknowledge my mother, Merle Rogers, and the late Leonie Zapparoli, the two women who inspired the book. Without their suffering there would be no book and no story to tell. I would like to thank my children, Daley, Maya, and Jonah, my greatest supporters and harshest critics. I would like to thank all of my dear friends and my whole family especially Judy Browne and Walter Maclean for their great love and tireless support.

I was able to find my voice and give structure to the novel in the very first, and only, writing course I took, so I would like to thank the instructor, Dennis Bock. To my readers, Kathy Tihane, Ann Choi, and Menbere Gabreselassie, thank you for being tough and not holding back. My thanks also to Dionne Brand, who in a few short meetings taught me a great deal; and to my editor, Colin Thomas, whose diligence, insight, humor, and incredible suggestions were invaluable. To Carolyn Jackson and Margie Wolfe at Second Story Press, I thank you for championing my book and saying yes when so many others said no. I would also like to acknowledge the support of the Ontario Arts Council.

Lastly, I would like to thank that thing that we call divine inspiration, all the beautiful books I've read, and all the ones still to read.

About the Author

CHRISTENE A. BROWNE is an award-winning filmmaker. Born in St. Kitts, Browne moved with her family to Regent Park, Canada's oldest and largest low-income community, in 1970. There she became involved in making videos, participating in and then leading the Regent Park Video Workshop Project before going on to attend Ryerson University's film program. Browne's first dramatic feature, *Another Planet*, was the first feature film to be directed by a Black woman in Canada. In 2007 Browne completed *Speaking in Tongues: The History of Language*, a documentary series that looks at the History of Language from prehistoric time to the present day. In 2011 Browne was awarded the Documentary Filmmaker prize at the Women's International Film and Television Showcase Visionary Awards. She lives in Toronto with her three children. *Two Women* is her first novel.